UNMARRIED

BOOKS BY EMILY SHINER

EMILY SHINER

UNMARRIED

bookouture

Published by Bookouture in 2025

An imprint of Storyfire Ltd.
Carmelite House
50 Victoria Embankment
London EC4Y 0DZ

www.bookouture.com

The authorised representative in the EEA is Hachette Ireland
8 Castlecourt Centre
Dublin 15 D15 XTP3
Ireland
(email: info@hbgi.ie)

ISBN: 978-1-80550-091-9
eBook ISBN: 978-1-80550-090-2

Hey girl, this one's for you.

PROLOGUE

If this house weren't so big, I might not have as easy a time sneaking around it, but Mitch is in the shower, and he can't hear me poking around on the first floor. Of course, the reverse is true, and he could be sneaking up behind me—

I whip around, but nobody's there.

My heart hammers in my chest, and I take a deep breath to try to slow it down.

The staff is gone.

Hannah is at her home.

The two of us are alone in the house. I'm safe... well, as safe as I can be when I'm in the house with my husband.

I cock my head to the side for a moment to listen for water, and when I hear it running, I hurry into the living room. How many times have I snuck through this house looking for proof of what Hannah told me?

It's not that I trust her or believe every word out of her mouth, but I'd be stupid not to at least consider that what she told me might be the truth. I press myself up against the wall and pull out my phone. In a moment, I have an incognito tab open, just in case Mitch decides to come behind me and look at what I was googling.

It's silly to hold my breath as I wait for the results to load, but I don't exhale until the text fills the screen.

Toxic when consumed in large quantities.

Dizziness makes me close my eyes and sink to the floor. Poison. He poisoned her.

As much as I want to believe Hannah was lying, it looks like she was telling the truth.

ONE

AIMEE

Dale's been dead and buried for three weeks, and I'm about to get married.

Not only that, not only am I going to get married just weeks after my fiancé died, but I'm marrying his best friend.

The man who was there when my fiancé died.

The man whose sister wanted me dead.

The man who knows my deepest, darkest secret and obviously isn't afraid to use it against me.

I take a deep breath and smooth down the front of my dress. I didn't pick it out, exactly like I didn't pick out my ring, the music, the flowers, the cake. It was like Mitch snapped his fingers and a wedding popped into existence.

Instant Wedding: You Only Need a Bride!

My dress is heavy. It's beaded, with a long train. I'm sure it's gorgeous, but I've barely glanced in the mirror since putting it on. Even during the fitting, I felt like I was looking down on myself, watching someone else try on a dress. I've heard of people having out-of-body experiences when they're under a lot of stress but never thought it was something that could happen to me.

Even when I lost my twin sister, I didn't feel this immense stress. Maybe it's because I could see a way out. Even though everything was terrible, I knew there was a way for me to have a good life.

But right now, dressed like this, about to marry a man who has the power to ruin the life I worked so hard for, I can't see a way out. The only thing I know to do is walk down the aisle to him, take him as my husband, try to survive.

I've survived this far. I've taken my twin's name, lived her life, and left behind who I really was. Nobody would look at me and doubt my ability to survive, but the truth is I'm tired. I'm great at pretending to be my twin, and right now I feel like I don't know myself.

Even now, with a floor-to-ceiling mirror available, I can't bear to look at myself. I don't want to see what will look back at me: me, dressed in a dress I didn't choose and don't want, holding flowers I hate, a ring I don't want on my finger.

I should run.

The thought hits me like a ton of bricks, and I actually take a step backwards like I was punched. Ever since Mitch told me what I had to do, I've been following his directions, being the perfect girlfriend, fiancée, almost-wife. I dress the way he wants me to, act in a way that is pleasing to him. All the time I'm hiding the truth of who I really am and pretending to be another person.

Do I want to do any of this? No. Of course I don't, but I don't have a choice. He has me, as men say, by the balls.

But what if the only reason I couldn't see a way out was because I was afraid to make one? What if I knew the way out all along, but I was terrified to actually take steps to find it because I knew failing would be worse?

I push the thought of the agreement I signed out of my mind. Surely it wouldn't hold up in a court of law, right? Even though multiple lawyers worked on it, I have to believe it would get thrown out.

I signed it under duress.

"Get out," I whisper to myself.

My bouquet falls from my hand and hits the floor, but I don't stop to pick it up. I step around it, my heart beating out an erratic rhythm as I press myself up against the door. This is a huge Catholic church, one I've never been in before, and Mitch stashed me in this room like he knew I wouldn't have the guts to escape.

Surprise, Mitch. I'm out of here.

It shouldn't be shocking. I was trying to run away when I agreed to go with Dale to Florida. The whole purpose of the trip was for me to break things off when we got home and for my friends to have already moved me out of our place.

I was trying to escape then, only Mitch caught me. After Dale died... well, he didn't give me any choice but to marry him. And now I'm here, and it's time for me to run again.

My feet ache in my heels, and I kick them off. Immediately, I'm four inches shorter, and I reach around my back, straining as I try to find the zipper so I can slip out of this dress. As I fumble, my fingers brush a long column of buttons, and I freeze.

There's no zipper. Instead, there are around two hundred tiny buttons that had to be painstakingly done up while I stood there, unable to comprehend what was actually happening to me.

No way can I get out of the dress on time. I'll have to make a run for it while wearing it.

Back to the door and I lean up against it, pressing my made-up face as tightly against the wood as I can to hear what, if anything, is going on in the hall.

There's silence out there, and the only sound I hear is the thudding of my heart. Taking a deep breath, I step back. Grab the handle. Twist.

It's locked.

Panic flares in me, hot and fast, and I jerk the handle back and forth. Both hands now, and I lean back like my weight will be enough to pop the door open. It doesn't budge.

No. I have to get out.

I whirl around, my eyes flicking about the space as I search for another escape. No other doors, no hidden ways in and out, only—

There. Huge floor-to-ceiling windows that look like they open into a courtyard. I reach them at a run, then fumble open the latch.

The window swings wide under my touch, barely groaning as the hinges work. A breeze races past me, and I shiver, then gather up my train behind me and take a step into my freedom.

That's it. That's as far as I get.

One step, then a hand closes down on my arm.

TWO

HANNAH

"My goodness, were you really going to run through the cemetery in a three-thousand-dollar dress?" Aimee's slouched in the chair in front of me, pouting like a little kid. I picked her flowers up and put them in a vase of water so they didn't wilt before she marries my brother, but did she say thank you?

No, she did not, but I can deal. She's under a lot of stress, and you can tell, just by looking at her, that she's one small inconvenience away from a complete and total breakdown.

Somehow, I have to make sure she holds it together, not because I care about what her wedding photos look like, but because I need her to help me get what's mine.

"Is the thought of marrying Mitch really so repulsive that you'd rather run through a bunch of dead people?" She doesn't respond or even look at me, so I reach out with my toe and gently nudge her. "Earth to Aimee. Hello, Aimee. You better perk up for your nuptials or your future hubby is gonna be pissed."

That does it. Her head snaps up, and she stares at me. "Oh yeah? Would his feelings be hurt? Wouldn't want that."

"No, you wouldn't," I shoot back. "He's easier to deal with

when he's happy. I would know." I soften my words with a smile.

She doesn't respond.

Sighing, I walk back over to the window and look out. Honestly, did she really think she was going to make a break for it? This cemetery stretches on for what looks like miles, and a woman in a wedding dress would be a pretty obvious target, no matter how fast she thought she was going.

But that's Aimee for you. Or, rather, *Steph.*

She's great at impulse, at leaping before she looks, all of that. But she needs to learn to think things through, especially now.

"Are you going to stand up and try to stop the wedding?"

Is that... *hope* in her voice? She really hasn't learned anything yet, has she?

I turn around before answering. "Do you seriously think I'd go against Mitch and do something stupid like that?"

Her shoulders slump forward a bit. Anyone else and I might feel bad for her, but not Aimee. Not now, not ever.

"Honestly, I want you to marry my brother," I continue. She raises an eyebrow, and I lean closer to her. "I need your help with something. It's... important to me, okay? I helped you before, and now I need you to return the favor."

She's going to say something in return. Her mouth is opening, and anger flashes across her face, but before she can come up with a response, there's a knock on the door.

She freezes and seems to sink even further down into the chair. I roll my eyes and hurry to it. Instead of joining whoever knocked in the hall, I stand in the doorway so I can monitor Aimee and make sure she doesn't try to make another run for it.

"You're dressed. Good." Mitch eyeballs me, then glances past me into the room.

"Hello to you too. Oh, and you're welcome for hanging out with your bride-to-be. You're also welcome for me keeping her from pulling a runner, by the way. But no need to thank me. I'm happy to be of service."

He glares at me. "She wouldn't."

"She would, and she almost did."

"I have someone watching this door."

"Out the window, Einstein." His eyes flick past me again and land on the windows for a moment before he looks back at me. "Yeah, those windows. She must be so excited to marry you."

He ignores my barb, which is what he always does. It's darn near impossible to get under Mitch's skin. The man seems to wear an invisible coat of armor, and he lets insults bounce right off of him. Doesn't mean I'm going to stop trying.

And speaking of wearing things... I hate to admit it, but he looks great. The two of them together could feature in a top bridal magazine, which goes to show you that money really can buy whatever you want.

My dress is gorgeous too, I guess, although sage isn't really my color. It's strappy and shows off my body, which I like. No way am I going to hook up with any of the groomsmen Mitch has standing up there with him, but I wouldn't mind having a little fun at the reception.

"Ten minutes," he tells me, then raps his knuckles on the door like we're speaking in code. "Can you watch her for ten more minutes?"

"You bet." I wasn't joking when I told Aimee that Mitch is easier to deal with when he's happy, so I smile. "Don't you worry about a thing, okay? I've got things completely under control over here. I want you to focus on the amazing life the two of you have built together and how much you two love each other, and—"

"Stop it." He leans forward, his mouth right by my ear. "You two got off on the wrong foot, didn't you? Don't make me tell the police that you were going to kill her."

I don't respond.

"You're my sister, but you need to understand one thing, Hannah. If you hurt her or scare her or do anything to make her feel like she's not welcome or the most amazing woman in the world, I will make you suffer for the rest of your natural life."

"You'll kill me?" I scoff, hoping he won't realize how terrified I am.

"No. I won't kill you. What kind of monster do you think I am? But I will do everything in my power to make sure that you wish you were dead. You think me taking your inheritance was bad?"

I hate him.

Yes, he promised our parents he would transfer half of the money to my name after they died, but he didn't. And he swore up and down that he'd split the proceeds with me from the sale of their house, but did he? No. They trusted him but never thought I was reliable enough to handle my own money. And now look. I have nothing. He's given me *nothing*.

I'm seething now, but I can't do anything to shut him up. My hands clench into fists, and I grind my teeth together to keep from saying something stupid.

"Believe me when I tell you that you'd rather be dirt poor than deal with what I will put you through. It'll be your own personal hell, Hannah."

"Blood sticks together," I blurt out. "Remember? How many wives can you have die before the cops—"

"Do not mention her anywhere near my future wife."

I close my mouth and nod.

"And don't think for a moment that you have more dirt on me than I do on you. You don't want to play this game, sister."

With that, he turns and stalks off. No greeting Aimee, no telling me he still loves me even though he can be a jerk. He's here and then he's gone, and it feels like the temperature has dropped ten degrees.

I slam the door and whip around to look at Aimee. She's staring at the wall, her face completely expressionless. "That's who you're marrying," I tell her. "Do you hear me? That monster!"

Nothing.

"Look at me!" I rush to her and drop to my knees in front of her. She doesn't respond, doesn't adjust her gaze. She's looking past me, and I reach out and grab her chin, twisting her head so her eyes lock on to me. "You really think you can survive being married to him?"

Nothing. No response. She's not breathing any harder than she was a moment ago. Her cheeks aren't flushed. It's almost as if her body is here, but her mind is somewhere else.

A chill works its way up my spine at the thought.

"You listen to me," I tell her, and even though she doesn't react, doesn't respond, I keep talking so I can make my point. "Mitch isn't some rich savior sweeping in here on a white horse to protect you and love you for the rest of your life. He gets bored easily."

There. A twitch by her eye. She's still not focused on me, but she's listening, I can tell.

"And when he gets bored, people die. What do you think happened to his first wife?" I pause to give her a chance to respond, but she doesn't. "Being quiet? Being boring? Staying out of his way in the hopes that you'll outlive him? None of those things are going to help you. You want to know how I know?"

Did her breathing hitch? Just once, just a little.

I'm whispering now so she has to focus on me. "Because he told me how he killed her. I tried to save her, but I was too late. I promise you, Aimee, when he gets bored with you and wants to kill you, I won't be able to stop him. Unless you help me first."

THREE

JACKIE

A Month Later—Monday

Boone's Farm wine will always remind me of college. I fell in love with the cheap bottles when I was too poor to buy anything new. Since finding it and getting trashed that first night on the Strawberry Hill wine, it's been a favorite.

Even when I had more zeros in my bank account and could afford the top-shelf stuff, Boone's Farm had a special place in my heart. Then I lost all the money I had, and...

Here I am.

"To Mondays," I say, pouring two glasses of wine. I cap the bottle and put it back in the fridge, but if I'm being honest with myself, we'll probably pull it back out sooner rather than later. Putting it away after pouring a glass gives me the illusion of being perfectly in control, but it was a rough day at work with grumpy customers and corporate changing opening and closing procedures, and I don't mind having something to take the edge off.

The first sip of cool wine makes me sigh; the second makes

me sink into my sofa and turn on the TV. I lean forward and hand the other glass to my work friend, Katy.

"Cheers to a long day," she says, touching her glass against mine and then taking a sip. "Thanks for having me over."

"Of course." I drain part of my glass, then force myself to stop drinking. It's one thing to get sloppy drunk on my own, but it's another entirely to get wasted in front of someone. Katy and I have been friends since I started working at the grocery store with her a year ago, but this is only the third or fourth time we've hung out.

Besides, *in vino veritas*, right? And I'm not really keen on coming clean about my past.

"So tell me about this place." She gestures around the room with her glass. "It's cute, but it really doesn't seem your style."

"That's because it's not. I rent it fully furnished, so none of the furniture is mine."

She picks up a throw pillow that reads *Happy Wife, Happy Life*. "Not yours?"

I shake my head.

"That terrifying clown picture when you first walk into the house?"

"Definitely not mine. Have you not read *It*? I swear, when I come home late at night, I can see its eyes move as it watches me."

"Take it down." She lifts her glass to her lips and takes a sip. "You could put it in storage until you move, right?"

I shrug. "There's no basement, the closets are tiny, and the attic is full of boxed-up holiday decorations. Really, there's nowhere to put it, so why bother? I try to ignore it the best I can. Besides, if anyone were to break in, they'd probably see it, panic that I'm more dangerous than they are, and leave." In addition, I'm used to being in spaces I'm not allowed to decorate, but I don't tell her that.

"Only a freak would have a painting like that," she agrees.

"But isn't it weird, living in someone else's house and using their things?"

Again, I shrug. "It's better than having to buy everything to fill a place. You think you'd remember stuff like a can opener and toothpicks, but I know I'd forget. This way, I didn't have to do that."

"Well, I think it's weird." She drains her glass and sets it down on the coffee table with a thunk. Seeing hers empty, I finish my wine and grab both glasses before hurrying into the kitchen to refill them.

Once they're full, almost to the brim, I put the empty bottle in the recycling and take in the kitchen. On some level, Katy is right. It *is* a bit strange to live in someone else's house and to use their things. The only things I brought with me when I moved in were my clothes. Of course, the food is mine. I obviously have to shop for that, but nothing else in here really belongs to me.

Even the outside of the refrigerator is mostly bare. A few local restaurants give out magnets when you order from them, and I've stuck them to the fridge, but besides that, there's nothing.

No family photos. No artwork done by little kids. No wedding invitations. Heaving a sigh, I hurry back into the living room.

"Remind me again about your family," Katy says as she takes her wine glass from me. "Do they ever come visit you?"

"Nope." I take a sip. "I don't have any family."

"Your parents are dead?"

I nod. "And I'm an only child. I have friends, but that's it."

This time, she doesn't say anything, probably because there's nothing to say. Truth be told, I don't know how I'd handle the situation if the roles were reversed. It's obvious how pathetic I sound; how terrible and useless my life seems.

But really, this is great.

I've had more and lost it. The thing about having less is that you celebrate what you *do* have. When you get something small, like a bonus at work or some fresh flowers blooming in the planter outside, you rejoice in them. And as for dating? No thanks. I've seen how some men treat the women in their lives, how they control them and grind them down, and I have no interest in going through that.

This place, even though it probably looks like crap to Katy and anyone else driving by, is the best place I've ever lived. I'm happy. I'm in control.

And even though I might have had more before, nothing in the world could ever make me go back now.

FOUR

AIMEE

Saturday

Mitch links his fingers through mine and gives them a gentle squeeze, pulling me out of my thoughts of Dale and the trip to Florida and back to the pool in front of us.

The water is clear, bright, and sparkling. The sun overhead is just warm enough on my skin that I'm starting to sweat, and the Loro Piana bikini I have on fits like it was made for me.

And here I thought that the little black bikini I took to Florida was a revenge bikini. Yeah, no. That thing was from Quince, and while I looked really hot in it, what I have on now rivals any tiny scraps of fabric I've put on my body before.

"You almost ready for lunch?" Mitch's voice is low and thick, and it hits me he must have fallen asleep out here while I was daydreaming. I turn my head to the side to smile at him.

"You think it's ready?" I have to disengage my fingers from his to glance at my watch, and I'm surprised to see that it's past noon. It's easy to lose track of time when we've spent hours each day out here by the pool after our wedding.

After what happened in Florida, Mitch didn't want to go on

a honeymoon, so we've been staycationing at his house. For weeks. I told him it was excessive; he told me he couldn't bear to be away from me.

Truth be told, I think he wanted to keep an eye on me.

Our house. It feels insane to call it that, especially since I feel like a visitor here. And as much as I'd love some freedom to poke around, he hasn't let me out of his sight. I'm going crazy waiting for him to go back to work. According to him, since we didn't take an actual honeymoon, he needed to be home with me as long as possible, but that ends soon. Thank goodness.

"Yeah, it's ready." He points towards the house, and I shield my eyes from the sun with my hand, squinting so I can make out the chef standing on the back deck. He's not waving or calling to us—that would be too tacky—but somehow conveyed to Mitch that our food is ready.

"Great. Let's go." I groan a bit as I sit up, then grab my Kindle from where I put it down by my lounge chair. When he suggested we lie out by the pool, I'd been fully intending to get some reading done, but my mind kept wandering back to the Florida trip.

Back to how it felt when I drugged Hannah.

When Mitch told me he was on my side and would help me.

When Dale died.

It doesn't matter if I'm trying to sleep, watching TV, or reading a book, I keep seeing Dale go over the railing. I hear him scream, then I hear the way his scream was cut short.

I hear how his body sounded when he hit the ground, how his head thunked against the pavement.

And then I hear other people freaking out.

Throughout it all, the one question I keep coming back to is why? Why did Hannah decide to hurt him? What did he do that pissed her off so badly she was willing to kill him?

She made the decision to hurt Dale. I can't make it make

sense. And then, for her to warn me about Mitch before I walked down the aisle to him? And to have the gall to ask me for my help?

I don't know if I believe her that he killed his first wife, even though she was convincing. I keep going over it in my head, trying to see it from all sides, but I can't make it make sense.

It's very possible she lied to me to mess with me. I need to find my own proof. One way or another.

Mitch takes me by the hand, yanking me from my thoughts as he helps me to my feet. We walk to the house, leaving behind the pool, the cabana, the gazebo in the backyard. This place is a dream, much nicer a place than I ever thought I'd live in.

I guess that's what happens when you're a neurosurgeon, huh? You make the big bucks; you get to buy the big house. It doesn't seem to hurt when your parents were loaded and died, leaving you, one of their two children, a buttload of money.

And, yes, that's the technical term. *Buttload.* No, I don't know how much it is, but it's the only thing that makes sense, that could make it possible for anyone to own a place like this, although his mid-six-figure salary doesn't hurt. He calls our neighborhood "Doctors' Row". Our neighbor to the right is a cardiologist. There are a few anesthesiologists down the road, a pulmonologist, and an oncologist. I can't think of a neighborhood that's more prepared for a medical emergency.

Mitch hands me a bathing suit coverup before we walk into the house. The AC is on, and I'm grateful for the soft fabric on my skin keeping me from being chilled. We pass the kitchen, and while he doesn't look to see what's on the menu, I can't help but glance in. Instead of seeing our food though, my eyes fall on the chef.

I'd love to get him on his own so I can talk to him, but so far I haven't been able to. I really need Mitch to go back to work so I can poke around the house without him catching me.

"Have a seat," Mitch tells me as he pulls out a chair for me.

We're in the dining nook, which is where he usually prefers to eat unless there's company over. There's really no reason to eat in the formal dining room unless we have a dozen guests joining us. The room's huge and great for entertaining, but it can feel really lonely.

"Thanks." I sit and smile at him as he sits down across from me. A moment later, our chef swoops in and lifts the domes from our plates at the same time.

"Garlic-chili shrimp bowls with fresh avocado, grilled corn, tomatoes, pickled red onions, and cotija." He turns around and takes two glasses from the person behind him. "Prickly pear margaritas to keep you cool. A salted rim for you, sir." The fish-bowl margaritas look too large on this small table, but if Mitch thinks the same, he sure doesn't show it.

He smiles at the chef—Peter?—and then motions for him and the other staff to leave.

My stomach rumbles, and I grab my fork, about to spear a shrimp when Mitch speaks.

"Don't you want to say what you're thankful for today?"

My mind races. "I thought we did that at dinner."

"I think it would be a good idea to do it at every meal. Don't you want to be a grateful person?" He sits still, his hands in his lap, watching me.

I put my fork down and smile at him. "You're absolutely right." My mind races as I think about what he might want me to say to him. I've always been good at guessing what people want to hear, and I'm glad that my skill has transferred over to dealing with Mitch as well. "I'm thankful for spending a lazy morning with you by your pool. Tonight's going to be a crazy night, and it was really nice having some quiet one-on-one time with you. I mean, a party for me? That's so kind of you. I know this was a lot of work for you to put together with all the moving pieces."

He beams at me.

Nailed it.

"That's what I'm thankful for as well, Aimee. You know, it's not everyone who can find such a blessing in another person's company like that. So many people need... things." He lets out a soft sigh, like he can't believe other people would dare to want more than they have.

I fight to keep from looking around the room. There are huge floor-to-ceiling windows overlooking the pool and gazebo. The silverware we're about to use? Yeah, it's real silver. The plates? Some sort of china. I don't know much about really nice things, but this house is loaded with them, and it's laughable that Mitch doesn't see it.

"You're absolutely right," I say because I really don't know what else there is for me to add to this conversation. I'm starving and want to dive into my lunch as quickly as possible, not talk him through some kind of stupid existential crisis. Mitch has never wanted for anything in his life.

He finds what he wants.

He pursues it.

He takes it.

Like me.

"Well, shall we eat?" He picks up his fork and lets it balance on his finger for a moment before stabbing a shrimp. I watch, barely paying attention as he chews it and takes another bite. And another. "Aren't you hungry?" he asks, and I snap back to the present.

"Of course I am," I tell him. "This smells amazing." And it does. I'm sure it tastes amazing too, but I barely register the spice when I take my first bite. "I was thinking," I say, after I swallow, "that I'm ready to go back to work. I miss nursing. I miss my patients."

He doesn't look at me. "No."

"No?" My head jerks up, and I stare at him.

"Correct. No. You don't need to work, and you're not going

to. What, you want people thinking I can't afford for you to stay at home? Nursing is in your past. Our marriage is your future."

I stab a shrimp and shove it in my mouth, so I don't say something he's going to make me regret, but my mind is racing. Mitch thinks he's in control, and right now, he is. The problem is that he knows exactly how to get what he wants. If not with money, then with coercion.

Blackmail, some might say.

I feel backed into a corner, but others would say that I agreed to this, that I signed the contract even though I didn't have to. That I'm lucky. That Mitch is amazing, he's kind, he's thoughtful, he's a hard-working man. And yeah, a lot of those things are true, but that doesn't mean he's *good*.

It doesn't mean I want to stay married to him.

It certainly doesn't mean I trust him.

What it does mean is that I have to figure out some way to get away from him. I have to consider what Hannah said.

He works really, really hard. I'd never say that he doesn't deserve the amazing things he has in his life because of the time and effort he's put into his career. The people he surrounds himself with love him. His patients adore him. He's changed lives. *Saved* lives.

But even though he's all of these things, you can't say that he's just a man.

I'm worried he's also a murderer.

FIVE

HANNAH

You know what really pisses me off about my brother's house?

That it's his and not mine.

But that's all going to change.

Mitch has to die for me to get anywhere near the money my parents should have given me. I can wrap my mind around that. And you know what? He deserves it. Sure, he's a great surgeon who's saved the lives of a lot of people, but he's a terrible man.

Since he stole my inheritance and obviously has no desire to give it back, I'm going to have to take it.

The look of surprise on Aimee's face when she sees me walking towards her makes coming to help with the party setup worth it. No, I don't want to be at my brother's house three hours before he has a party, not when the staff he hired can handle it all on their own, but I want to talk to Aimee alone. I need her to see that I'm on her side.

"Aimee," I say, my voice carrying through the foyer. Cold marble floors look amazing, but they make sound carry like crazy. "You're not dressed yet? Don't you want to be in full hostess mode? Let me take over while you get changed."

She doesn't respond, but I didn't really expect her to, not

when my brother is standing right next to her. I see the way he takes a small step forward, like he wants to put himself between us. It's laughable, really, to think that he believes he needs to protect her.

He thinks he's the reason she survived our trip to Florida, but he's wrong. The only reason she's still here is because I changed my mind at the last second. I'm a woman. Changing my mind is my prerogative.

Besides, Dale had to die.

"Hannah, you didn't need to come here this early." Mitch walks forward and hugs me, his cologne thick in my throat. "I hired staff. I don't need you to be a party planner."

"Better than a party pooper," I say, throwing Aimee a wink over his shoulder. "But what kind of sister would I be if I didn't come support you, big brother?"

"A normal one." He lets go of me and takes a step back so he can appraise my outfit. Not that there's any way anyone, not even him, could find fault in it.

It's a custom black dress, perfectly designed, cut, and sewn to fit my body. I love the way it skims my curves and how it flares out a bit when I turn. Paired with impossibly high, strappy heels, I know I look a treat.

Small earrings don't compete with the pearl necklace I have on. Of course, it's the pearl necklace from Dale. I never take it off. What? You think I was going to get rid of it? Dale was a jerk, yes, but his taste in jewelry was impeccable.

I glance at Aimee, wondering if she's had time to consider what I told her. I'm hoping she'll be my ally, but I haven't had time to talk to her about it. Mitch has very strict rules about how she and I are allowed to interact.

"Well, you and I have never really been normal, have we?" I grin at him.

"Hannah," Mitch warns.

"I know, I know." I waft my hand between us to clear the

air. "We're at a party, and you want me on my best behavior. See, but I didn't sign anything that officially keeps me in line." It's a dare, and all three of us know it.

We're the only ones in the foyer, and there's no way Aimee doesn't hear every single word. If there were a butler or some other staff standing here, of course I'd keep quiet. I'm not stupid.

I like pushing his buttons.

"If you can't play nice, you'll have to leave." He grabs me by my elbow and spins me around so we're walking back towards the front door and away from Aimee. I know what he's trying to do. He's trying to contain our argument so she doesn't hear what we're saying.

Really, I get it. The life that Mitch has built could blow up were I to light the fuse. Aimee can't light it. She can't do anything, in fact. Her hands are tied. For a moment, I wonder if she wants me to burn it all down for her. Sure, her fancy life might be over, but she could leave here, hide in some Podunk town somewhere, lick her wounds.

She certainly wouldn't be sleeping in a king-size bed on organic cotton sheets that were probably woven by fairies, but at least she'd have her life back. To an extent.

She'd be Steph, not Aimee.

Would she lose her nursing license and degree? I don't know if her college would take back her diploma once they learned she wasn't even the twin accepted to their nursing program in the first place. I know it's insane, but I've spent a lot of hours thinking about what would happen to her and how I could facilitate the worst possible ending.

But that was before I figured out how useful she could be and how much danger she was in. Nobody should have to suffer through being married to Mitch, and I'll make sure Aimee is free of my brother... as long as she helps me.

"Listen, I'm playing nice," I tell him, and he stops perp-walking me to the door. "But remember that I'm still healing from what happened in Florida. You and Aimee moved on, but I really cared for Dale." Can I get a single tear to run down my cheek? I try to think about something sad, but Mitch barking out a laugh interrupts my train of thought.

"You didn't care about him. You only wanted to use him to get to Aimee."

"Fine." I cross my arms and lift my chin so he knows I mean business. "I didn't care about Dale. You're right. But you want to know who I did care about?"

"Let me guess. Your high school sweetheart?"

"That's right. I cared about Brian." I stab Mitch in the chest with a finger to drive my point home. "So you and Aimee can live here and play house and act like everything is hunky-dory, but I haven't healed from his death."

"Then see a shrink." Mitch grins at me, but there's nothing friendly in his smile. "I'll even foot the bill, but let me tell you something: Aimee is mine."

"I don't want her. In case you missed it, she didn't have anything to do with Brian's death, so hurting her wouldn't accomplish anything. You know the one thing I want."

"Shut. Up. My life is finally what I've always wanted. I will not allow you to screw it up. Do you understand me?"

Sweat breaks out on the back of my neck. If I really start sweating and have to change my dress, I'm going to be pissed. "You're crystal clear," I tell him.

"Good. If you don't think you can play by the rules, I'm sure I can have something drawn up to make sure you do." With that, he whips around and stalks off to talk to Aimee.

I stand perfectly still, watching the two of them. It's a good threat. Mitch knows how to throw his weight and his money around to get what he wants, and I know he'd love nothing more than to have me sign some stupid piece of paper saying that I'll stay in line and won't screw him over. He would love to make me promise to be the perfect sister and not ruin this perfect little life he's planned out.

Aimee certainly doesn't seem interested in rocking the boat. Besides almost running for it at the wedding, she seems to have settled into married bliss. That, or she's doing a great job pretending, but without talking to her, I can't tell. It infuriates me that I have no way of knowing what's really going on in her head. She could have run. Hid. Yeah, her life would be different. It would *feel* like it was over, but she'd still have a life.

Instead, she did the stupidest thing she ever could have possibly done. The more I think about it though, I realize she didn't really have a choice, not in that one final decision she made.

Going to that high school party and walking off with some guy who had been in prison? Stupid.

Stealing her sister's identity? So dumb.

Orchestrating a trip with Dale so her friends could move her out of his apartment and she could screw him over one more time? Insanity.

But there's one thing she did that is easily the worst thing she could have, even though she didn't have a choice in the matter. It's one decision she can't change. Can't hide from. I've thought about it, tried to see it from different angles, and considered her options, but she really screwed up this time.

She married my brother. She signed the agreement. And now, I have to help her.

SIX

AIMEE

The buzz of our guests reaches me on the second floor, but I'm in no mood to hurry downstairs. Instead, I pause in the hall bathroom and check my appearance one more time.

My hair? Perfect.

My makeup? Professional.

The dress I'm wearing costs as much as what I used to pay for rent for my small but overpriced apartment, but the fabric is a bit itchy, and I pluck at my waist to try to get a little breathing room.

"Aimee?"

I ignore the person calling for me. There's a finite number of rooms in the house, so even if they have to go room by room to find me, find me they will. And although I know I need to go downstairs and play the role of the perfect hostess, I'm not ready to do that yet.

I want to hide out up here a bit longer, not pretend I feel comfortable in a house full of Mitch's friends, work buddies, acquaintances. I've seen the guest list, and this place will be crawling with doctors, lawyers, businessmen. They're all rich, they're all powerful, and they all support my husband, which is why they're here to celebrate our marriage.

Even if I had the guts to tell one of them that this marriage is a sham, they wouldn't believe me. They're rich. They're in control. And, in contrast, I'm nothing. A complete nobody—someone who should be thankful I got to marry into this lifestyle, not someone who should be complaining.

I won't let myself cry.

Without looking away from my reflection, I turn the tap to cold and grab the hand towel. Once it's wet, I wring it out and place it on the back of my neck. I don't have a headache yet, but I'm sure to eventually, so I open the door under the sink, grab some Tylenol, and pop two.

There. I'm as prepared as I'm ever going to be. This night has been creeping up on me for two weeks now, and even though I really hoped I was going to get away with not having the party or at least not showing up to it, all my hopes were obviously misplaced.

"Aimee?" There are heavy footsteps out in the hall, and I freeze, then drop the sodden towel into the sink. I'll deal with it later. Tonight, maybe, if I can get away from the party early enough.

Or tomorrow. It doesn't matter. None of this matters.

Plastering a smile on my face, I turn and open the door. Click off the light. My stomach twists, and my pulse races, but anyone looking at me would think I was the epitome of calm. I look completely in control and not at all like my world is falling apart.

I don't glance to my right because I don't want to see the person who was calling me. Instead, I hurry down the curved staircase, my hand on the wide banister, the thick runner muffling the sound of my heels. The staircase ends in the foyer of our home, and I nod to the butler standing there, square my shoulders, and follow the sound of the voices.

With this many people over, there's no way to contain them to one room—or even one area of the house. They sprawl like cancer, clumps of people in the living room, the kitchen, the library. Like aggressive tumors, they've spread to the dining room and even out onto the back deck. I don't know everyone, don't even recognize half of them, but I still have to make nice.

It's all part of the agreement, and even though I regret every single day that I had to agree to the terms laid out for me, it's the one thing I know to be a constant in my life.

I have a question about what I'm going to be doing on the weekend? Check the agreement.

I worry about what my future will look like in a month? Six months? A year? The agreement has the answer.

Any fears I have, any worries—any excitement over my future—have all been addressed, thanks to the agreement. A lot of people get songs stuck in their head, but I have the agreement. I live and breathe it, the pressure of it weighing down on me, the knowledge that I have no way, yet, to get out from under it the only constant in my life.

A woman with long black hair stops me. Her hand flutters against my arm like she's afraid to touch me for too long, but she's standing directly in front of me, so there's no way that I can get around her.

Naomi? Naila? Natalie? Mitch told me her name at the beginning of the party, and I'd thought then that she looked familiar. Still, I don't know who she is, only that I feel like I've seen her before.

"Norma," she tells me, obviously reading my mind before giving me a smile. Well, as much of a smile as she can possibly give. There's enough Botox in her and all the other women here to kill an elephant, I'm sure of it. No doubt she was beautiful before having work done, but too much can change someone's face and almost make them unrecognizable. "We met before, but it's been a while, back when you first got back from Florida."

Her voice drops on *Florida*, like it's a curse she needs to be very careful when using.

"Norma, yes." I sound gracious even though I never would have been able to place her as a lawyer. With a name like *Norma,* you'd understandably expect her to be about eighty years old, but she's pushing forty and dresses like she's thirty. "I'm so glad you could make it tonight."

I'm actually not. I wish she and everyone else were gone, but she has no way of knowing that. Nor does she have any way of knowing that when I think of her, I think of the agreement, and I have to fight down the hate I feel.

Not that she knows exactly what kind of document we were signing. When you have a few lawyer friends Frankenstein it together, nobody really knows the full extent of what's on the pages.

Except, of course, the poor idiots who sign it.

"I wanted to tell you I'm going out on my own. Starting my own firm. Contract law is fascinating, of course, but I really want to be in the courtroom." Her eyes are locked on me. She oozes intensity.

I suddenly feel very small.

"That's great," I tell her, but I have no idea why she feels the need to tell me this. "I hope it goes really well for you. That you get plenty of clients."

"Me too." Her hand is still fluttering against my arm. She's too afraid to commit and really squeeze, brave enough that she won't back off and let me go. "I want to be the lawyer people turn to when they need help. When *women* need help."

I stare at her, my mouth dry. It suddenly feels like all the moisture in my body has been removed, and even though I know I need to say something, I can't get my tongue to work.

Is she... suggesting something? Offering something? My ears are pricked for the sound of anyone walking up behind me, but the only thing I hear is the whooshing of my heart.

Does she know that I'm trapped?

No. As much as I like to think that she does, that she's here to help me, that she's offering because she not only knows what I'm going through but wants to make sure I get the help I need, the *freedom* I need, I can't assume anything.

And what if I were to trust her and it all blew up in my face? No way do I want to admit it, but that could easily happen. Nobody in this house is loyal to me.

I wish I had a friend here. I want someone on my side, someone who would help me, someone I could confide in without worrying about who they would tell, but I'm alone.

Norma, as much as I'd like her to be on my side... she's not. She's a spy. She's testing me. That has to be what she's doing.

Goosebumps break out on my arms.

"You remind me of her, you know," she says, and I stiffen.

"Her?" I need this woman to spell it out even though I'm pretty sure I already know who she's talking about.

As if to make sure nobody will overhear us, she leans forward, her lips close to my ear. "Mitch's first wife."

Ice trickles down my spine. "How do I remind you of her?" I keep my voice just as low, hoping she'll confide in me.

"You're innocent. And you have no idea what you married."

Not *who* I married. *What* I married.

"Tell me more," I say, but as I do, a group of people walk closer to us. They're laughing and drinking, and we both automatically move away from each other.

"You can call me when you decide you need me," she says. She's speaking slowly, like she can tell I'm having a hard time focusing on what she's saying. "I'm here for you."

No. She's not.

I want to trust her. I want to believe that someone in this new fresh hell of my life is on my side, but how can I? I don't know her, but apparently she knew Mitch's first wife.

And that woman is now dead.

But before I can come up with a good way to extricate myself from the situation, to tell her I don't need her help, that it won't be necessary, to figure out a way to ensure she doesn't go behind my back and tell anyone that I'm plotting something, an arm loops around my waist.

It's Mitch.

He found me.

SEVEN

JACKIE

"I'm telling you, his death wasn't an accident," Katy says.

We're in the grocery store break room taking our last breaks before closing up for the night. Dinner, you might call it. My feet are killing me after pulling a double today, but she's full of energy and is pacing back and forth, her new sneakers eating up the floor before she dramatically turns around and heads back in the other direction.

"You say that about every death that makes the news," I tell her, then take a bite of my bologna sandwich. Delicious? No. Cheap? Yes, and I don't mind fueling myself with calories that aren't really tasty. That's all food is, when you think about it. Calories to ensure you can keep going during the day. Who cares if they come from steak or bologna?

Not me. Not anymore.

"Okay, you've got me there." She stops pacing and shoves her cell phone in front of my face. "But look at him, Jackie. He was really cute."

"Cute people matter more than not-cute people?" My voice is dry, and she rolls her eyes the way I thought she would.

"Oh, come on. Remember that death I followed last year for a while?"

I swallow, thinking, then nod. "You mean Henry James?"

"That's the one. I knew from the moment I saw the article online that he didn't die of natural causes, and I was right."

"If I remember correctly, the article you saw online had the headline *Henry James Didn't Die of Natural Causes*."

"You're yucking my yum."

"No, I really don't care about tragedies befalling random people. Besides, you know as well as I do that people get drunk and do stupid things."

She falls silent, and I feel my gut twist. "Hey, I'm sorry. I didn't mean to bring up your husband. It's just that alcohol and life don't really mix."

"No, you're fine. He shouldn't have been drinking and driving. He's seriously lucky he didn't take someone out with him. Just an old tree." She pauses, then perks right back up. "Seriously, though, Jackie, I have a funny feeling about this one."

"Okay, gimme." I pop the last bite of sandwich in my mouth, then grab the phone from her. She's right, even though I'm not going to admit it because she'd be a real pain in my butt if I did, but the guy is cute. *Was* cute. He looked like he lived at the gym, all muscles and a stupid smile. I flick my finger on the screen to scroll, but I don't have time to read the article before the break room door swings open.

Automatically, I drop my hand to the side and tuck the phone down where our boss, Gary, can't see it. Phones are allowed in the break room, but he's so anal about not seeing them out on the floor that it's second nature to hide them when he comes poking around.

His eyes flick to the movement of my hand, but he doesn't say anything about me using a phone. Instead, he turns to Katy. "Your break was over a minute ago."

She scoffs, then glances at her watch. "Your clock must be running fast. I have another minute and a half."

Gary taps his foot on the floor, and Katy rolls her eyes.

"Okay, yep. I'm coming. Gimme that," she whispers before taking the phone from me and tucking it in her pocket. "I'll see you at the registers."

I nod, then give Gary a smile as he follows Katy from the break room. The door closes behind them, and I glance at the time to make sure I'm not going to run over and get in trouble too.

Five minutes.

Stretching, I get up and throw my trash away, then pull my phone from my pocket. No messages. No missed calls. No emails.

I'll be honest, it was difficult at first to be alone, to know that other people were in constant contact with friends and family and that I didn't have anyone I could reach out to. Yeah, I have Katy, and she's great, but it's taken a long time for me to feel comfortable letting her into my life.

Even so, there are a lot of things she doesn't know about me. I keep them hidden, tucked away, little secrets that might not seem like a big deal if you knew one or two of them, but would change your perception of me if you knew all of them.

Oh, and they'd send me to jail.

But I try not to think about that.

EIGHT

HANNAH

This party is ridiculous, but at least I know what Mitch is up to. He's trying to show everyone here at home that he's got things under control, that he's nothing to fear, that he had nothing to do with Dale dying when we were in Florida.

Like throwing a huge party will be enough to prove he's innocent. I get it though, I really do. If I had a career to worry about, I'd want to make sure everyone knew I wasn't a threat as well.

But I don't care what any of these people think about me, and I highly doubt they're here to show Mitch that they support him. They're here to get a peek at the trio who survived the trip, the man who was there when his best friend died and then married the dead man's fiancée. They're morbid, full of questions and curiosity, and I hate them all.

All evening I've kept one eye on Aimee. She looks lost, perpetually confused. She floats from room to room, her head moving like it's on a swivel, and only stands still when someone stops her. I think she'd keep moving until she couldn't walk another step if people would stop interrupting her.

Right now, she's in the library by the grand piano. She holds a flute full of champagne, but she's had it so long it's stopped bubbling, and I'm sure it's grown warm. Not once have I seen her take a sip of alcohol. But she has poured a fair amount down the kitchen sink when she thought nobody was watching.

"Good for you," I mutter, then I drain the flute in my hand. That's what, four glasses of champagne? Five? I don't know, and it doesn't really matter. A tux-clad server appears, and I put the empty flute down on his tray before grabbing another and taking a sip.

Bubbles dance on my tongue, and I close my eyes for a moment to enjoy them, but, just as quickly, I open them back up. The last thing I want is for Aimee to disappear somewhere. She'd love nothing more than to find a little hidey-hole and tuck herself away from the party, but that's not part of the agreement.

I haven't seen the entire thing, of course. Just little bits and pieces of it when Mitch was getting it all organized. I'd love to read the thing in its entirety because then I'd know exactly what she got herself into and how I could help her get back out. Unfortunately, he has his copy hidden away somewhere, and digging around his house tonight in an effort to find it could end poorly for me if I were to get caught.

In his mind, as long as he kept things separate, nobody could piece it all together. He and Aimee are the only ones who know exactly what they signed, although I know a few pieces of it.

And judging by what I know, there's no way I'd have ever agreed to sign something like that. Then again, Aimee was desperate. I haven't asked her, but I'd wager she was as desperate as the night she stole her twin's identity.

Another sip.

Aimee has wandered out of the living room and down the hall. The lights are off in that part of the house, making it clear that Mitch doesn't want anyone going down there. She walks quickly, her head down a bit like she doesn't want to make eye contact with anyone who might stop her.

I down my champagne and put the empty glass on the coffee table. It would create a ring if left there, but I'm sure one of the servers will grab it before there's a possibility of condensation reaching the wood.

My eyes are on Aimee as I follow her. What in the world is she doing? Is she—?

Aimee has stopped in front of the door that leads to the basement. It's tricky to see her using only the glow from the party behind me as a light, but I watch as she grabs the knob and twists it hard from side to side before leaning back on it like she can brute-force it open. It's impressive, really, how she holds on to her champagne with one hand and doesn't spill a drop.

"He keeps it locked," I tell her.

She jumps and turns to me. "Hannah. What are you doing?"

"Just wondering why you'd willingly walk away from your party." I lean against the wall and watch her. "You can try all you want with that door, but even I don't know where the key is. It's a non-starter."

Her shoulders slump forward.

"It's okay." I step closer to her and pluck her flute from her hand so I can take a sip. Yep. Warm. Still... I only pause a moment before draining it. All this champagne is going straight to my head, but I can't seem to stop. "Mitch has a thing about basements, so I don't think there's anything down there anyway. Don't worry your pretty head about getting in there, and certainly don't let him catch you trying."

"Thanks." Her voice is flat.

"Anyway, we should get back before he clocks you as missing. Wonderful party, right? Aren't you having a blast meeting all of Mitch's friends?"

She blinks at me. "It's incredible."

"Great. Come on. Walk with me for a minute." I loop my arm through hers and pull her across the room to the double doors that lead out onto the back deck. They're thrown wide open, a lovely breeze flowing into the room. Yes, there are people outside, but most of them have had a lot to drink, and I know they won't pay us any mind. When I trip, she's steady enough on her feet to catch me.

How much champagne did I drink?

"Where are we going?" She tugs back, but I'm driven by champagne and frustration. Mitch never lets her out of his sight, and this has been my first real opportunity to talk to her on my own since the morning of the wedding.

Weekly brunch dates between the three of us don't count. No matter how close I came to being honest with her, no way could I have talked to her as candidly as I desired.

The agreement might hang directly over *her* head, but I'm in its shadow.

"Out. To talk."

On the deck, I pause, then kick off my heels. I wait to give Aimee time to do the same, but when she doesn't, I shrug and pull her into the yard. There's a gazebo here, all lit up with Christmas lights, and, surprisingly, it's empty. I lead her to it, then sit her down before standing in the doorway.

"Okay." She crosses her arms and stares at me. "You got me out here, Hannah. Why? What do you want from me?"

I stare at her. She seems remarkably calm after what I told her at the wedding.

"I thought it would be a good idea to check in on you."

She takes a deep breath before responding. "I couldn't be happier to be married to your brother."

"Liar." Standing in the door was the best way to prevent her from making a break for it, but I still go sit next to her. When our knees touch, she quickly angles hers away from me. "Did you think about what I said at your wedding?"

Aimee swallows hard. "I don't want to believe you."

"But you do?" My heart beats faster as I wait for her answer. Finally, she nods.

"I'm worried that you were telling the truth. He's..."

Aggressive.

Controlling.

"Demanding," she finally says.

Yeah, that too.

"I can help you, and you can help me, okay? I know, after our start in Florida, you probably don't want to trust me, but I'm on your side. I promise."

She doesn't look at me. Her jaw is tight, her eyes locked on the bench across from us.

"But, Aimee, listen—" My voice cuts off when I see who's watching us.

"But what?" When I don't immediately respond, she clears her throat. "Hannah?"

I jerk away from her grip, my eyes locked on the person walking up to the gazebo. Talking to Aimee was stupid. I knew it when I approached her, but I honestly thought I could get away with cornering her by herself for a few minutes. I needed to know what she thought about what I'd said and if she was willing to help me. I wanted to see if she was going to follow along with the agreement, if she was going to continue to play ball.

My signature might not be on the actual paperwork, but I know exactly what role I'm to play.

Mitch made it very, very clear that I'm not supposed to spend time with Aimee on my own, and judging from his expression, he's pissed that I disobeyed him.

NINE

AIMEE

Mitch slowly unzips the black dress I have on, his fingers tracing along my spine until the dress falls and puddles around my feet. Without speaking to him, I step out of it and stride slowly—confidently—to the bathroom.

I feel his eyes on me. They're greedy, just like his hands, but there are rules to our agreement, and I don't have to worry about him following me into the bathroom, or to bed.

Not tonight anyway.

In the shower, I turn the water on as hot as possible. My skin instantly reddens when I get under the spray, but I don't turn it down or step out. Instead, I squeeze shower gel onto my washcloth and scrub away the night.

Yes, I carried around a flute of champagne for most of the evening, but I didn't actually take a sip. I'm allowed to drink. Mitch has told me I can have alcohol as long as I don't get sloppy and stupid, but honestly, the thought of letting my guard down isn't appealing at all.

I'd rather abstain.

Hannah was drunk though. I think about the confidence oozing out of her as she pulled me outside so she could... what? Remind me that Mitch is dangerous? Yeah, I know that. The only benefit of my marriage to Mitch is that he's protecting me from her turning me in to the cops or hurting me. If she had her way... well, she's acting like my friend, isn't she, so maybe I'm wrong about her. But why in the world should I let her get close? She wants me to help her, and I want her help in return, but I'm scared. More than anything, I want out of here, but in order to do that, I need some freedom. Money, a car, and time to get away are all luxuries I don't have.

I shiver and turn under the hot spray, letting it hit me full in the face. Let's say that the showers in jail probably don't get this hot. We'll leave it at that.

After I've boiled and basted in the hot water, marinated in a plethora of shower gels and shampoos, and finally rubbed a delicious oil all over my skin, I pull on my soft flannel PJs and step out into my bedroom. As I suspected, Mitch is sitting in the chair by my bed.

Not *on* my bed. It's not in the agreement.

"Can we talk?" He's relaxed, his tie loosened, looking for all the world like a man who's about to have a wonderful conversation with the wife he loves.

But I know the truth, and so does he.

"Of course," I tell him, then perch on the edge of the bed as far away from him as I can get. "The party was amazing. Thanks so much for throwing it for me."

He inclines his head to me but doesn't respond. Probably because we both know that the party wasn't really for me. It was for him to parade me around, to show his friends and colleagues that not only was he innocent of any wrongdoing for what happened to Dale in Florida, but that he was stable. Settling down but not settling.

"You deserve all the best in this world." He spreads his hands like he's inviting me to look around the room and take in all that he gave me, but I don't have to. I've seen it all for weeks now.

The hardwood floors that are professionally cleaned so they seem to shine. The thick rug that probably costs more than most people pay for a car. And what about the four-poster bed, the closet full of expensive clothes, the French doors that open onto a huge balcony so I can overlook the gardens?

It's insane. It's everything I ever dreamed of having when I was a little girl. In fact, I don't know a single person who wouldn't want to live in a house like this. Of course, it all came with a price.

He's not finished speaking, and he leans forward, resting his elbows on his knees so he can get a better look at me. I feel like a bug under a microscope, but instead of wincing away from his stare, I smile back at him.

It's something new I'm trying because I think it'll throw him off. If nothing else, it should make him think that I'm happy here, even though I hate it more than anything. It might buy me some alone time to snoop. To escape.

"What did Hannah want to say to you?" he asks, and the question is so predictable that I have to fight to keep from laughing. "I saw you two outside, and you know you two—"

"I asked her about your first wife," I say, the words out of my mouth before I can stop them. "I want to know about her."

"You asked her *what*?" He stiffens. "What did she tell you?"

"Nothing. She said that it was a conversation for you and me to have. Mitch, I want to know about her. You never talk about her, and I can't help but think that's weird."

"My first wife is none of your business." He stares at me and waits for me to nod before continuing. "She is in the past. *My* past. Not yours. Do you understand?"

"I do, but she helped make you who you are." I reach out and take his hand. "I owe her for helping turn you into this amazing person."

"She's dead, Aimee. What she did or didn't do when she was still alive doesn't matter. Don't mention her again."

Okay. "Right, I'm sorry. I don't mean to step on toes. It's just—"

He yanks his hand from mine before I can finish my thought. "I don't want to talk about her, and I don't want you looking for information about her, do you understand?"

"I do."

"Good. Then let her rest in peace."

My face hurts from smiling at him, but it's the only way to hide how upsetting this conversation is. Why won't he talk about her?

Because he killed her.

I push that thought away. "Of course," I tell him. "That's all on me. I'm sorry, just..." I mime drinking, and he laughs, then relaxes. "I think I needed reassurance, that's all, but I know how much I matter to you. How much you care."

"We had a whirlwind romance," he says, and his voice grows soft.

I feel my stomach clench, not because I think he's going to try to go back on the agreement, but because of the way he proposed.

Not down on one knee with a ring like Dale did. Certainly not after reading me amazing poetry or telling me he loved me or while we were on vacation in some remote, tropical place.

But on the plane back home, Dale's body in the cargo hold. Mitch had held my hand, the two of us in the back row, joined only by Hannah. When I'd asked about the car they drove to Florida, he informed me he'd hired a driver to bring it back to Vermont for them.

I'd thought at first that we were so lucky to be flying home on a mostly empty flight so I didn't have to talk to anyone, but then he'd demanded a seat next to me, he'd held my hand in his, and he'd told me he wasn't going anywhere.

Growing up, I'd told myself repeatedly that I wouldn't be the type of person to be pushed around by a man. I never would have let one of them talk to me the way he does, do what he does.

So what happened?

I can tell you what happened.

I became Aimee.

And even though I thought she was dead and buried, if I'm going to find out what happened to Mitch's first wife, if I'm going to survive him, I need to push him closer to the edge. Make him make a mistake. I need to find proof of what he did.

In short: it's time to become Steph again.

TEN

AIMEE

Sunday

Mitch is swimming before breakfast when I make my way down the stairs.

It's a bit after six, and while I'm tired, I'm already fully dressed. My hair is perfect, and my makeup looks great. Mitch made it clear to me that he never wants to see me in the morning if I'm not dressed and ready to impress.

When I'd argued that sometimes it was nice to lounge around in pajamas and enjoy a slow start to the day, he'd happily reminded me of the agreement I'd signed and that I had to do what he asked.

For now at least.

I can't stop thinking about what Hannah told me—that Mitch killed his first wife. And then I think about how cagey he was after the party last night when I asked him about it. I don't like that he wouldn't tell me anything, even if it was to lie to me. He's smart, and I'm sure he can think on his feet, so the fact that he shut me down the way he did last night is upsetting.

But I'm not going to sit back and ignore the fact that he's a giant walking red flag.

In the downstairs hallway, I pause, but I don't hear him in the house. Mitch can't hide his presence. Even if I don't see him, I know when he's inside. It's as if the air itself moves, like him existing in these four walls causes a disturbance I can pick up on.

But he's still outside, and that's why I rush down the hall to the kitchen. Breakfast smells amazing, as always, but I'm not skulking around to try to get an early bite to eat. I want something, but it isn't muffins.

It's information.

"Hey, Peter," I say, doing my best to sound casual. "How're you doing this morning?"

He's standing with his back to me, and when he turns around, he's already made me a cup of coffee.

How does he do that?

"Good morning, ma'am. Did you sleep well?"

Ahh, I see what he did there—instead of answering my question, he turned it around for me to answer. "I did. Are you having a good morning?"

"Of course." The smile he gives me is brilliant. "Unfortunately, breakfast isn't quite ready, but if you give me a little bit longer, I'll be ready to serve you both."

"Oh, I'm not hungry yet," I tell him, then take a sip of my coffee. I keep my eyes locked on him as I do. "How long have you worked for Mitch?"

"Almost six years." His answer is instant, and while there isn't any bite to his words, it's clear he doesn't like this conversation. "Is there anything special you want to request for lunch or dinner? The menu is planned, but I'm sure Dr. Ellis would be willing for me to make some changes."

"No, everything you make is perfect. I was wondering, how well did you know Mitch's first wife?"

Peter pales. Even though he barely moves, I see tension grow in his body. His shoulders roll forward a bit, and he stares at me before forcing his face to relax. "Not very well."

"But you were here when they were still married," I say. "When she was still alive."

"That is true, but not everyone wants to speak to the staff like you seem to."

There's a dig there, I'm sure of it, but I ignore it. "Please don't think I'm being rude," I tell him, aiming for a different tactic. "I know you hear and see more than you let on, and I was wondering—"

"I have nothing to say about the prior Mrs. Ellis," he says. "But I can tell you that I'm very happy you're here, and I know Dr. Ellis is as well. Now, if there's nothing in the kitchen I can help you with, I need to get back to work." He tilts his head to the side, and my gaze follows the movement to see the pile of fruit he still has to cut.

"Of course," I tell him. "Don't let me be in the way. But if you ever want to talk, or ever remember anything—"

"Breakfast will be ready shortly, Mrs. Ellis. And I'll make sure to bring some coffee to top up your mug. Now, if you'll excuse me." He turns away from me, leaving me standing in the door.

"Okay. That was a strike," I mutter to myself as I turn away from the kitchen. I wander down the hall, one ear pricked for the sound of Mitch coming back into the house. There's nothing though, and I breathe out a sigh of relief as I walk into the library.

Of course Mitch has a huge set of leather-bound classics. They take up floor-to-ceiling shelving on the far wall. Other bookshelves boast souvenirs from travel, photos of family and friends, and...

Are those photo albums?

I'm barely able to keep from running as I hurry across the

room. Sure enough, I'm rewarded with pictures of a younger Mitch when I open the first book. There's him and Hannah as little kids, both in bathing suits, about to jump into a pool.

And there he is graduating high school. College. Medical school.

I flip faster now, skimming past photos of him out with friends. I finish the album and replace it before removing another and starting the process over, but as soon as I flip open the front cover, my heart drops.

Our wedding photos. They're gorgeous, sure, but not what I'm looking for. A quick flip through the album tells me that the entire thing is full of photos of the two of us. I put it back on the shelf and pull the first album down again.

This time, I spend more time looking at the photos, but in every one where there's a group of people, Mitch stands away from the women. His first wife—whoever she is—isn't in this album.

My heart sinks as I put the album back on the shelf. Surely he had photos taken of his first wedding, right? They have to be here... or *were* here, I guess. I can't wrap my mind around him getting rid of every photo of his wife, but it seems like that's exactly what happened.

I swallow hard and step back from the shelves. My head turns as if it's on a swivel as I look around the library. Surely there's a photo of her somewhere in this house. He wouldn't erase her from memory, would he?

Although, if what Hannah told me is true, then removing her photos from the house isn't the worst thing he's done. It doesn't come close to being the worst thing he's done. I feel like I'm choking, and I force myself to take a sip of my coffee to try to calm down.

So he doesn't have any photos of his first wife around the house. Big deal. Wouldn't most second wives be thrilled to know there wasn't the specter of the first missus watching over them?

Maybe, but that's not how I feel. It's not comforting, the fact that his first wife has been erased from existence in this house. It's terrifying. Even though I didn't find what I was looking for, I did come to realize one thing: I've got to get out of this house. Somehow, I have to figure out a way to escape, to save myself, before he does to me what he did to his first wife. Even if that means trusting Hannah.

That thought is on repeat as I leave the library. I don't know how I'm going to get out of here or even survive Mitch, but I have to—

Wait. What was that? Is someone at the front door?

ELEVEN
JACKIE

Sunday rolls around, and I actually have it off. Most of the employees at Fresh to Go live for their days off, but since I don't have anyone in my life to spend time with besides Katy, I don't mind the long hours when I'm asked to work doubles.

Besides that, I need the money. It's not like before when I had disposable income. Sure, the house I lived in wasn't ever going to be mine, and I knew I didn't belong there, but I made it work the best I could.

I kept telling myself that millions of other people had it worse than I did, that I could do anything difficult for a while, especially if it meant I had an out eventually. I made sure everything ran as smoothly as possible and kept everyone as happy as possible.

It wasn't always easy.

It's 10 a.m. before I bother rolling over and getting out of bed. I used to be an early riser, and it almost makes me laugh to remember the long hours I would put in at the gym even before having breakfast. It's crazy how different my life is now.

Some people would say that it's worse, but I think it's better. I'm in control. I'm the only person I have to answer to.

My front porch is only big enough for a single rocking chair, and I perch in it while sipping my coffee. Scrolling through the news when I first get up is probably a great way to get brain rot, but I want to know what's going on out there in the rest of the world.

The local news is boring, which is what happens when you live in a small town. After a moment, I pop over to a national news site. There's political drama, and an up-and-coming starlet showed her underwear at an awards show. With a sigh, I prepare to thumb off my phone when a headline catches my eye.

It's that guy on vacation who fell off a balcony while drunk and died. Katy had been all about it yesterday, but she loves true crime and always thinks there's more to a story than what's really going on. I adore her and I love her chipper attitude when we're working together, but I remind her over and over that not everything is a conspiracy.

Sometimes bad things happen, and there isn't a reason. There's no greater force in the universe conspiring for or against people.

Still, I click on the link. Take a sip of coffee. My eyes flick back and forth as I take in the news. A couples' retreat, according to the paper. Two couples, all friends, all out drinking and having a few laughs and then...

He fell and died.

Bad luck. I turn off my phone and set it down on my lap. As soon as I finish this cup of coffee, I'll make another and then go for a walk before it gets hot. Texas is steamy pretty much all year long, and while I don't love the heat, I wanted to live somewhere new.

Right as I drain my final sip of coffee, my phone rings. It's face down next to me, and I hesitate before answering it. It's probably work wanting me to change my schedule.

Three rings. Four. I grab it and answer.

Katy's breathless. "Remember that guy I told you about who was on vacation and fell to his death?"

"I read the article on him," I tell her. I stand, then let myself into my house. My screen door slams shut behind me, and I miss what she says at first. "Repeat that," I tell her. "What did you say?"

"I said that I just saw a new article about that guy, Dale. He was engaged to one of the women on the trip, right? But his fiancée, or ex-fiancée, I guess, recently married the guy's friend who went with them."

"That's so weird." I pour some coffee and stir in sugar. "Wasn't it two couples on a retreat together? What happened to the other girlfriend?"

"No idea, but that's not the wild part. Do you think they were cheating? Why would you get married that quickly after the guy you were going to marry dies?"

"They were probably cheating." I blow on my coffee and take a sip. "Do you think they killed him?"

"I do." She sounds confident, and I can't help but smile. "The police have cleared the three of them of all wrongdoing, but that seems like a load of crap to me. What if they took him down there to off him?"

"Where were they from? I didn't see it in the article."

"Vermont."

I swallow hard as I walk back outside to my porch. "So the armchair sleuth thinks it was a murder, but the police cleared it?"

"Yeah, but I did some digging," she says, and I laugh.

"Of course you did. You missed your true calling to be a detective."

"Right? Forget bagging groceries. Call me Sherlock. Anyway, the guy who didn't die—the one who just got married to the ex-fiancée? You'll never believe this."

"You're killing me with the suspense." I lower myself into

my rocking chair. On second thought, it's getting kinda toasty out here. I should have gotten up earlier if I was really going to take a walk. After coffee, I'll read inside with the fan on.

"Well, this isn't his first marriage. His first wife died. And his new wife? She was in a terrible accident as a teen. Her sister and another guy died. Tell me the two of them didn't conspire to murder Dale."

"Yeah, maybe. It is weird. I'm sure there will be a podcast about it eventually."

"Probably. And maybe I'll be the one to start it. I'm brainstorming titles already. Want to hear them?"

"Hit me."

"*Death in the Everglades*. Although, to be fair, they weren't really at the everglades, so that's not a great contender. *Florida Murder*. That one is clear and to the point."

I chuckle. "What about using their names in the title? Like the so-and-so story? Then people don't have to do a lot of googling to find your podcast. It pops right up." I take a sip of coffee.

"Genius. You're a genius. You're right! Do I use the dead guy's name? Dale? Oh! No, I'll use the happy couple's names because the entire thing is weird. How about *The Happy Couple: Mitch and Aimee Ellis*?"

I freeze. She keeps prattling on, but I'm not really listening to what she's saying. My heart beats faster, and I feel my coffee mug tip forward. A moment later, hot liquid splashes on my knee, but I don't pay it any attention.

"I'm sorry," I say, cutting her off. "Did you say Mitch Ellis?"

"Yeah, and you should look him up. He's insanely hot. And a doctor. But really, people who go through medical school have to be a bit insane. I'm not giving him a free pass because he's a hot doctor. If anything, it makes me even more convinced he's a murderer."

Mitch Ellis.

"I have to go." I'm rude and cut Katy off, but I don't care. "I'm sorry, but I drank too much coffee, and my stomach is—"

"Don't tell me, don't tell me. I hate hearing about people being sick. Call me later. Or I'll call you. I'm digging into this guy. One dead wife and then he marries someone else's fiancée? Please. Give me a break. No way is this guy good news."

I hang up on her. My hand shakes, and my coffee mug falls to the porch as I stand up. I hear it shatter, feel the last of the coffee splash on my feet, but I don't stop to clean it up.

In the house, I run to the bathroom. Dropping to my knees, I pull my hair back from my face. And then I vomit.

TWELVE

AIMEE

My skin prickles as I step back from the front window where I've been watching Mitch talk to Hannah. It's hard to make out every word they're saying thanks to the super-thick-and-very-insulated windows he had installed all throughout the house, but I can read their body language and pick out a few words here and there.

The heavy curtain I'm standing next to barely moves when I brush against it on my way across the living room. The last thing I want is for either of them to suspect that I heard something I wasn't supposed to, but I'm dying to know everything about my husband. I'm grateful he didn't catch me snooping in the library because no matter how often he tells me that this is my home, I know he wouldn't want me digging through his past. And from what Hannah said to him just now, she's worried for me.

She's trying to be there for me, but he doesn't want that to happen. He doesn't want us close, and I'm sure I know why. It's not because she wants to hurt me—the two of us got over that in Florida, or least she says she did. No, it's because she knows the truth of what he did, and he doesn't want her to tell me.

Which means I have to talk to her.

When the front door swings open, I'm curled up in a leather recliner by the fireplace. There's no fire lit, of course, since it's summer, but I can only imagine how cozy this place will be in the fall and winter.

Of course, that's assuming I'll still be here. I'm great at pretending that I like Mitch and our life together, but whenever I have a moment of quiet, I'm planning my exit.

"Aimee, there you are!" Mitch walks right up to me and lightly places his fingers under my chin to lift my face to his. The kiss he gives me is claiming, and I fight down revulsion at the feeling of his lips on mine. "Hannah's here and would love to spend the day with you since you don't have plans."

"I do have plans," I tell him, brandishing my Kindle. "I want to rest up after last night's amazing party and read."

"Mommy porn?" He clicks his tongue disparagingly at me and shakes his head.

"It's not—"

"I told you to use my library." Before I can stop him, he reaches out and plucks my Kindle from me before tucking it under his arm. "Twain, Shakespeare, Steinbeck. That's who I want you to be reading. Not... whatever this is."

"Monster smut," I tell him.

"My wife," he tells me, leaning close and hissing the words at me, "will not read *monster smut*. Do you understand me?"

I blink at him, and a chill steals over me. Is this the dark expression he wore before his wife died? Before he... killed her?

"Completely." I fold my hands in my lap and stare up at him. I'll find where he puts my Kindle and get it back. I'm locked in this prison cell, but I still have ways to rebel.

"Good. Now, Hannah is here to spend some time with you. She told me she misses you and wants to hang out more than you two do." He gestures for her to approach, and she does, a small smile already playing across her lips. "I don't know what the two of you will do, but—"

"Girl stuff," Hannah interrupts. She bumps Mitch out of the way with her hip and, to my surprise, he lets her.

Interesting.

"Well, I'll leave you to it," he says but lingers for a moment, staring at the two of us. I keep a smile plastered on my face until Hannah shoos him from the room, then turns to me, a smirk on her face.

"You excited to spend time with your new sister?" she asks, and I feel my stomach drop. "It's been so rude of Mitch to keep the two of us apart when I think both you and I know that we're going to be great friends."

"So excited," I tell her. And I am excited to actually get to talk to her about Mitch and his first wife, but I'm also terrified of what she might tell me and what she wants me to do. "What were you thinking?" I stand up while I speak, ignoring the fact that I'm at a clear disadvantage here. The irony of me losing my phone in Florida and not being able to call my friends and now not being allowed a phone even though we're in the same town isn't lost on me.

I miss my friends. I'd do anything to see them or chat with them. Tears burn my eyes, and I blink them away.

"Shopping. I figured you'd been held in this prison of a house for long enough. I'd go crazy only having Mitch to talk to and thought you might need a break." She whips out her phone and taps on the screen. "But before we go, we need to exchange numbers in case we get separated."

I pause. After a moment, I admit, "I don't have a phone."

Her head jerks up so she's looking at me. "No phone?"

"Nope." I pop the *P* like that will convince her that everything is fine. "I don't need one, and—"

"My brother took it, huh?" She clicks off her phone and

slides it back into her pocket. "He's controlling, in case you haven't noticed."

Duh.

"We didn't think I really needed one since I don't leave the house without him. And if he needs me, he can always call some of the staff. They're always around."

Hannah stares at me. "You can't seriously be that naïve, Aimee."

Shock makes my mouth drop open as I stare at her.

She sighs. "Come on—you're going to catch flies if you stand around like that. We're going shopping."

I pause. "I don't—"

"Whatever it is, I don't care. Get in the car."

Thirty minutes later, we pull up to a shady strip mall on the outskirts of town. The car ride over was blessedly quiet, but Hannah breaks the silence as soon as she parks.

"Stay here. I don't know what cameras this place might have, but Mitch is the type to go behind you and track what you were doing. It'll be better for both of us if he doesn't figure this one out."

Then, before I can stop her, she's out of the car. The door slams, and she strides confidently into the closest store. Two of the front windows are broken and have been covered with plywood. The sign above the store hangs crooked and has been tagged with spray paint so many times I can't make out what the place is called. I shift in my seat, then reach over and lock the doors.

Just in case.

Fifteen minutes pass before Hannah appears at the side of her car. She unlocks it and slides in before tossing a paper bag in my lap.

"Hide it," she tells me, and I hurriedly open it and slide my hand inside. "If he finds it, you tell him you found it on the ground. Or it fell from the sky. I don't care what you tell him, but if you point the finger at me, I swear to you, I'll break it off."

My fingers close around a phone, and I pull it out, my heart already beating faster.

"I bought a year-long plan for you, so it's ready to go. Also, I programmed my number in it so you can reach me. Don't be stupid about it. Don't set up your old social media accounts on it because Mitch will notice if there's any new activity on them, and he'll come for me after he comes for you." She pauses, thinking.

"Thank you—" I begin, but she cuts me off, one hand held right in my face.

"Nope. Don't thank me. Get it through your head, Aimee, and help me. I need your help with something. Think of this as an olive branch. Proof that you can trust me. But if you turn on me, you'll regret it. Don't get greedy." She starts the car and backs out of the space before flinging us into traffic.

My mind races as I think about what could be so important she was willing to risk everything to get it. "You want money, don't you?"

She nods, her jaw tight. "Yes. Mitch took it from me, and I can't get it. But you can."

My stomach rolls. "He'll kill me. If he really killed his wife like you said—"

"He did."

"Then there's nothing stopping him from hurting me as well." That's my big fear. I don't know why he wanted to marry me so badly, but I have no reason to think he'll want to keep me around, that he won't get tired of me, that he won't kill me.

"I'll keep you safe."

Yeah, right. "Only if I don't turn against you, right? Is that the deal?"

She slows to a stop at a red light then turns to look at me. "That's the deal. I'll protect you, but only if you help me. What do you think? You get free of Mitch, and I'll get the money he stole from me. Feel like teaming up again?"

Again. The last time we teamed up, someone died.

THIRTEEN

HANNAH

Aimee hasn't said a word about the phone I bought her. She sits next to me in my car, her head turned so she can look out the window, both of her hands clamped tightly around the phone.

It's not a really nice one. It's not new or super speedy or anything, but it'll do the trick. The camera is old, the memory is kinda busted, and since it's a used phone the guy probably got in a drug deal, there are scratches on the screen.

No way do I think anything he sells from under the counter is actually legal, but I don't care. As long as Mitch never knows about my visits here, I won't have to deal with any repercussions. Although, to be fair, her new phone is such crap that Mitch might not care that she has it.

Yeah, right. He'd come for me, I know he would, and even with the dirt I have on him, I don't know if I'd be able to get him to back off. The trophies tucked away in his room are enough to get him sent to prison indefinitely. He doesn't know how carefully I've planned for the possibility that he might turn on me, how prepared I am. Murder trophies that would send him to prison forever should be enough to keep him off my back, but he's not always rational, is he?

He'd be rational if he were dead, and that's the thought I cling to.

But there's one thing it has that makes buying the phone and giving it to Aimee worth the couple hundred cash I paid to buy it and set it up.

The tracking app.

Of course, the only places she's been since getting married are the house or out to eat with Mitch, but it's not like I can put a tracker on my brother's phone, can I? He's no idiot, and there's no way he'd ever let his phone out of his sight long enough for me to do that.

But he loves having Aimee nearby, so if I can keep an eye on her, then I can keep an eye on him. It won't help me when he's at work, but it will when they're out of the house together.

Excitement makes my palms sweaty, and I glance over at Aimee to make sure she's still not paying attention to me. When I'm sure she won't notice, I let go of the steering wheel and wipe my hands on my jeans.

We pull up to the mall, and I kill the engine and turn to Aimee. Slowly, like she isn't sure if she should, she meets my gaze.

"Please tell me you have a credit card," I say, and her face flushes. "Are you kidding me? He took your credit card?" Anger rips through me. Any man that controls a woman like this is problematic, even when the woman in question is one I have a strange history with.

"Okay, that's fine. I'll foot the bill. Just... we'll have to talk to him about getting you a credit card, okay?" I grin at her and see confusion written all over her face.

Of course, she adjusts her expression after a moment. It's clear she doesn't really want to let on how much she doesn't understand. I don't have to read her mind to know what she expected when I invited her out.

She thought I'd be mean. That I might bring up Florida. That we would get into a fight.

But that's what Aimee hasn't figured out yet. Even if I wanted to come for her, I couldn't. Not easily anyway. She's no longer the little girl in Florida who didn't have anyone on her side. As much as I hate to admit it, she has Mitch on her side now, and he's determined to keep her safe.

She's under his protection.

And while that might sound good at first, she has no idea how much of a danger my brother really is.

FOURTEEN

AIMEE

Do I trust Hannah not to go back on her word if I help her?

Gosh, I want to, but my first instinct is not to. But then I remember that she didn't hurt me in Florida. She saved me when Dale turned into a bigger threat and she realized the truth: I didn't kill Brian.

She's self-serving, but maybe that will work to my advantage. If nothing else, maybe I can get out of this marriage with her help. It's worth a shot. I have to be careful. Watch my back. Make sure a target doesn't suddenly appear on it.

This is the first time Mitch has left to run errands without me since we got back from Florida. I guess if you're counting staff, I'm not really alone, but the chef in the kitchen and the cleaning lady in the living room shouldn't bother me upstairs.

I dump the shopping bags on my bed and yank on a pair of new black leather leggings. Mitch will hate them, but they're similar to the ones I wore in high school, and they make me feel like... well, me. Even though the ones I wore in high school cost ten bucks and these cost ten times that.

Once they're on, I stalk out of my bedroom to Mitch's.

Not sharing a room was one concession he was willing to

make, and thank goodness for that because if I had to roll over and see his face every morning before I'd even had a chance to pee, I might snap and murder him right then and there.

And while that might be how this marriage of inconvenience ends up, I'm not going to prison yet.

And I'm not going to die.

I refuse to let this man kill me. Hannah's warning about his first wife ricochets around in my head. He was married before, but where are the photos of her? I sure didn't find any in Mitch's photo albums. Where's the art she picked out, the feminine touches I'm sure she left in his space?

If she died a natural death, those touches would still be here, right? If he lost her and grieved her, he'd want proof of her around.

But there's nothing in the main part of the house. No photos of her on the wall. Not a single thing that would make anyone believe there was another Mrs. Ellis before me, and that worries me.

Peter didn't even want to discuss her, and why is that? Is it because he's scared of Mitch? I've seen him get angry, and who's to say that he never lost control of that anger? Without knowing for sure what happened to her, I don't know how careful I have to be.

I have to know the truth, and worry and concern mingle in my mind as I stand outside Mitch's bedroom. There might be answers in here, but part of me is terrified about what those answers might be.

I take a shaky breath and snap on the light to his bedroom before pausing in the doorway to take it all in. The four-poster bed with dark-navy bedding is just what I expected, and of course he has a huge dresser that probably cost more than my college tuition. Without thinking about what I'm doing, I run my fingers along the edge.

No dust. Nothing out of place.

The bedside table has a book, an empty glass for water, ChapStick, and a sleeping mask to block out any light that the heavy-duty military grade curtains can't handle.

There's a huge plant in the corner of the room, but I ignore it. It's probably some almost-extinct species he bribed someone in a lab to grow for him. Instead of wandering around the rest of the room, I open the first drawer of his dresser.

Socks and underwear perfectly folded.

I slam it shut and work my way through the drawers, but there are only clothes, and they're all perfectly stacked. Instead of messing them up to feel better, which is kind of what I want to do, I close the drawers and eyeball the closet.

Before I can take a step over to it, though, something catches my eye.

Right above the first drawer, but under the top of the dresser, there's a small lip. I freeze, then lightly grab it. It pulls out with a whisper, and my heart starts beating faster as I see what's inside.

Money, mostly. Stacks of it, all bound with paper straps like they came directly from the bank. There are some coins too, resting on the velvet bottom of the drawer. My eyes flick across from side to side, taking in a really nice Rolex and a pair of huge diamond earrings.

But that's not what really catches my attention. There, in the back, tucked behind some of the cash, is a photograph. My fingers tremble as I pluck it from the back of the drawer.

It's of a woman, half-turned away from the camera. She has thick brunette hair down to her shoulders but has tucked it behind her ear. There's a giant diamond sparkling there, and my eyes flick down to the earrings I found in the drawer.

This has to be his first wife.

Excitement grows in me, and I flip the photo over, hoping to find something written on the back. Maybe her name, or the date, but there's nothing. Disappointed, I flip it back to get a better look at her.

She's beautiful. Why wouldn't he have anything around the house that might remind him of her?

Maybe because he doesn't want to be reminded of the woman he killed.

Our wedding portrait hangs in the dining room directly above the table. It's strange for me to sit there and eat and stare at my face knowing full well that the smile I'm wearing in the photo is fake.

But this smile? This woman? She seems happy.

I think about what Norma told me at the party. That I remind her of Mitch's first wife. Innocent. That neither one of us knew what we married.

But I did know who he was, and I said *I do* to him anyway. Still, it's not like I had a choice—not when I worked so hard to take over my twin's life after she died. I built this new life of mine from the ground up, and marrying him was the only way I could save it at the time. But now I have my feet under me, and now I'm ready to break free from him.

I shiver and place the photo back in the drawer, then carefully slide the drawer back into place. It feels like a small victory —to find anything that proves that another woman lived here before me, but I still have more questions than answers.

And there's no way Mitch will give them to me.

Sighing, I turn to his closet. It's got double doors, and the automatic light inside clicks on when I open them. My heart sinks when I take in what's behind the doors.

There are rows of clothes on both sides of the closet. The row on the right has expensive suits, all organized by color. I can easily imagine him standing here in the morning as he debates between charcoal, navy, or black.

Thrilling choices.

On the left hang his jeans, his button-downs, his ties. Shoes stand in a perfect line on the floor. Everything has a spot, and is in its spot, and even though I want to dig through his clothes to see if there's anything in here that might answer some of the questions I have, I'm afraid to mess anything up.

He's neater than I will ever be. Neater, even, than the real Aimee ever was. Regret fills me as I back up and close the closet doors.

Still, I must be missing something. There's no way that the only sign of the first wife is a single photo of her tucked in a drawer in his dresser. Even a psychopath would keep more than that, right? Peter already shot me down when I asked him about Mitch's first wife, but there's more staff here. I have to corner them and find out what they know because I'm not finding anything here.

Mitch's room is perfectly curated to look like the person he wants to be. Clean. Orderly. Always in control. But even those people have skeletons in the closet. You have to find them.

Sighing, I turn to the door to leave. I honestly thought Mitch would keep anything that reminded him of his first wife close to him. In his bedroom would be the perfect place for him to make sure he had an eye on them, but I'm either wrong or totally missing it.

Right as I reach for the light switch, I accidentally kick the baseboard.

And it moves.

FIFTEEN

HANNAH

My brother has never been quick to answer my calls, but today he picks up on the first ring.

"I dropped your little princess off at the house about an hour ago," I tell him. "She's all yours again."

"You were supposed to let me know immediately when she got home," he tells me, and I roll my eyes.

"Oh, please. I was busy and you're at work getting ready to hit the ground running tomorrow like a good little doctor. What, you think sweet little Aimee is going to get into trouble if you don't know exactly where she is at all times?"

Even though I can't see him, I know exactly what face he's making, and a thrill shoots through me. I love needling him, especially now that I've convinced him I'm necessary for his wife's mental health. He may not have wanted me to spend time with Aimee, but even more than that, he doesn't want her to suffer. I guess he does care about her in some way.

I didn't like that he told me I couldn't spend time with her, so I made it very, very clear to him why ostracizing her from anyone other than him was a bad idea. And you know what? He believed me.

"If you want to hang out with her, you need to follow my rules."

"And if you want her to be happy, you need to let her have friends. Or is that not your goal? Do you not care if she's happy?"

"What the hell is that supposed to mean?"

"Just that you seem to find wives disposable. How long were you married before your first one died?"

He hangs up on me.

SIXTEEN

AIMEE

I drop to my knees, my heart pounding.

Holding my breath makes me feel like my hands are steadier. Carefully, I work my nails along the edge of the baseboard, then tug it out. Each centimeter it pulls out gives me a bit more space to grip it, and I adjust my fingers, then give one final yank as I exhale.

The baseboard pops right out of the wall.

The piece of baseboard isn't long, only about six inches, but that's enough space for him to tuck something in there. I take a deep breath and stick my fingers in a few inches.

Nothing.

I have to reach deeper, but it's pitch-black in the hole and gives me the creeps.

"Get over yourself," I mutter, then shove my fingers inside. At first, there's nothing, then my fingers close on an envelope.

I can't help but grin as I pull it out. It's not sealed, but the flap has been tucked into the envelope. There has to be something important in here—something he didn't want anyone to find, something that might be the key to me getting out of here in one piece.

My fingers tremble as I pull the flap free and dump some papers out on my lap. There's a sliding sound, then a bangle slips free from the envelope and lands on my knee. I'm breathing hard and stop to listen to make sure he hasn't snuck home or one of his staff hasn't come up here to check on me. I don't know that they would, but there's always the chance they're hired not only to keep up the house but also to spy on me. Is that why Peter refused to talk to me? Is everyone in this house against me?

My heart beats faster at the thought, but I think I'm safe. There's no sound, no footsteps on the stairs. I glance around the room to verify that there aren't any cameras in here I need to be aware of, but there's nothing.

I pick up the bangle and turn it so I can look for any inscription but don't see one. It's pretty, simple, and thin. I can't tell if it's real gold, but whoever wore it had style. Since it doesn't offer any clues as to where it came from or who it belonged to, I slip it back in the envelope.

A bit more confident now, I turn my attention back to the papers in my lap. There are only a few, and I pick the first one up to examine it. It's a death certificate, and I feel my breath catch in my throat.

"Jo Ellis," I whisper, running my fingers down the paper. I've seen death certificates before, even held the one for my twin after our parents left it out on the kitchen table by accident, but this somehow has more gravity.

I've never met the woman this belongs to, but I feel like I know her. To be in this terrible situation and know that she went through it as well, it's like we're... not *sisters* exactly but in the same club. The smile on her face, the way her skin crinkled around her eyes—seeing her photo has made her feel human, made her feel real, made her feel like someone I can relate to.

She feels like *me*.

She was twenty-eight when she died. Tears spring to my

eyes. That's young. Too young. I wonder if she ever got to travel or if she really knew what love was like. I wonder about her friendships and if she kept her friends even when she was married.

How alike are we really?

I put her death certificate down and pick up the next piece of paper. It's Mitch and Jo's wedding certificate. My eyes flick to their wedding date.

She was only twenty-six when she married Mitch. Almost twenty-seven technically, which means... I grab her death certificate and skim it until I find the date she died.

They were only married a little over a year before her death.

The fear I felt before over being Mitch's wife and what that means for me hits me full force. It's like someone punches me in the chest, and I drop both pieces of paper and lean over, grabbing my stomach and squeezing.

This man is a monster. He came across as charming, if a little overbearing, at first, but the more I'm getting to know him, the more I'm learning there's something dark lurking below the surface. As if the agreement he made me sign wasn't bad enough, his first wife barely made it to their first anniversary before she died.

Before he killed her.

The thought is unbidden, but now that I've had it, I can't get it out of my mind. Hannah put it there, and she would love to know that she's in my head right now, but I can't quiet her voice. How did he do it?

Did he shoot her? He sure looked comfortable with a gun when we were in Florida, and I have a good feeling that wasn't the first time he's held one.

Or did he choke her? His hands are huge, and there's no doubt in my mind that he could easily choke the life out of someone if he was angry enough. I've only seen flashes of his anger, but they've been enough for me to know with certainty that I never want to have it fully directed at me.

There are so many ways to kill someone, and now that I've opened this Pandora's box and started wondering about what really happened to Jo, I can't stop thinking about it.

She's dead, he killed her, she's dead, he killed her, she'sdead-hekilledhershe'sdead—

"Enough," I say, my voice loud and firm in the silence of his bedroom. With my mind racing like this, ready to go off the rails, I'm sure to do something stupid. The last thing I need is to act strange around Mitch and clue him in to the fact that I suspect something about his past. This bracelet? It had to have been hers. This is his little cubby of trophies, and the thought that he's kept all of it to remind himself of what he did to his first wife is terrifying.

Calmer now, I grab the death certificate and look at it again, reading slower this time. After a minute, my eyes snag on two words.

Drug toxicity. He poisoned her. My heart beats faster when I think about what that probably was like for her and how scared she must have been.

Moving quickly, I stuff the death and marriage certificates back into the envelope, then grab the final piece of paper to put in it as well. The last thing I need is to keep falling down this rabbit hole and wondering what, exactly, I married.

Not who.

But before I can stuff the paper in the envelope, I realize what it is. A photo of an older couple with their arms around each other. Maybe there's a name on the back. I turn it over. But shock makes me drop it.

No names. No identifying information.

Just two locks of hair taped to the back.

SEVENTEEN

JACKIE

I'm in my car before lunch and before I've had a chance to think about what I'm going to do. My mouth is minty fresh after I brushed my teeth three times, but I can still taste the sourness of my vomit. I grab my water from the cupholder and take a huge swig.

Then another.

I feel feverish, but when I press my hand against my forehead, I'm sure I'm not sick. Not with a virus anyhow. Before I crank my car, I dial a number and drum my fingers on my steering wheel while I wait for him to answer.

"This is Gary," my boss says, his words clipped. Efficient.

"Gary, it's Jackie. I'm sorry to do this, but I need to take a week or two off work."

There's a pause, and while I know we didn't get disconnected, I still pull the phone away from my face to make sure. Satisfied, I press it up against my ear again and wait for him to respond.

"You're kidding, right? You're my best employee, Jackie." He lowers his voice. "Don't tell anyone I told you that, of course, but I don't know what I'd do without you around here.

Everyone else acts like this place is just a paycheck, but you really seem to care."

"I'm sorry, but I'm having a family emergency," I lie. "I'd rather not go."

"You don't have any family."

His response is immediate, and while it shouldn't, it hurts.

"It's an aunt," I tell him. "A lawyer called, and she's on hospice, but she wants me there because I'm the only other living relative and apparently there's a dog named Taco I'm going to have to take care of even though I'm allergic, but what do you do? It's family, and—"

He cuts off my rambling lie. "Fine. Go. When do you think you'll be back?"

I bite my lip. "It depends how long it takes until she dies."

Silence.

"That was insensitive of me. I'm sorry. You go, Jackie, and take all the time you need. Your job will be here for you when you get back."

"Thank you." My voice is tight, and I know I sound like I've been crying. "You're a good boss, Gary. I'll let you know how things progress and when it looks like I'll be able to make it home."

And then I hang up. My head is spinning as I back down the driveway and pull out onto the main road. No, my little rental doesn't look like much, but it's home, and it's the only place I've felt safe and like myself in years. Leaving it hurts, and I don't want to do it.

But if Mitch is up to his old games, then someone needs to stop him. And I'm the one person in the world who knows him better than anyone else. I spent a long time around him and in his house, sussing out his secrets.

And then I had to run.

My stomach is in knots as I press down on the gas. Flying would be faster and have me in Vermont tonight, but there are several reasons I don't like being in the air. Driving to Vermont is exhausting, but from what I saw online, Mitch and Aimee have already been married almost a month and a half.

Has he hurt her already? I'll sleep in my car at a rest stop and push to drive as quickly as I can. If all goes well, I'll be there this time tomorrow.

I have to hurry.

If I hurry, I can save her.

EIGHTEEN

AIMEE

Mitch left his phone on the kitchen counter when he popped out to his car to grab something. Today has been a fever dream as I try to figure out what to do about my new husband. No way can I trust him, but I have to make him think I'm on his side for as long as possible—at least until I can get away.

Was Hannah telling me the truth when she told me he killed his first wife? I'm afraid she was.

No matter what, I don't have time to worry about it right now.

I have to learn everything I can about him so I have the best opportunity at making it out of here in one piece. He's so secretive, so unwilling to let me in. I know that chances are good his phone is wiped clean of anything about Jo, just like the rest of the house, but I have to look. And truth be told, I'm curious. You know what they say about curiosity.

It ensures you learn the truth about the man you married.

I didn't get caught poking around in his bedroom or photo albums, and I have to hope I won't get caught poking through his phone.

I grab it and hurry from the kitchen into the huge walk-in pantry. If he catches me in here with his phone, he's going to be pissed, but I might buy enough time to look through it without him catching on.

A girl can hope anyway.

That all depends on whether I'm able to unlock it. I try his birthday, my heart sinking when the phone shakes and the screen clears. My birthday? Same result.

"This better not be it," I whisper, then type in our anniversary.

Nope.

One more shot. I'll give it one more shot, then I have to put it back. How many times can you try a password before the phone locks you out completely? I'm not entirely sure, but maybe five? Hopefully five.

The date of his wife's death.

There's a soft click, and the phone unlocks. Before I can let myself really mull over the implications of him using the date he killed his wife as his phone's PIN, I tap into his messages.

It's empty.

Emails? Empty.

Fine. What about his browser history?

Cleared.

My palms grow sweaty, and I open his photos, but I need a password to view them. My heart sinks when I type Jo's death date and the folder doesn't open.

What about Dale's?

Nope.

The door from the garage slams, and my head jerks up. As I rush to the kitchen, I press on the side button, locking the phone. I put it back on the counter without breaking my stride and hurry to meet him.

"Get what you needed from the car?" I ask. I'm already reaching out to help him with whatever it was he got when I see what's in his hands and my arm drops back by my side. "Is that...?"

"Hermès." The company's bright-orange paper bag is repulsive. I've never wanted anything like that, never thought I was the kind of woman to carry a designer handbag. I'm much more of a discount-store-purse gal, especially because I tend to be hard on purses and wear them out.

You don't wear out an Hermès. Even without ever wanting one, I know that.

"We have a party next weekend. An invite for an invite, so to speak. You can't be caught dead with the kind of purse you used to carry." He smiles at me and holds out the bag. "Take it, Aimee. I want to see what you think."

I carefully fix my face. "This is amazing, thank you." I lift the box out of the bag and pull the purse out. It's tucked inside a cloth bag, and I carefully hand that to Mitch so I can look at the purse he bought me. He's watching me intently, his lips slightly parted as I turn it over in my hands.

"Oh, wow, it's—"

"A gold Kelly with gold hardware."

"You know," I say, opening the purse and taking a peek inside, "there's a Walmart version of this. They call it the Walmès, and you really can't tell the difference between it and the real thing..." My voice trails off when I look up at him.

"Don't ever compare anything I give you to something from Walmart again," he tells me, each word clipped, and I'm nodding before he finishes speaking.

"Right," I say. "That was dumb. This is obviously so much nicer." The purse feels unnatural in my hands, but I force myself to smile at him. If he wants to spend a stupid amount of money on a purse, who am I to argue with him? I take a deep breath for courage before speaking again. "Did Jo like purses like this?"

"She had taste, so of course she di—how did you know her name?"

I freeze. "What?"

"Her name. How did you know her name was Jo? I've never told you."

"You did," I lie. "You were tired, and it was late, and—"

"No, I didn't." He uses one finger to lift my chin so I'm looking at him. "Have you been snooping?"

Ice runs down my spine. "No. I promise you—you told me her name."

It takes him a moment to respond, and the entire time he's staring at me. I take a deep breath and force myself to keep eye contact with him. I have to hope that even if he has an inkling of what I've been up to that he'll ignore it. He's dangerous, yes, but he's also head-over-heels in love with me. Or, at least, in love with the idea of me.

Either way, his obsession should keep me safe. For now.

When he does speak, his voice is low, his words dangerous. "Maybe I haven't made myself perfectly clear, but you are my wife now."

Oh, I know. No matter how much I wish it weren't true, this is my life. For now.

"I don't want you digging into my past. I don't want you mentioning Jo again. Furthermore, as my wife, you need to hold yourself to certain standards. They dropped when you were with Dale—we both know that."

Okay, ouch.

"You need to do better. While you were out with Hannah, I came home from work and went through your closet. I threw away all the purses you brought with you when you moved in with me."

Wait, what?

I guess I would have known that if I'd bothered putting my new clothes away, but they're still bagged up on my bed. Still, I open my mouth to interrupt, but he holds his hand up to keep me quiet and keeps talking.

"I don't want to be cruel to you, Aimee. And I certainly don't want you to think that I'm not on your side or that I don't care about you. I *do* care about you, and that's why I did what I did." His phone buzzes on the counter, but he's on a roll now and doesn't stop to look at it. "Tough love is a real thing, and I know it can be difficult to be on the receiving end of it, but believe me when I tell you that your life will be better for it in the long run."

I don't know what to say. There have only been a few times in my life that I've been speechless, but this is definitely one of them. The absolute gall of this man to act like he's doing what's best for me when it's clear he's only trying to make his life as easy as possible is infuriating.

Instead of screaming at him and throwing the stupid purse on the ground, I take a deep breath. "You threw out my purses?"

"You're welcome." He pauses, his eyes flicking down to my hands before landing on my face once again. "Let up your grip on the Hermès, darling. You're going to hurt the leather."

I don't care about the leather.

But telling him that will only result in the two of us getting into a row, so I do what he tells me to and relax my grip.

"Good girl. I know this has been an adjustment, but I've tried to give you some time to yourself, some time to understand that this really is the best option for you. You're still holding on to your old life, but that can change. It *will* change." His eyes flick to my leggings, and I see the way his jaw tightens, but he doesn't remark on them.

"I liked my old life."

"Your old life was a joke." He reaches out and lightly touches my cheek. The feeling of his fingers on my skin burns, and I fight to jerk away from him. "Listening to Dale talk, you were an idiot. A gorgeous idiot, sure, but not someone who really had a lot of brains. But that's not true, is it? You're not stupid, no matter what he said."

I can't speak. Dale thought I was an idiot? The thought that the man I loved, the man I wanted to marry, would think of me that way is a stab to the heart. Or is Mitch trying to hurt me? I stare at him as I try to think through the possibility that this is one way for him to manipulate me.

I'm lying to him. Who's to say he's not lying back?

"You needed a strong male figure in your life to take control. Dale wasn't that guy. He might have thought he was. But when you and I connected on the beach in Florida and you made it clear that you were as interested in me as I was in you, I knew I had to step in."

My stomach churns.

No way did I ever think that this was how my life was going to go. All I wanted was to get revenge on Dale for how he treated me, but Mitch is making it seem like I'm the reason for what happened. That it was me coming to him that caused him to decide to *take care of me.*

"I know this is a lot to take in." His phone vibrates again, and he grabs it from the counter and taps on the screen, a smile flirting with the edges of his mouth. "Good. They're on time. Leave that here, Aimee, and come to the living room. I have something important to attend to, but I got you a little treat. You'll love it, I'm sure." With that command, he strides out of the kitchen.

He doesn't look back. For a moment, I think about making a run for it. I have this stupid purse that I could probably sell for some cash. I have the phone Hannah gave me. But I'm not prepared.

I can't go to my friends, not when I know he'd look there first. I don't have connections outside of town.

With a sigh, I put the purse down on the counter.

"Aimee! Now!" His voice carries to me from the living

room. So, like the dutiful wife he thinks I am, I follow the path he took.

I have to make him think I'm on board. That I... love him.

And then I'm going to do to him what he did to his first wife.

NINETEEN

HANNAH

All afternoon I keep an eye on Aimee's dot. Each time I tell myself that I can go longer without looking to see where she is, I end up tapping the little tracker app so I can check up on her. It's not that I'm dying to know what she's doing—I want to use her to keep an eye on my brother. I have a plan for him; it's just not time yet to implement it.

I have no idea what she's doing. After buying her a phone and taking her shopping, I dropped her off at the house and sped away, not wanting to stick around in case Mitch somehow found the phone I gave her. Of course, Aimee told me she would hide it from him so he'd never know about it, and maybe that's what happened.

Maybe it's tucked into a shoe in her closet and she's out with Mitch right now. Surely nobody would be able to find a burner phone tucked in the toe of one of her boots.

"Come on!" I slam my hand down on the kitchen table. When I was buying her a phone, there was a small concern in the back of my mind that this plan might not work out the way I wanted it to, but I'd dismissed it out of hand.

And now it's back, rearing its ugly head in full force.

Of course she's not going to risk taking her phone with her when she and Mitch leave the house. I suddenly have a really good feeling the little dot representing her will never leave the confines of the property, which means I have to come up with another way to track him.

Okay. I made a mistake. Dropped the ball. But I can fix this, I'm sure of it.

I might not be as flush with cash as my brother, but I still have enough to get the tools and toys I need. There are pieces of jewelry with trackers in them. I have a good feeling that if I bought her something, told Mitch it was an olive branch, and gave it to her, that he would put his foot down and make sure she wore it.

Do I need to track her every movement? No, I guess I don't, but the working relationship we have is tentative. As much as I'd like to trust her, I can't—not completely. Not yet, and maybe not ever. Sure, I'm going to work with her, but uneasy alliances aren't my thing. I'm much more of a solo gal, and feel like covering all of my bases with her and hoping to keep an eye on my brother at the same time is a good move.

Sighing, I roll my shoulders back to release the tension in my neck. Ever since their over-the-top wedding, where I had to stand there in a custom dress and act like I was happy for the two of them, I've been tight and uncomfortable.

A good massage is what I need. Maybe a little wining, dining—

My phone buzzes, and I lunge for it. It's a picture message from Mitch, sans words, of a security company truck in his driveway.

The message is clear. He's installing more cameras or a better security system or *something* that will help him keep his precious wife safe. I scoff and send back a thumbs-up emoji, then I pause and think.

This could be beneficial.

My fingers fly across the screen as I respond.

I've been wanting to beef up the security here. Will you send them this way next?

It's a bit of a long shot. Mitch has always been the type of person to want to keep his finds to himself. I hold my breath, afraid even to breathe, but then he responds.

I can do that.

Good. I slowly exhale, but he isn't finished.

Always chasing what I have, huh?

Jerk.

I don't want to give him the satisfaction of knowing that I read that message, but I have to respond, or he might punish me by not sending the security company, so I drop a heart in the chat, then turn off my screen.

Okay. This is good. It isn't foolproof by any means, but I'm desperate, and desperate times call for desperate measures, so I'm willing to do whatever it takes to get the results I want.

Half an hour later, I'm fresh out of the shower. I've spritzed on some Firebird Snowdrift, fixed my hair and makeup, and put on a dress that not only clings to my curves, but enhances them. No way will any guy showing up on my porch think I lounge around the house looking like this, but that's the point.

When the doorbell rings, I take a deep breath, then hurry to the foyer and fling it open. My heart is hammering hard in my chest, and I feel more nervous than I do on a first date.

Probably because the best outcome from a first date is a

great lay, while the best outcome from this working the way I want it to is being able to see every single one of Aimee and Mitch's movements in the house. It's obvious why I want to keep an eye on my brother. And as for Aimee?

Someone like her, who's willing to take her dead twin's life, then work with me to kill her fiancé, she's not going to go down without a fight. As much as I wish I could guarantee we're on the same page, I have to be careful, and the best way to do that is to keep an eye on her.

As the door swings open, I plaster a smile on my face and lean on the doorframe before popping my hip out a bit. That's one thing a lot of men don't understand about women: when you're sexualized from the time you're a little girl, you learn how to use that sexuality. Good or bad, it's ingrained in us. I don't think about how I'm standing. I just know that the man on my porch will let his eyes roam over me.

He'll smile.

Even if he's got a girlfriend or is married, there are going to be thoughts going through his head that he can't control, and I fully intend to capitalize on them.

Gosh, I hope he's cute. I hope he's hot. I hope he hits the gym as much as I do and—

I've been playing it coy, looking down so he can get his fill of me before I make eye contact. I want him to be thinking about my body, then see my face and realize that I'm one hundred percent the total package.

My eyes drag up his body.

So far, so good.

He's in jeans that cling to his thighs. His shirt is tucked in, which makes him look a bit like a nerd, but it's probably company policy. His arms though? My eyes linger on the way his biceps strain against his shirt. He has a clipboard held in front of his chest, but judging by the rest of his body, I have a pretty good feeling his abs and pecs are going to be out of this world.

I'm congratulating myself on a job well done. I don't want additional security cameras around *here* and certainly don't have the cash to pay for them, but having this man on my porch and in my life is going to make the cost worth it.

That's what's running through my mind. Until I get to his face, that is. As soon as my eyes lock on that, I realize I might have really screwed up.

TWENTY

AIMEE

I've been oiled, kneaded, and massaged to the point where I feel more like a pile of putty than a human, but even my masseuse with the hands of a deity can't make me forget about the conversation Mitch and I had.

He thinks he owns me. He thinks he can control me and that there isn't anything I can do to stop him or gain my autonomy. And the worst part? The part that gives me a headache and makes me worry I might really be screwed?

I think he's right.

Mitch knows everything about me, and that means he's in control. Not only that, but the more I poke around, the more I believe Hannah. I think he's a murderer, and that means I'm in danger.

Sighing, I wipe my hand across my forehead to clear away the sweat that's beading there. To add insult to injury, there's a security team downstairs installing more cameras, more sensors, more ways for him to watch me, to keep an eye on me.

And there isn't anything I can do about it.

"How do you feel?" Mitch's voice drags me from my

thoughts. I'm currently wrapped in a fluffy white towel and sitting on the edge of my bed while I try to think things through. "Is your head on straight now?"

I nod. "Yes. Thank you, that was amazing."

"Good. They'll be here once a week to take care of you. I want to make sure you get the care you need and understand that this is where you belong." He sits down next to me, and my heart kicks it up a notch.

Lazily, like he doesn't have a care in the world, he drapes his arm around my shoulder. I stiffen but force myself to relax. If he can pick up on how uncomfortable I am with him touching me, I worry he'll guess that I found out the truth about his first wife.

"Tell me how it went with my sister earlier today." His tone is conversational, but it feels like there's a current of danger under his words. Dr. Mitch Ellis isn't used to being denied what he wants.

"She was really nice," I tell him. "We went to the mall and bought some new clothes." I shift, turning to look at him, but his arm stays firmly around my shoulders. "I meant to ask you and completely forgot when you gave me the Hermès, but is there any way I could get a credit card?"

He frowns, and I forge ahead.

"Hannah was nice enough to pay for everything for me, but I don't want her spending money out of her own pocket for the two of us to hang out. I know it's a lot to ask, but—"

"How much did she spend on you?"

I swallow. "Almost two grand."

He nods. His face is impassive. If I could get inside his head, I might be able to tell what he's thinking and better plan for how to respond. Right now, though, I have no clue what's going on upstairs.

"Two grand?" He pulls his phone from his pocket and taps on the screen. I watch as he opens Venmo and selects Hannah's name. "Glad you're feeling more comfortable here, Aimee, but next time you need to ask."

"Right." I dip my head like I'm chastised and then look up at him from under my lashes. "You're totally right, Mitch. I'm sorry."

He presses a kiss against my forehead before I can pull away from him. "Good to see you're not going to make things difficult," he murmurs.

I muster up my courage and speak before my brain has the chance to tell me to shut up. "Did she?"

Even though he doesn't move, I feel him stiffen. He had been relaxed, at least a little bit, but now he's stiffer, his muscles tight, like he's in fight or flight.

And someone like Mitch? He doesn't run.

"Who?"

"Your first wife." As I speak, I reach out and lightly rest my hand on his thigh. It's not high enough to invite anything, but it feels like something a wife would do if she weren't trying to start a fight. "I want to be better than her. I want—"

"I told you I don't want to talk about her, Aimee. When someone is out of my life, they're gone. Removed. Old friends I don't talk to? You'll never hear me mention their names. My dead wife? I don't want her ghost lingering in our marriage. Do you understand what I'm saying to you?"

"I do. I just—"

"Need to drop it." He pauses. "Why are you so interested in her anyway? She doesn't matter."

"She *did* matter. And I'm interested because you loved her," I tell him. "I don't even know what happened to her! She's the elephant in the room, and nobody will talk about her, not even—"

"Not even who?"

I shake my head, my mouth clamped tightly shut.

"Aimee, who did you ask?" When I don't respond, he stands up. "Hannah?"

"No."

His eyes search mine, then he shakes his head. "Which of the staff did you try to talk to about her?"

How did he know? A thin sheen of sweat breaks out on my skin. I no longer feel soft and protected in my towel—it clings to me, soaking up my sweat as I hold it against my body. I'm uncomfortable, but I don't dare move.

"Who. Did. You. Ask?"

"Peter," I whisper. "But he didn't tell me anything, Mitch, I promise you! He wouldn't answer a single question. He—"

What I'm saying falls on deaf ears. Mitch spins away from me and stalks to the bedroom door without another word. Before I can think through what's happening, he's through it, his footsteps loud as he pounds down the stairs.

I drop my head into my hands and groan. Adrenaline courses through me, making me feel jittery and uncomfortable. No way can I continue to sit here any longer, and I turn and dig through my new bags of clothes.

It takes me a minute to realize what's wrong. I bought five new pairs of black leggings, and except for the pair I had on before my massage, they're all gone. Rage rips through me as I pull everything out, digging deep into the bags for anything black, anything that would make me feel more... *me*.

But there's nothing. My hands shake as I yank on a pair of jeans and a dark-blue top and rush into the bathroom. There, I close the door and brace my hands on the counter as I look into the mirror. I could be a good girl, put on light eyeshadow and pink gloss. I could, once again, turn into Aimee.

Or I could be Steph.

My hand shakes as I add more mascara and a swipe of eyeliner. I want to smudge the eyeliner and do a smoky eye, but I pause.

Not yet. Not when he's close to the edge.

Instead of bright-red lipstick, I grab a nude that Aimee would have worn.

I'm using my dead twin as armor, at least for now.

Aimee's the armor, and I'm okay with that. But Steph is the weapon, and Mitch has no way of knowing that I've already decided I'm going to become her again.

TWENTY-ONE

HANNAH

Patrick Long sits across from me in my modest living room, a glass of whiskey in his hand, a wry smile on his face. Drinking on the job is usually frowned upon, but he assured me that it wasn't going to be a problem if he stayed and had a drink with me.

He told me he could easily make it seem like our meeting about additional cameras in and around my house took longer than possible. That nobody would question how long he was here as long as I signed on the dotted line. Then he grinned at me, showing me all his teeth, and told me it was going to be fine because he was the boss.

That gave me chills.

No way can I afford this. Not really, not when I'm faced with actually having to get a real job. The thought is disgusting, but it's one I have to consider. With dear old Mom and Dad's investments mostly in Mitch's name, I'm screwed.

And, sure, he bought me this house, but there's no comparison between the life I'm living and the one he has. It irks me— no, it *burns* me, makes me want to lash out at him and hurt him, but I can't very well do that when all of his money would go straight to Aimee if something were to happen to him, can I?

I have to make sure she thinks she really needs me and that she isn't going to turn on me, because if something happens to Mitch without her being all in on helping me, no doubt she'd take the money and run before his body even had a chance to cool.

That's what I would do anyway, but I made it clear that if she helps me, I'll help her.

Which brings me, of course, to Patrick.

Patrick Long, master of opening locked doors and a veritable ghost in the night. Our paths have crossed a few times since we casually dated in high school. Okay, fine. It was more than *casually*, especially on his end. He was more interested in me than I was in him, and claimed I broke his heart.

The fact that he was the one updating Mitch's security system isn't lost on me. This man has never held down an honest job in his life, and I doubt he woke up one morning and decided he was finished with his life of crime.

They tell you that crime doesn't pay, but Patrick is living proof it does. Not that he wears a lot of designer labels or does anything to show off the money he has in the bank. He's smarter than that, of course. You don't get to where he is without having some street smarts.

"So you're the one in charge of updating my brother's security system," I say and take a sip of my whiskey. It's Macallan 32, a bottle I nicked from Mitch. "That seems suspicious, if you ask me."

"Suspicious?" He grins at me. His teeth are perfectly straight and white. The man may have gotten veneers or may have won the genetic lottery, it's hard to say. Whatever the case, he looks like he walked off an Armani walkway. Minus, you know, the company-issued polo and clipboard on the sofa next to him.

"Pat—can I call you Pat?"

"Absolutely not. We're not teenagers anymore, *Hanners*." He bristles and takes another sip of his whiskey, but his eyes never leave my face.

"Well, *Patrick*, I'm sorry if I have a hard time believing that you're suddenly on the up and up. The last time I saw you—"

"I helped you get your hands on a gun. *Illegally*, I might add. How did that work out, by the way? Were you able to take care of whoever was bothering you? Because I saw the news, Hannah, and from what I saw, Dale didn't die of a gunshot wound."

I ignore him. "The last time I saw you—"

"You pushed him, didn't you?" He gives a little nod, like he's pleased with not only his ability to ferret out the truth, but also with me taking control of the situation. "Atta girl. I always knew there was more to you than meets the eye."

"Would you listen?" I slam my glass down on the coffee table between us, and he holds his hands up like he's surrendering. "You're the worst, you know that?"

"And yet you offered me such a lovely drink. Why do you think that is?"

"I didn't kill anyone, so let me set the record straight on that. In case you didn't notice, I'm not in jail. No arrest record."

"Me either, darling, but don't think for one moment that it's because I haven't killed anyone. I'm good enough that I've never been caught. Just like you." He grins at me, and my stomach flips.

Offering him a drink was stupid, and now I have to figure out how to handle him.

And Mitch, so I can get the money I deserve.

And Aimee, so I can keep it.

"Let me guess—you're working for a bogus security company because it allows you access to expensive homes where you can take your pick of what things you want to boost?"

"Boost? I'm not in the stolen car business. And you will obviously find this difficult to believe, but my company provides excellent service."

"Your company?"

"I started it."

Of course he did. "And after providing excellent service, you steal things."

He shrugs, a smile playing on the corners of his mouth.

"You're the one in charge of installing systems so you can make sure all the areas you need covered are covered. And this allows you to really scope out the place and see if it's worth your while. What if it's not?"

"Then my company provides the best security monitoring this side of the Mississippi. Frankly, I'm disappointed that you don't seem to understand that. Not everything in life is black and white."

"So you're Robin Hood," I ask.

"Not exactly. You think I'm stealing gold bars and distributing them at the soup kitchen?" He shakes his head, then looks around my living room. "You know, I can get you a really nice setup in here. No *boosting* necessary."

He doesn't think anything I have is nice enough to steal. I mean, he isn't wrong, but it pisses me off that he'd make a snap decision like this. I want more from life. I want the money I was promised.

"You're planning on stealing from my brother, aren't you?"

"I'm covering all of my bases, and he's one of the many high-net-worth clients I've reached out to recently." He drains his whiskey and sets his glass down next to mine. "Now, darling, if you're finished, why don't you show me your areas of concern, and I'll talk to you about how I can put your mind at ease."

My mind is not anywhere near at ease. In fact, it's been

racing since I figured out what he's really doing when he installs security systems. Part of me wants to loop him in on my plan, but the other part of me knows one very important fact about criminals: they only look out for themselves.

Still, there might be a way for me to get him on board. And although it'll involve me depending on him a little, if I keep him at arm's length, I can still make sure I come out on top.

"Hannah? You ready?" He slaps his palms against his thighs and moves to stand up, but freezes when I speak.

"How would you like to make more on one job than you normally make in a year?"

Slowly, like he doesn't have a care in the world, he sits back down. He reaches out, takes what's left of my whiskey, and drains it. Then he looks me right in the eyes and says the words I hoped he would.

"Tell me everything."

TWENTY-TWO

AIMEE

I pushed Mitch too hard earlier asking about his first wife, but I'm not the one who paid the price.

Peter is gone. I came downstairs for dinner only to see him walking out the front door. He never left before dinner was over, but as he walked through the door, a small woman in a white chef's coat brushed past him.

Fired. Mitch fired him, and it was because I tried to talk to him about Jo. My stomach twists when I think about the expression on his face, how we locked eyes for a moment, how sad he looked.

I'm the reason he lost his job.

We've just finished dinner—a steak for Mitch and a small salad for me so I can lose the last five pounds he thinks are so offensive—and he's stripping down for his shower. Downstairs, one of the cleaning staff should have finished picking up the kitchen. She'll let herself out the front door and go home until tomorrow morning.

But what will Peter do?

"I want you to join me," Mitch tells me, but I shake my

head. I know what day it is. I know I have duties I have to perform, but I also know I'm not going down without a fight.

Sure, it's in the agreement, but after the way this afternoon went, I want to feel like I have some semblance of control over my life, even if it's not real.

Mitch frowns. "You know what today is. You know—"

"I'm aware." I chirp the words to sound not only completely unbothered but also like I don't have any tricks up my sleeve. "Believe me, I haven't forgotten. But I'm not ready for a shower yet. I thought I'd hit the elliptical for half an hour or so."

His face relaxes. Even though he gets Botox regularly and doesn't have any frown lines, I've quickly learned how to tell when he's tense. But my lie works. Instead of trying to force me to do what he wants, he reaches out and lightly strokes my cheek.

"Good girl. I'm glad to hear that my suggestions haven't fallen on deaf ears. Only lose a few pounds, okay? Not too many. I don't want to be married to a skeleton." His hand drops to my side, and he gives me a squeeze.

It takes all my self-control not to either pull away from him or slap him in the face.

"I'll see you after my shower," he tells me. "Make sure to drink plenty of water with your workout."

"Of course." I close the bathroom door behind me and sigh with relief, then hurry to my room to change into workout clothes. It's not that I'm actually going to exercise right now, but the last thing I need is for him to realize I was lying to him.

After pulling on some shorts and a sports bra, I hurry downstairs. The staff, including the new chef, has left for the day, and the house feels subdued. It's almost like it's sleeping, like it's waiting for the next day to begin.

In the kitchen, I dig through the cupboards. I don't do the grocery shopping, and while I can offer ideas of what I want to see on the menu, all my suggestions for cookies and ice cream have fallen on deaf ears. After today, I need sugar.

No, chocolate. I need chocolate.

Thank goodness there are chocolate chips stashed in the back of the cupboard, and I open the bag. Before grabbing a handful, I hurry back to the stairs and listen for his shower.

Still going.

With a handful of chocolate chips in my mouth, I run to my bedroom. It's probably overkill, but I'll hide them in a box of tampons.

One more handful, then I brush my teeth twice, stash the chocolate, and start yanking out drawers. My bathroom is fully stocked with every type of makeup or beauty supply I might need, but that's not what I'm looking for.

A sleeping aid would be great. Something I could use to knock Mitch out would not only remove the pressure of the night but give me some time to myself where I could just... exist. Unfortunately, though, there isn't anything like that in any of the drawers.

I'm also missing laxatives. Not that he'd ever eat a brownie, even to save his life, but I like to think I'd be able to figure out some way to drug him with them. I did slip Hannah the roofie in Florida.

The memory of that makes me smile, and I stand, closing the top drawer with my hip. Sure, we're working together now, but I've never been so pleased with myself as when I managed to drug her. I want to trust her—I need to be able to—but I don't. Not yet, not even when she promised to help me.

Still...

If we're going to work together, there has to be some trust, right? I want my freedom. I want enough cash that I can set out on my own without having to worry if I'm going to afford the first and last month's rent of a new place. I'd like a car that's reliable but not flashy, and to change my name, if that's what it would take.

But do I really think she's going to let me walk away after we kill Mitch?

A laugh bursts out of me. Yeah, no, not if she has to throw me under the bus to protect herself. Hannah may want to team up with me, but she's only ever on one person's side—her own.

That thought drives me to my closet. I was lucky today that Mitch didn't come in here and poke around after I finally hung up my new clothes. If he'd found the phone I stashed in a boot, I can only imagine he'd have gone apoplectic. As sneaky of a hiding place as it seemed at the time, I need to figure out another one.

His water is still running, and I drop to my knees and pull the phone out. It's on silent, and I swipe my thumb across the screen to unlock it.

The only number programmed into it is Hannah's, but she's not who I want to talk to. I want to reach out to my friends. I miss them so badly it hurts, but I'm afraid to reach out.

What if they showed up? Mitch would be charming to them, I'm sure he would. But would he punish me?

Would he kill me?

With a sigh, I swipe my thumb across the screen again and tap Hannah's name to call her before I can stop myself. She answers on the first ring, and I wonder for a moment if she was sitting by the phone waiting for me to call.

But no, that would be crazy.

"Aimee. How are you?" Hannah sounds unconcerned, not like someone who asked me to help her kill her brother.

"I'm fine," I lie. "Mitch is in the shower, and I was thinking about what we talked about."

"You mean getting rid of him?"

Sweat trickles down my back, and I stand up and close the

bathroom door before turning on the shower so nobody can overhear me. "Yeah, that."

She exhales hard. "I hope you're not getting cold feet."

"No, nothing like that. I was looking for any information about Jo, and—"

"Why would you do that?"

I freeze, my mind racing. "Because I wanted to know something about the woman he killed. I wanted to know how much danger I'm in."

"A lot. More than you realize. Aimee, you trust me, right?"

"Of course I do."

Well, only a little, but only because I don't have any other choice, only because there isn't anyone else I can turn to right now.

"Good. Then listen to me. He killed her. Jo was amazing. She was such a good person, and he wiped her off the face of the earth."

"I thought—"

"What, that learning about her would make things click for you? That you could talk to Mitch and get him to confess?" Her laugh is humorless. "No, trust me, digging into his past isn't going to do you any good. Let her rest in peace, and you and I can get justice for her."

A thought hits me, but I don't voice it. "You're right," I tell her. "Sorry for bothering you."

"You're not a bother. Just be careful, okay? You and I are a good team; we have to stick together."

"Totally." I tell her goodbye and hang up, then tuck the phone deep into a drawer behind some socks.

She said she wants justice for Jo, but I know she really wants her money. If she wanted justice, she'd take any proof of Mitch being a murderer to the police. Wouldn't that be the better option? We could have him locked up, and then I'd give her her money before putting this town behind me.

There's no reason he has to die, not unless it comes to it. Not unless I have no other choice. Right now, I need to be careful. I'm walking a tightrope between the two of them, and I've already made him angry. I need freedom to dig into his past and into Jo. I need him to give me space, and I'm not going to get that by making him so mad he fires his staff.

Mitch is smart. He's not going to suddenly let me off my leash when I haven't given him a reason to do so, which means I won't have an opportunity to dig deeper into his secrets.

I have to give him a reason to do so.

If I can get him to trust me, even just a little bit, then I'll have more time and space to poke around the house and learn more about him. It'll be difficult because I've already started pushing his buttons with my clothes and questions, but there has to be something.

Some olive branch I can give him.

Something that will cause him to overlook the fact that he's angry with me.

Some way to—it hits me. Yeah, it'll upset Hannah, but I can smooth it over with her. I can explain that I had to throw her under the bus to get him to trust me. She's not completely irrational. And while she definitely won't like what I'm about to do, I feel like I have to hedge my bets. She thinks I'm all in on her plan and that I'm completely on her side, but that couldn't be further from the truth.

I'm not letting anyone in this family kill me.

It's risky, I know it is, but there's only one good way I can think of showing him exactly how trustworthy I am.

TWENTY-THREE

HANNAH

I'm in my pajamas when the doorbell rings once, twice, three times. It's immediately followed by someone banging their fist on the door, and I freeze, unsure of what to do.

Patrick left a while ago, and although I'd like to think he'd be on my side if something terrible were to happen, I have to remember that he's the kind of guy to only really worry about one person: himself.

"Hannah, I know you're in there!" Mitch's voice carries down the hall to where I'm standing at the base of the stairs, one hand on the railing, my foot actually on the first step. "Let me in right now or I'm going to break down the door!"

Crap.

My mind races as I try to think through what could have him so fired up. Mitch does a great job at making sure people think he's level-headed. He's Dr. Cool and Collected, at least around his patients and contemporaries. In person though? When you really get into the family drama? Yeah, he tends to let out his real feelings a bit more than he should.

Case in point, the fact he's about to break down my front door.

"Chill out, I'm coming!" I yell at him as I scurry down the hall to the door. Did he hear me? Maybe, but maybe not. He's still slamming his fist against the door. I have to hope he has the self-control to keep from slamming it into my face.

He must hear me unlock the door because he immediately falls silent. Slowly, as if I'm strong enough to slam the door in his face if he makes a wrong move, I open it, peeking through the crack. "You trying to get my neighbors to call the cops?"

He plants his hand on the door and shoves it open. My feet slide back as I lean against it to keep him outside, but I'm not strong enough. He's in my space now, and he whirls on me, his eyes wide, his hands clenched into fists. "What were you thinking?"

My mind races. I've done a lot of things he has every right to be upset about, but I don't know which one he knows. He's the one who sent Patrick over here this afternoon, so no way do I think he's mad at me about that.

Unless, of course, the scumbag double-crossed me, but he's smarter than that. The only person who could—

Aimee.

It's a risk, but it's one I'm going to have to take. "She told you about the phone, huh?"

There's one moment where I think I really screwed up, that Aimee didn't come clean with him about the phone at all and that I've played right into his hands, but the way his face darkens even more tells me I hit the nail on the head.

"Explain yourself. Now. Then tell me why I shouldn't do to you what we did to Dale."

Now is probably not the time to remind him that he, *technically*, didn't do anything to Dale. I was the brains *and* the brawn behind that operation, but I'm not saying anything. Not when he looks ready to rip my head off and punt it down the hall.

"Aimee's scared," I say, lifting my chin and daring to look him in the eyes.

"Scared? No, she's not. She has everything in her life handed to her on a silver platter. For the first time since she was born, someone is worshipping the ground she walks on. Scared? Try harder."

"I'm serious. You don't see it because you're so in love with her you can't see anything but how amazing she is." Thank goodness I'm not Pinocchio. "But she's lonely."

"Lonely. Right."

"I'm serious." He's still upset, but he looks like he's calmed down a little, and I'm grateful for that. "You're everything. You're great at your job, you're stupidly rich, you only have to snap your fingers and people bring you whatever you want, and she's left in the house without anyone to talk to. I bet you told your staff to leave her alone, didn't you?" He winces, and I know I'm right. "Can you imagine what that's like for her?"

I'm talking out of my butt right now, and I hate that Aimee has backed me into this corner. Did Mitch find the phone on his own? Or did she offer it up to him as some sort of olive branch? It doesn't matter right now, but I want to know if she's still on my side. Unless she has a really good reason for what she did, I'm leaning towards not relying on her. I have to be careful.

"She didn't tell me any of this."

He's still upset, but there are signs he's calming down. He's still braced against the door like he's trying to keep me from escaping, but his shoulders have relaxed a bit. His hands are no longer clenched into fists.

He has such a massive blind spot for his wife it's ridiculous, but it's that very blind spot that should get me out of this.

"You're her husband, not her best girlfriend. Of course she's not going to tell you every little problem. She wants you to be glad you married her. This is all new to her. She signed the agreement you wanted, she fell into a life that she's never dreamed of, and she needed human connection." I swallow hard, knowing this is my chance to really drive it home. "Did you look at the phone?"

There's an expression on his face that's there and gone in a breath.

"You didn't. Let me guess—you broke it and now are here to figure out what was going on?"

"I didn't break it."

Thank goodness. I have to hope that she'll be allowed to keep it. This is my one shot at keeping an eye on her if he ever allows her to leave the house. And at the rate I'm going, that might be something I can figure out how to make happen.

"My number is the only one programmed into it," I tell him. "She knows you don't want her talking to her friends right now, at least not until you two have settled into a good routine. No social media apps are on the phone." *She better not have downloaded any.* "It's a lifeline for her to reach out to me if she's alone in the house and scared or lonely. That's all it is."

He sighs and runs his hand through his hair. "You should have come to me before giving her something like that."

"Why? Because you would have let her have it, no questions asked?"

He glares at me. "Because she's my wife. I don't get left out of any decisions regarding her. Do you understand me?"

"Of course. And I'm glad you can understand I did what I did because I care about her. I care about you. I want the two of you to have a long, happy marriage, and the only way for that to happen is for both spouses to have an outside person to talk to. I want to be that person for her."

And... scene.

Mitch is still for a moment, letting everything I said sink in, then he gives me a stiff nod. "Fine. I'm going to let her keep the phone."

A flash of triumph shoots through me.

"But I'm not happy with you. You should have come to me instead of undermining the relationship I'm building with her."

"You're absolutely right, and I'm sorry. I promise you—it won't happen again. Anything I want to do with her or give her, I'll run by you first."

"You need to stay away for a while," he says, and my heart drops. "She has a phone, so you two can stay in touch, but I don't want to see you around the house for a few days. Give the two of us time to really find our routine and for her to open up to me."

I have to stop my mouth from dropping open.

"I need verbal confirmation that you understand, Hannah. You can call and text her, but don't come by."

"Of course." Now it's my turn to clench my hands into fists. "I'll stay out of the way until you deem it appropriate for me to come by."

"Good. I knew you'd understand." And with that, he opens the door and steps out into the night.

No apology. No *I'm sorry I acted like a maniac in front of your neighbors.* No thanking me for taking care of his wife.

Just him telling me I can talk to her, but I have to stay away from her.

Fine. That's fine. A few hours ago, the thought of being kicked out of his house and banned from the property would have been enough to drive me mad, but that doesn't matter now.

Because Patrick and I came to our own agreement.

And soon I'll be able to see everything that goes on inside their house.

TWENTY-FOUR

JACKIE

Monday

I haven't spoken to anyone from Mills Fort, Vermont, since I left in the middle of the night.

Nobody knows where I went. Nobody knows that I'm back. I pull my baseball cap down lower on my face and adjust my oversized sunglasses before getting out of my car. This motel is run-down, looks like it has roaches, and has become invisible to most people driving past it.

In short, it's perfect.

With a sigh, I lock my car doors and head to the front office. Knowing my luck, I'll recognize the person working the front desk, but the teen barely looks old enough to drive and checks me in without glancing away from their phone for more than ten seconds.

In my room, I sit on the edge of my bed and sigh, then dig my phone out of my purse. It's too early in the afternoon to drive by Mitch's house, so instead I DoorDash a pizza and hang out until it's delivered.

Four hours later, I pull on a black long-sleeved shirt and get back in my car. Vermont used to be home to me. I felt safe here.

And now I want to run right back to my little place in Texas.

Instead of angling my car towards the interstate, I turn into town, eschewing the main roads to take back ones. Twenty minutes later, I'm pulling into one of the nicest neighborhoods in town.

My skin feels tight, and my ears are pricked for any sound coming from Mitch's house. From the road, it's difficult to see all the way up the driveway, but I take my time, driving past it once before circling back and parking down the street.

It hits me that my car doesn't fit in here. Even the staff working in these homes have nicer vehicles than the old Corolla I'm driving. A woman taking her perfectly groomed Yorkshire terrier on a pre-bedtime stroll heads in my direction, her eyes lingering on my car longer than I would like.

Sweat beads on my forehead, and I drag my eyes away from her to look back at Mitch's house.

It doesn't look like he's moved. I can't imagine he would. I remember how he used to brag to everyone with ears that his house was the best in town, that he deserved it, that nobody else could ever have as nice a place as he did.

And you know what? He's right. It's two stories with a full attic and basement, but I never went into those spaces, and neither did he. While the inside of the house is gorgeous and looks like something out of a magazine, his landscaper deserves the real praise.

The driveway loops around a huge fountain, the flower beds closer to the house scream with color, and the grass is perfectly edged. A sidewalk leads to the left around the house to the backyard, where the huge deck was designed for entertaining and sunbathing. Past the deck is the pool, a sixty-foot-long behemoth with a hot tub.

Every house in the neighborhood is nice, but his—

My eyes snap to the woman walking the terrier. She's joined now by another Lycra-clad woman, this one walking some kind of doodle. The doodle is lunging at the end of its leash to get to something on the sidewalk, but the two women are too busy talking to pay it any attention.

And then the first one raises her arm and points at me.

I gas it, speeding past them as my heart thumps in my throat. Without turning to look at them as I drive by, I'm not sure if they're still watching me, but I'm terrified they are.

Back on the main road, I start driving across town to the motel, but then I stop. Yanking my steering wheel, I pull into a gas station and park in the back part of the lot. It's shadowy here, and the only creature who notices me is a small cat that flicks its tail at me before jumping a low wall.

My stomach is twisted. My heart pounds in my chest. Nausea washes over me, and I take deep breaths to try to calm down.

That's the closest I've been to Mitch in... how long? Would he recognize me after so long since he's seen me? It's a silly thought—of course he would. I lived to serve him, to cater to his every whim, no matter how ridiculous. But how much attention did he really pay to me?

Not much.

I'm out of my car without realizing I'm on the move. His neighborhood is right down the road, but instead of walking to it, I hurry into the one next to it. It's smaller, without any street-lights. I can get closer this way and hopefully avoid stares from the neighborhood watch.

There's a huge backyard behind the house, perfect for when he threw parties. His house stands out, looming over the back-yard. The lights are on, and the entire thing seems to glow. I can almost see into the upstairs landing, and I stand on my tiptoes to get a better look. He's in there somewhere, probably cozied up with her.

His new wife.

Maybe the greasy pizza for dinner wasn't the best idea. I press my hand to my mouth and take a deep breath to calm down. It's one thing to come to Vermont to see if Mitch is up to his old games, but what if he is? Am I going to approach him?

No. I can't do that.

But his new wife... Aimee? Is that her name? The picture I saw of her online looked so sweet. She can't possibly know what he's capable of.

Could I save her?

My palms are itchy, and I wipe them on my pants before cutting through someone's backyard. I can't get caught, but I want to get closer. I want to know.

There's a tall security fence that surrounds Mitch's back-yard, and I walk up to it, using an old stump of a downed tree as a stool so I can peer over the top. From here, I can't see anything clearly.

I have to get closer.

Thank goodness I work out a little. My breath is loud in my ears as I grip the top of the fence and slowly drop into the back-yard. Once my feet are both on the ground again, I freeze, my heart pounding in my ears.

If Mitch were to find me, would he call the police? The thought makes me chuckle.

No, not Mitch. He's the type of guy who wants to handle things himself. If he had any idea I was snooping around, I know he'd handle me himself.

I keep my head low as I hurry across the backyard. Every step risks the floodlights turning on and catching me in their beams, but I push on. Finally, I'm at the back deck. I take the stairs quickly, crouching lower, then press myself up against the house.

What am I doing?

Aimee's face appears in my mind.

Saving her. Saving Aimee.

I'd bet anything that Mitch killed Dale. And then for Aimee to turn right around and marry him that quickly? There's no way that was love. I really don't think they had a relationship.

Knowing Mitch the way I do, he planned it out. He scoped her out, stalked her, hunted her, whatever you want to call it. And then, when she was in his sights and didn't have any way of freeing herself, he snagged her for his own.

He's done it before.

Anger flares in me, hot and fast, but I push it down.

There's a small fake brick tucked in the real ones on the side of the house, and I run my fingers over it before gently sliding it out. Excitement grows in me when I dip my fingers inside the exposed hole and pull out a key.

I ran away from Vermont. I saved myself. Tried to forget what I'd seen.

But Mitch is the type of guy to leave a trail of bodies in his wake, and I'm not going to sit idly by while he adds Aimee's to the pile.

I can't. My conscious won't let me.

I heft the key as I slide the fake brick back into place. I'll make a copy and return this one as soon as I can. Then, right as I'm about to run back across the yard to my car, the outside lights turn on. There are loud voices, and I shrink into the shadows.

TWENTY-FIVE

JACKIE

Tuesday

Aimee's gorgeous.

I have no good reason to be shopping at the expensive grocery store down the road from her house, but I couldn't help myself. I need to make sure I'm right and that she's innocent in all of this. I need to know for sure that Mitch is the problem, and that's why I've been following her.

She makes her way through the fresh veggies, glancing at piles of avocados and displays of bananas but doesn't pick any up. Her basket hangs empty on her arm, and I'm confident I know the reason.

Mitch has a chef, and his chef does all the cooking. The way Aimee is wandering around, however, you'd think she loves being in the kitchen. She picks up a ripe peach and sniffs it, then puts it in her basket before beelining out of the fresh produce.

I duck behind the dried fruits before carefully following her as she strolls down the candy aisle. She plucks a candy bar from the shelf, then drops it into her basket. Now she's in a hurry, and I have to walk faster to keep up with her as she uses self-checkout. In the parking lot, she tosses her receipt in the trash, unwraps the candy, and puts the wrapper in the trash as well.

Then she's in her car.

I'm running now, terrified I'm going to lose her. When a little girl gets in my way, I dance around her, my eyes locked on Aimee's black Escalade. She should be easy to keep up with—the traffic at this time of morning is relatively light.

Sure enough, by the time I pull out onto the road behind her, I can still make out her vehicle. She stays on the main road before abruptly turning into the park.

"Where are you going?" I ask, then reach out and turn down my radio so I'm not distracted.

Aimee parks up front, near where the local moms park to take their kids to the playground. I pull in a few spaces away from her, then pop on a pair of sunglasses and get out of my car.

Aimee's easy to follow. She has on a teal athleisure set, and her brunette ponytail swings when she walks. I trail behind her, but when she picks up the pace, I realize I'm going to lose her.

Laughter and shrieking from the playground draw my attention for a moment. There's a group of little kids running around chasing each other, and I pause to watch them. I never had the chance to have children, no matter how badly I wanted them. The girl leading the pack has dirty blonde hair, like mine, and I feel my breath catch in my throat.

She's running hard, pumping her little arms and legs, but then she darts around the slide and the spell breaks. I snap back to the present and turn to look for Aimee.

The path is empty.

I swear louder than I mean to, and one young mother shoots me a dirty look. Rather than sticking around to apologize, I hurry away from the playground, my head turning left and right as I look for Aimee.

She has to be around here somewhere.

But she's not on the main path. It winds its way by a small creek, and while I'd normally slow down and enjoy the view, my heart races as I chase after her. I'm like a dog with a car, unsure of what I'll do if I actually catch the thing I'm chasing but determined to have the best possible shot at it.

Another turn, then another. I'm running now, heedless of the fact I have on jeans. Around another bend, then I see her.

She's bent over like she's catching her breath, but she must hear the way my sneakers slap on the path because she jerks upright and turns to face me, her eyes wide.

"Oh sorry," I say, stopping a few feet from her. "I didn't mean to scare you."

Her eyes flick down my body, taking in my outfit, but when she looks at me again, she smiles. "Strange outfit for a run."

"Yeah, well. I wasn't planning on breaking a sweat today." I run my hand through my hair, well aware of how short it is. I never wore it this short when I lived here, and I'm hoping nobody will recognize me.

"It's a good day for it." She moves off the path to give me space to pass her.

I'm not done talking to her. There has to be more. "Hey, your wedding set is gorgeous," I tell her, gesturing at her hand. She looks confused but holds her left hand up between the two of us. "That's quite a rock. He must be quite a man."

"He is." There's a frigid air about her now. She'd been friendly, smiling and relaxed, but now she stiffens. Her words are clipped, and she tightens her jaw.

"Did you help him pick it out? Because you have great taste."

"I didn't." She drops her hand to her side, angling it so I can't catch another glimpse of her rings. "I have to go. Have a good morning."

Then she takes off. If I'd thought she was making great time before, I hadn't seen anything. She practically flies away from me, even though she doesn't break into a run. In a moment, she's around the curve and I can't see her.

I scared her.

There's a bench by the path, and I walk over to it and drop down into it. My goal in talking to her hadn't been to scare her, I swear. I just...

What?

With a sigh, I rest my elbows on my knees. I don't want to admit why I followed her here and why I was running after her, but the truth is obvious.

I wanted to talk to her.

I wanted to get to know her.

I wanted to see if she knows her husband is a murderer.

I've been watching long enough—I have to get into that house.

TWENTY-SIX

AIMEE

The ladder rung under my foot creaks, and I freeze.

I count to ten. Exhale slowly. If someone heard me, they'd come running, but nobody's calling my name, nobody's trying to stop me.

Nobody's asking me why I'm going into the attic.

It's been a couple of days since I went to Mitch, as contrite as possible, to tell him about the phone Hannah had bought me. I had a good feeling that he was going to be angry, but the amount of rage that rolled off him wasn't something I'd expected.

I didn't tell him about the phone to screw her over. It was insurance for me: to make him think I'm on his side after pushing so many of his buttons and to hopefully make him turn a blind eye to me going through his things. All of the cameras he installed have had me on my best behavior, and I've been too afraid to poke through the house until today. It's a risk, but it's one I have to take. Coming clean with him was supposed to make me feel like I had some control, but even so, I've been terrified.

Are the staff watching me? I fear they are, and that's why

I've been on my best behavior since the weekend. The last thing I want to do is make him angry at me. Truthfully, though, I never would have guessed how angry he'd be. All's well that ends well, though, because they apparently worked things out, and he came back a lot calmer than he was when he left.

He was in such a good mood, in fact, that he gave me the phone back and told me I was free to text and call her—but only her—whenever I wanted. The caveat? That he was free to check my calls, texts, and internet history whenever *he* wanted. Knowing that, I have to be careful if I look anything up. I know I can use a private browser or delete my history, but I don't put anything past him. Mitch didn't just give me the phone; he also gave me permission to leave the house—as long as I only go to pre-approved locations, that is. I was confused but was too nervous to ask him exactly what happened when they chatted.

All I know is that she's not dead, he's not here, and I'm alone.

The new chef is at the store picking up ingredients for dinner. I'd try to talk to her, but I'm afraid to get her fired.

The cleaning crew is here, dusting, mopping, and polishing the place until it shines. They studiously avoid making eye contact with me when we're in the same room, but when I turn around, I know they're watching me. I feel their eyes on me, and I'm careful not to step a toe out of line.

And Mitch? He's at work. This is the best time for me to snoop without getting caught... as long as the staff isn't watching me, that is.

I climb a few more rungs of the ladder, then pause and tap my back pocket to make sure I have my phone. Not that I'm expecting calls or texts, but I might need the flashlight in the attic.

Immediately, it beeps, and I freeze.

It's Hannah. It has to be Hannah. Mitch has my number,

but he texted me an hour ago telling me he was heading in for a difficult case.

I hesitate, trying to decide whether I even want to pick it up. Knowing it's my sister-in-law, I'm inclined to ignore it, but curiosity gets the better of me.

Doing a little exploring?

I'm so surprised I almost drop my phone, but I manage to keep my grip on it at the last second.

I'm assuming you're poking around. That's what I would do if I were in your shoes and my new hubby was at work.

Relief rushes through me. Okay, that makes a lot more sense. She doesn't *know* that I'm getting into the attic; she only assumes I am because she'd also be looking for any dirt on her husband.

Just taking it easy actually.

No reason to really get into a conversation with her. I keep it short and sweet and then shove my phone back into my pocket before climbing another rung. At least it doesn't seem like she's angry with me for telling Mitch about the phone she gave me.

My phone beeps again.

Well, if you get nosy and dig up dirt on Mitch, let me know.

I close my eyes and take a deep breath before typing out my response.

Not today :)

This time, after I send the text, I turn my phone on silent and shove it back into my pocket.

Just a few more rungs and I'm in the attic. Carefully, I stand, then run my hands over the ridge beam in front of me. My fingers slide across the hard plastic of the switch cover, and I grin as I find the light switch and turn it on.

Man, this place is *clean*. I shouldn't have expected anything different, I guess, but I'm still surprised. And it's huge. Empty space stretches out in all directions, and I pause for a moment to take it all in. To my right, there's furniture covered with sheets, but to my left are boxes that are taped up. I head to the left, ignoring a few empty baskets on the floor as well as a table lamp.

I'm not entirely sure what I'm looking for, but I'll know it when I see it. A diary? A journal? Something that tells me Jo was here, or something that details her life and marriage with Mitch.

I want to know if things with Mitch got bad long before he killed her, or if there are warning signs I should look out for. Hannah hasn't told me exactly when she wants to kill Mitch, and I refuse to be a sitting duck.

I drop to my knees by a box and rip off the tape. The sound is loud in the silence of the attic, and I glance at the hole in the floor where I climbed up. The ladder is extended to the floor in the hall right outside my bedroom, but the cleaning crew finished on the second floor.

I should be fine, at least for a little while.

The tape I crumple into a ball and stuff into my pocket before opening the flaps of the box. My heart picks up the pace as I lean forward to see what's inside. It's—

"Dishes?" I frown and run my fingers along the edge of the plate in question. I may not know much about nice china, but I have a feeling this stuff came with a hefty price tag. Maybe Mitch got tired of using it—it is a bit floral for his taste—or maybe—

"Maybe it was their wedding china and he boxed it up after he killed her." I frown in disgust and close the flaps before turning to another box. Surely there's something up here of Jo's, something personal that will prove to me not only that she existed but give me a clue of what's to come.

The tape rips off easily, and I throw it to the side before opening the flaps. My movements are jerky and uncoordinated because I'm excited to know what's in it, but I'm also terrified of getting caught.

What's inside makes me freeze.

Baby clothes, all with the tags still on them. I swallow hard as I think through the implications.

Did Jo get pregnant and lose the baby? Did she want a baby and Mitch didn't? Or is it possible that he wanted a baby and she knew better than to have one with a psychopath? I can imagine her sneaking away to a doctor to get a birth control subscription, utterly terrified of what would happen to her and her child if Mitch became a dad.

Tears spring to my eyes, and I wipe them away.

I wish she were still alive. I have so many things I want to ask her, but the only way to get answers is to keep snooping. Rocking back on my heels, I stare at the pile of boxes in front of me. It's daunting, and I feel myself getting frozen with inaction.

I could spend hours up here.

Days.

There has to be a better way to find something—anything—about Jo. I feel like something is chasing me as I rush back to the ladder, turn off the light, and climb down into the hall. The ladder snaps back into place with a soft click, and I pause, leaning against the wall as I try to catch my breath.

The attic is too overwhelming, but there has to be some-where else I can look. Somewhere more important. Some-where... private.

Excitement fills me as I rush back down the hall to my bathroom. Inside, I turn the shower on and run the overhead fan to make some noise so the staff will think I'm in the shower, then I tiptoe back downstairs to Mitch's office. He doesn't lock it—doesn't lock any of the doors in the house actually—which is something he promised should make me feel like I was welcome to be with him at any time.

No thanks.

I put my hand on the handle and pause, trying to get my heart to slow down. I want to be able to hear any sound in the house, but that's difficult when my heart is hammering away like this. Mitch should be home in... I check my watch. Two hours.

The chef will start dinner soon.

Now's my chance.

I take a deep breath and open the door.

TWENTY-SEVEN

HANNAH

Well, if this isn't better than reality TV, then I don't know what is.

After poking around in the attic, Aimee snuck into my brother's office. Really, I didn't think she had it in her. Being able to watch her on camera suddenly became more important, especially if she's digging for anything she can use to get out of this marriage on her own.

I need her help. She better not turn on me, or I'll make her regret it.

I followed her through the house via the cameras Patrick set up. Even though Mitch only wanted a few put up around and inside the house, Patrick really went above and beyond the call of duty when I asked him to and promised to make it worth his while. Of course, Mitch doesn't know about all the cameras, and it was easy enough for Patrick to lie about needing some updated parts, show up at his house, and install the extras.

I had Patrick add it to my tab, which is something I'm going to have to pay off sooner rather than later. That's fine. As long as my plan goes off without a hitch, the two of us will stand to make a lot of money.

Or... I will. Because my plan doesn't involve splitting my earnings with Patrick, no matter what I promised to get him to install the extra cameras at Mitch's house.

A big payday? Check.

Us pretending to date so he could keep an eye on me? Gross but check.

The man is shady, belongs in prison where he can't touch my money, and I'll do whatever it takes to put him there when this is all said and done.

Starting his own security company so he could rob people? Come on. It may have worked for a bit, but no way was it going to work forever. People were going to catch on eventually—I'm sure of it.

Unfortunately for me, Patrick wasn't able to install a camera in Mitch's office or bedroom. I'd wanted him to in case Mitch was hiding anything in there, but Patrick told me it would be too dangerous and he was sure to get caught.

With a sigh, I get up and walk to the kitchen to pour myself a glass of water. My throat is dry, and I'm stiff from sitting and watching Aimee for so long.

That little trick of texting her when she was going into the attic was a moment of brilliance. Her eyes got so wide! Even through the screen, it was easy to see how upset she was, and I'm dying to know not only what she was looking for, but what she found. I wasn't joking when I told her there was no way into the basement, but it looks like she took that energy elsewhere to snoop.

I didn't want to overdo it, of course. There's always the chance she'll figure out that I'm watching her through Mitch's new security system, and I can't have that. Patrick made it very clear that he would kill me if Mitch figured out he'd given me access to his home's cameras.

All that means is that I have to be careful what I do with the information I get. I can gaslight Aimee all I want to, but Mitch is off-limits, at least for now.

I drain my water and put the glass in the sink, then wander back to my computer. Mitch's office door is closed, but a quick glance at the last minute of recording tells me Aimee hasn't left and carefully shut the door behind her.

She's still in there.

Still poking around.

I'd love to know what she's finding.

And I think I know exactly how to get her to tell me.

TWENTY-EIGHT

AIMEE

Of course I've been in Mitch's office before, but never by myself.

It's one thing to wander through the main rooms of the house. The library, the dining room, the lounge... those spaces were all designed for guests to see them, and they all feel like him, but this is different.

It's darker. The light wood tones he prefers for the rest of the house have been swapped out. The blues are deeper. Richer. The curtains on the windows are heavy and thick enough that I think he could pull them shut and prevent any light from entering.

I've already closed the door behind me, but some part of me is screaming for me to open it and flee. I take a step back as my eyes sweep around the room, but he's not here. Nobody is here.

I'm safe. For now.

But my heart is pounding. I know if Mitch were to find out that I'd snuck into both his bedroom and his office, he'd be irate.

I take a deep breath and force myself to walk straight to his desk. Even without looking, I have a very good feeling the drawers will be locked, but I still tug on each one.

They don't budge.

To the other side of the room then, where he has a small bookcase absolutely loaded with books. Mitch would never make it easy for someone to find dirt on him, but would he ever have imagined that someone would enter his office to poke around? Probably not. No way does he let anyone into his house without fully vetting them. Mitch isn't the kind of guy to take risks and make mistakes, and I doubt it's crossed his mind that he might have dropped the ball with me, especially since I told him about the phone from Hannah.

It was a calculated risk. She's got to be upset by it, but I had to do something to make Mitch think I'm on his side. This fine line I'm walking is dangerous, and I need both of them to trust me if I want the best possible outcome.

My fingers dance along the titles. Most of them are his college and medical school textbooks. There are a few classics here and there. So, nothing. Nothing pertinent to my search, nothing that would give me any insight into the man I've married.

I'm frustrated now, and I stomp over to the other closed door. Maybe a closet? Maybe I'll open it and there will be a huge bookcase right here?

But when I swing the door open, I'm surprised to find an attached half-bathroom. Reaching in, I click on the light. Not a single thing is out of place. The counter is clean, which I would expect after having the cleaning crew come through. The mirror is spotless, the sink wiped out.

I didn't even know he had this space in here.

Each drawer I yank open is meticulously organized. Rage burns inside me as I dig through the items, looking for anything I can use against him.

Until I see it: a bottle of sedatives.

Chills dance up my spine as I hold the bottle. It's a few

years old, according to the expiration date, which tells me he doesn't use them regularly.

Did he use them on Jo?

I slam the last drawer shut and grab the counter, my heart hammering hard as I pant. I don't know what I expected to find in here, but the man keeping me captive as his wife isn't perfect. What I saw behind his baseboard is proof enough for me that he's prone to dropping the ball.

Trophies.

I wonder if Hannah knows that Mitch has killed more people than just his first wife. I've seen enough true crime documentaries to be comfortable guessing that the items hidden behind his baseboard are trophies from people he's killed.

If Jo wrote anything down about how dangerous he is, I think I'll find it stashed away. Mitch isn't the kind of guy to throw something away, not if it could be used for him or against him. As soon as I have proof, I'll have the leverage I need to get away from here. To put him in my rearview mirror. To never return.

And if I don't find something that will help me gain my freedom? Then my only alternative is to believe that Hannah isn't going to screw me over and help her carry out her plan. I'm scared to believe she's not going to turn on me, even though she did give me a phone and Mitch agreed to let me keep it.

My phone.

What would Mitch do if I called 911? I barely have time to consider the question before the answer hits me full in the face. If he could control the narrative, I'm sure he'd spin some story about how I need professional help, how meds would ensure I wasn't feeling guilty over what happened to Dale, how he's taking care of me.

And if Hannah got involved? She claims to be on my side, but if push came to shove, do I really think she'd stand by me after I threw her under the bus with Mitch? I'm terrified to work with her, terrified to go against her more than I already have by telling Mitch about the phone. If I go against her, she could turn me in as Steph and take the life I worked so hard for away from me. Maybe she doesn't realize that she holds the one card that could bring this all crashing down. Or maybe she does and she's waiting to use it.

No matter if it's with or without Hannah's help... I need out.

I leave Mitch's office and close the door before coming up with a mental list of the next few places I want to poke around to try to find something I can use for leverage against him.

At the same time, should I be looking for some form of leverage against Hannah? There's literally nothing stopping her from turning me in to the cops except her brother. If I take him out of the equation, then that will leave her, and...

My head hurts.

There are too many variables to think through. I need to talk to my friends. I need their advice. I need—

Norma.

She said something about changing the direction of her career so that she can better help out women who are in a bad situation, right?

Does that mean what I think it does?

Excitement rushes through me. All I need to do is get in contact with her. If you hire a lawyer, they can't turn against you. There's client privilege, which means I could tell her the truth of what happened to me when I was younger and she wouldn't be able to go to the police.

The alternative, which is worse, is that she was at the party as a plant. Did Mitch ask her to test me to see how loyal I am to him? Is there a possibility that she only approached me and said what she did because he wanted to know how I would respond?

Fear is paralyzing, and without knowing for sure if she's really on my side, I know I can't call her.

A few hours later, Mitch is home. We're both in the library, but while he hasn't looked up from the book he's reading, I can't seem to focus. My mind is a ping-pong ball bouncing around as I try to work through what to do next.

"You seem distracted tonight," Mitch remarks. He doesn't even look up from his book when he speaks. "Everything okay?"

"Things are great," I lie. "Just a long day, and I'm pretty tired."

He levels his gaze at me over my book. "What did you get into today?"

Does he know?

Even though I didn't find anything in his office, no way would he be happy about me poking around in there. Did someone on the staff tell him I was in there? I'm mulling that over when I have an even worse thought.

A security company was over recently to make sure he has the coverage he wants around the house. Did he watch me on camera poking around in his office? No. Surely not. That's weird, right?

But what if he's had an eye on me all day and I didn't know it? I shiver.

"I was by the pool a lot," I say, watching him for any flicker of emotion on his face. "Had a Mai Tai. Ended up taking a nap out there."

"Sounds lovely." His voice is calm, but his next words are loaded. "What is on your face?"

"Eyeliner." I lift my chin a bit in defiance.

"You look like an emo kid."

I shrug. It's a small act of defiance, but I like getting under his skin. "I'm comfortable like this."

"My wife doesn't dress like that." He holds my gaze, but I don't blink. I don't move. I just stare at him. "Am I clear?"

"So clear," I tell him. *Pick, pick, pick,* I'm picking at his exterior, and I like it. "Mitch, there's one thing we haven't discussed, and I want to." I take a deep breath. "What do you think about kids?"

"I don't do kids." His answer is immediate, and his tone doesn't leave any room for discussion.

"Any reason? Did you and Jo never—"

"I don't do kids. What Jo and I did or didn't do isn't your concern, Aimee. I don't want children."

I pause. "Did Jo?"

"Did my first wife want children? You're really asking me that right now?"

I'm terrified, but I manage to nod.

"Yes." One word, one single word with more finality to it than anything I've ever heard before from him.

My heart squeezes. Those baby clothes in the attic—she bought them. She probably loved looking for them, and then he killed her and boxed them all up. But why not throw them away? As soon as I have the question, I know the answer.

Control. It's all about control with him.

"Don't ask me anything more about her. I thought I made it clear that I don't want to discuss her."

"You did. I'm sorry."

"Good. I want to help you with your weight loss, and I hired you a personal trainer. They'll be able to ensure you get the workout you need so you get results without hurting yourself."

The change in subject gives me whiplash, but of course he changed it right when he was getting uncomfortable. "Thank you. You're so attentive."

He'd looked back at his book, but his eyes flick to mine again.

I hold my breath.

"I don't miss anything, Aimee," he tells me.

TWENTY-NINE

HANNAH

Wednesday

It's a perfect morning for a walk, don't you think?

Aimee's on my screen dressed in a really cute matching athleisure set. I see the moment she hears her phone alert to her text, and a thrill races through me.

She's boring to watch, but I can't look away. Watching her wander aimlessly through the house, keeping tabs on her while she looks through cupboards and under beds, seeing them eat dinner, it's all gotten a bit yawn-inducing for my taste. I don't know what she's looking for, but she obviously hasn't found it yet.

So I thought I would shake things up this morning. By now, she might have forgotten about the first texts I sent her the other day. There's a very good chance she'll have relegated them to the part of her brain that doesn't deal with anything important.

You know, good on Mitch for springing for the really high-quality cameras. I can see everything, including the flush that's starting on her chest and will quickly make its way up to her cheeks.

She's staring at her phone and suddenly turns to lean against the wall for support. As soon as she's off the property, I'll lose sight of her, so I wanted to make sure she knows I know what she's up to.

The thought of living rent-free in her mind is too sweet for me to pass up.

There's a pause, then I see her typing. A moment later, my phone buzzes.

Sure is. That's what you're doing too, huh?

A laugh bursts from me, and I clap my hand over my mouth to stop it, then realize I don't care. Nobody is here with me. Unlike my spoiled brother, I don't have a full staff waiting on me at all times. Who cares if I laugh in my own house?

Exactly! Endorphins are good for you!

I giggle as I type my response because that couldn't be further from the truth. I'm still in my pajamas, crouched in my computer chair like a gargoyle, my half-eaten breakfast on the desk next to me. She has no way of knowing any of that, of course, and that I can lie to her without her ever knowing the truth gives me a buzz.

She texts again, then shoves her phone into the side pocket of her leggings.

I grin at my phone as her text comes through.

Well, have a good walk!

Then she's out the door, her ponytail swinging with every step. I grab my mouse and click, changing from internal views to external cameras so I can keep an eye on her. There she goes down the path.

Click.

I watch as she cuts down the driveway.

Click.

And she turns onto the sidewalk by the road. That's the last I see of her, and I sit back in my chair, satisfied. As much as I'd like to keep watching my screens to see when she comes home, I force myself to get up. The money from my parents isn't going to last forever, but I refuse to get a job. I've been living off the interest in my accounts as best as possible, but I need a big payday, and there's only one way I can get that.

Right now, it's time to shower and get dressed. Actually put on makeup. As much as leaving the house seems like a chore, I have someone to visit.

An hour later, I'm sitting in Mitch's office at the hospital. It's as neat and sterile as the last time I was here, only he has a new photo on his desk. It's him and Aimee at their wedding. He looks handsome; I have to admit it, but she looks rather like a deer caught in the headlights. I can't help but snicker at the scared expression on her face.

His office door swings open, and I put the framed photo face down on his desk. "Hey, brother," I say, my voice singsong.

Mitch stops in his tracks. He's still in his white coat and has a file in his hands. I don't know the exact details of what he does all day, but he usually ends up looking exhausted. Sure, he makes a ton of money, but he doesn't need it.

So why spend all day working and saving people when you could enjoy your life? That's something I'll never understand about my brother, no matter how hard I try. He likes the glory. That's the only thing that makes any sense.

"What are you doing here?" He drops the file on his desk and, in the same motion, pushes my feet to the floor. "Don't you have some children to scare or something?"

"Ha. You know, if you didn't want to feed into your God complex, you really should have considered being a clown. You have the sense of humor *and* the face for it."

He glares at me. "What do you want, Hannah? You never come visit me at work unless you need something."

"You're right, and that's not fair to you. Call me a crappy sister if you want, but I've turned over a new leaf and want to strengthen our relationship." I hold my hand up in the Boy Scout's gesture and wait for him to acknowledge me. He doesn't, so I continue. "I wanted to let you know I have a boyfriend."

He laughs. The jerk actually laughs. Without giving me a chance to respond, he turns to close his office door, then looks back at me. "What poor sap did you convince to date you?"

"Patrick Long," I tell him, then wait for a flash of recognition at the name. It doesn't come, and I'm honestly not surprised. Mitch is the kind of guy to use service employees but never really pay them any mind. If he'd recognized Patrick's name, that would have shocked me.

"How much are you paying him?"

He's not far off. No way would I ever actually date Patrick now, but he made it clear he wasn't letting me out of his sight until I'd paid off my debt to him. All the extra cameras he installed at Mitch's house came with a steep price, and since I won't get my money until Mitch is dead and Aimee comes through... I'm stuck with Patrick for a while. At least he's hotter than he was in high school.

Not only am I stuck with him, but he wants to be *involved*. He wants to spend time with me and my family to make sure I don't ditch him without paying, and although I don't love that, I don't feel like I have a choice.

"Gosh, you're fun. I'm serious, Mitch. He's a great guy, and I wanted you to know that we want to have you and Aimee over for dinner this weekend."

Now I have his full attention. At first, he'd obviously been distracted. He'd listened to me, sure, but it was clear he wasn't really hearing what I'm saying. Now, though, he looks right at me.

"Dinner. You want to host dinner?"

"I do."

"Did hell freeze over?"

"It did not. I want you and Aimee to meet him."

"And who is going to cook said dinner? Did you miraculously stumble into some inheritance I don't know about and hire a personal chef?"

I ignore the barb. "I'm going to cook it," I tell him, hoping I sound more confident than I feel. Of course, there's always the possibility that he might—

"Not a chance. If the four of us are going to have dinner together, I'm going to use my chef."

Ahh, there it is. I'd been hoping he'd take control and offer his house instead of me having to host. When you have to handle all the cleaning and cooking on your own, it's a treat to go to someone else's place.

"That's so noble of you to offer, but I don't want you to feel you have to do that."

"It's done. Saturday. Come at four; we'll eat at five. You know I don't like eating too late because it disrupts my sleep."

I fight the urge to roll my eyes. Of course I know that. Anyone who has a single ear and has met Mitch knows that the man has a sensitive stomach and can't sleep if he eats too close to bedtime. Me? Unaffected.

"Fine." I stand up and brush off my clothes like I'm irritated with him. "Fine. You always like taking control, don't you?"

"I like making sure things don't suck," he corrects. "Bring a nice bottle of wine."

And with that, I'm dismissed. I fight to keep a grin off my face until I'm in the hall and well away from his office. Mitch is so funny because he's like every other man out there. If you can get them to think that they're the ones who came up with a plan, then they'll run with it.

He banned me from being around Aimee recently, but the man can't resist showing off. Saturday can't come soon enough.

Not when I'm ready to kill him.

THIRTY

JACKIE

Friday

It's Friday night, which means Mitch and Aimee are out to dinner. He's nothing if not a creature of habit, which has only made my job of watching him easier than I ever thought possible.

Again, I park at the gas station right down the road. And again, I'm dressed all in black, only this time I'm more prepared for my night activities.

Instead of bringing my cell with me, I left it in the motel room, tucked under the mattress since there isn't a safe for me to keep it in. I have a small flashlight with me, a pair of rubber gloves, and, most importantly, the house key.

It feels heavy in my pocket as I scale the privacy fence and drop into Mitch's backyard. My baseball cap sits low on my face so nobody can identify me, but this time, I'll do better to avoid the security lights he has set up. Last time I was terrified that he'd seen me and was coming out to deal with me. But then I remembered: they're on timers.

He's always had a security system, but knowing Mitch, he

hasn't changed the code to disarm it. I'm feeling pretty confident as I push the original key back in its hidey-hole, slip my new copy of his key into the lock, and let myself in through the kitchen.

No beeping. No sirens. No bright lights flashing, but that's all to create a false sense of security for anyone who might dare trespass. I remember a huge dinner with friends one night where he bragged for the longest time that he would catch anyone who broke in on his own so he could deal with them.

I dart down the hall and reach the front door. This is where the alarm panel is, and I pull my flashlight from my pocket, click it on, then shine it on the panel. Just as I'm reaching to punch in the code, I remember the gloves.

Crap. I should have already had them on just in case.

The flashlight falls from my hand. I swear as the light bounces in different directions, then finally lands on my feet. Rubber gloves are hard to pull on when your palms are sweaty, but I finally do it, then grab the flashlight and punch in the code.

1-0-2-6.

His birthday. Of course.

There's a moment where I don't think the code is going to work, just a second's delay, but then the system turns off and I sigh heavily. I'm in, but my work isn't finished.

I'd love to take my time poking around the house, but instead I beeline for his office and sign into his computer. It's tempting to log into his online banking or to look through his personal documents, but I go straight to his security system.

A few clicks and I've disabled it for half an hour. Another click and I've pulled up the footage of me running through his house so I can get to the panel to turn off the alarm. I delete it, then turn off his computer monitor.

Spinning away from the desk, I set a timer on my smart watch for twenty-five minutes. The cameras are *down for main-*

tenance, or that's the message he'd see if he tried to log in now, so I need to get through the house and back out before anyone catches wise to what I'm doing. Surely, if Aimee is here of her own volition, there will be some proof of that. Likewise, if she's in danger, I should be able to find something to prove that she needs my help.

I hope.

"Where to first?" I ask. I stand and push his chair back to his desk, then walk to the bookshelf. It's been a long time since I've been in this house, but most things look the same. Besides, what interesting things am I really hoping to find tucked away in between his old med school books?

Nothing.

Upstairs then.

In the upstairs hall, I pause before opening the main bedroom door. My hand trembles as I turn on the light, but I force myself to do it and then take in the space.

There are no feminine touches. Frowning, I hurry to the bathroom and look inside, but no peach lotion, no mascara, no errant bobby pins litter the sink. I open the shower door and step inside, but there's no long hair on the wall, no floral shampoo.

He *is* married, right? So where's her stuff?

Back to the hall. At the last minute, I reach inside the main bedroom and click off the light, then I walk into the guest room. Even without turning on the light, I know I hit the jackpot.

A soft perfume lingers in the air. It's probably silly, but the space *feels* feminine, and I'm rewarded when I turn on the light.

The four-poster bed is a light wood with an off-white coverlet. There are multiple pillows at the head of the bed and a pair of folded silk pajamas next to them. I trace my fingers along the fabric. These PJs couldn't be more different from the flannel ones I wear.

My watch buzzes to let me know five minutes have passed,

and I snap to attention. Her closet is just what I thought it would be—groaning with designer clothes. I flick through her dresses, then turn my attention to her jewelry box. Drawer after drawer is filled with diamonds, sapphires, emeralds. There are a pair of ruby earrings that are absolutely stunning, and I almost pluck them out to look at them when something else catches my eye.

A pearl necklace, all the way in the back corner of the jewelry box, tucked out of sight. I frown and pull it out, the pearl dangling in the air in front of me.

Mitch hates pearls.

After closing her jewelry box and closet, I head to her bathroom. Everything in here is as neat as a pin. Just like Mitch's, everything has a place.

Five more minutes have passed.

I turn off the lights and run back into Mitch's room. Now I know that he and his wife have separate bedrooms, but I don't know what to make of that information. The Mitch I knew before never would have allowed his new bride to sleep in a different bed. There has to be a reason for it.

Maybe Aimee really can handle Mitch. That thought gives me hope, that I might have misread the situation, that maybe he's getting his comeuppance.

Back in his bedroom, I drop to the floor and look under his bed.

Nothing.

I hurry back to his closet and dig behind his hanging clothes. I push deeper, then my fingers brush something cold and metal.

The hair on the back of my neck stands up. I yank my flashlight from my pocket and shine it on the safe in front of me. My fingers tremble as I press the buttons on the mechanical lock. He didn't change the code on the security system, and I have to hope he didn't change it here either.

Three loud beeps, then a light glows green. I take a deep breath and open the safe, sure that there will be something in here to either put my mind at ease that Aimee is stronger than I thought or clue me in that she needs help.

A single manilla folder sits on the bottom of the safe.

My watch beeps that another five minutes have passed.

Without hesitation, I grab it and flip it open.

THIRTY-ONE

HANNAH

Mitch and Aimee are eating out at Flight, his favorite restaurant. It's what they do every Friday night, what he did with his first wife, Jo.

So why, then, did I get a notification that there was movement in his house? I'm curled up on the sofa in my PJs, a glass of wine at hand, but I ignore it as I tap on my phone to open up the security app.

I tap the little red icon, growing excited when I see the notification that there was movement on both the first and second floors. That's not a fan, or an open window causing papers to blow. That means—

Someone's in the house.

Excitement shoots through me, and I sit up, tucking my feet under me as I stare at the screen. Whoever it is moves quickly, obviously familiar enough with the layout of the house to hurry down the hall to turn off Mitch's alarm.

"Who are you?" I ask, peering closer at my screen. The person has a slight build, so I'm already guessing it's a woman. Their hair is either cut short or tucked up under the baseball cap they have on. I know it has to be luck keeping them from looking right at the camera so I can see their face, but I'm still frustrated as they hurry to Mitch's office.

And straight to his computer.

I lean forward like I'm going to be able to get a better look at what they're doing. The camera is set up like I'm looking over Mitch's shoulder, and I watch as they confidently type in his PIN. They navigate to his security system and delete the footage of them breaking into the house.

"Aren't you interesting?" I breathe the words, excitement building in me. "You're a busy little bee, aren't you?"

They hurry up to the second floor.

A tap on my screen and I'm watching the top of the stairs. Patrick offered to try to put a camera in Mitch's bedroom, but honestly? Ew. I settled for one right outside it as well as one in Aimee's. There's also a camera outside the third bedroom, what I figure might one day be a nursery, but there hasn't been any action on that one since I had it installed.

The person—*a woman, I'm sure it's a woman*—reaches the top of the stairs and immediately turns to the left to enter Mitch's bedroom. I swear as she walks out of frame, and I reach out to take a sip of wine.

Surely she won't be in there long.

I was right, and after a few moments, she appears at the door. I still can't see her face. She has it angled down to the floor, almost like she's afraid that she didn't do a great job keeping the security system from turning her in.

She pauses, then hurries to the second door. I take another sip of my wine, then put the glass down. I feel like I'm buzzing, like I'm high, even though I've never actually done drugs. Still, it's exciting to watch her move through my brother's house and to know that she's clueless that she's on camera.

Aimee's room. She steps inside. Traces her fingers over Aimee's pajamas. I think for a moment that she's going to look up at the hidden camera, but she's careful. I watch as she goes into Aimee's closet and bathroom.

She's looking for something. This isn't the trip of someone taking a stroll through another person's house. Not for a second do I believe she's a stranger.

She knows my brother. I'm sure of it.

But does she also know Aimee?

"It can't be," I whisper as the woman checks her watch, then darts back down the hall to Mitch's room. This time she's in there longer than before. I get nervous, wondering if I have time to drive over there and interrupt her.

Surely not. Surely, with the way she keeps checking her watch, she's not planning on sticking around for much longer. I'd love to head over there and catch her in the act, but unless she settles down and decides to hang out for a while, I don't have time.

But what do I have to lose?

Even though I know the chance of running into her at Mitch's place is slim, I find myself getting up off the sofa. Excitement washes over me as I throw a coat on over my PJs and slip on a pair of shoes. After exhaling hard, I hold my phone in one hand in front of me so I can keep an eye on the screen. With the other hand, I grab my purse and my keys. Let myself out of my house. Lock the door.

My phone snaps easily into the mount on my dash. I back out of the driveway, one eye on the road, the other on my phone.

What is she doing in his room?

The right thing to do would be to call the cops and tell them there's an intruder. I'm sure, if I gave them the address, they'd be there in no time flat, ready to protect the town's most beloved doctor.

But if I'm right, if I know who this woman is and can stop her on my own. I don't want the police involved.

No way. She's not even supposed to be alive.

THIRTY-TWO

JACKIE

What in the world is this contract?

My mind spins as I read through it. I'm skimming, sure, but even though I'm not reading every single word of it, none of it makes any sense.

My knees give out, but rather than sinking to the floor, I brace one hand on the wall for support. As I do, my watch buzzes.

Crap. Time to go.

If I'd brought my cell phone, I'd take pictures of the pages. Do I take this folder with me? Do I try to come back later? I feel like I've already pushed my luck by breaking in once. Coming back again, even if it's on a night I'm sure Mitch and Aimee will be gone, feels dangerous.

Without thinking about what I'm doing, I close the safe. There's a thud, then the lights blink red to let me know it's locked. Bile burns the back of my throat as I push Mitch's hanging clothes into place, then I back out of his closet and close the door, the folder tucked under my arm.

I have to hurry. In a few minutes, his security cameras will go back online, and any movement in the house will result in a call to the cops.

I race downstairs. As I'm hurrying towards the back door, I trip, my toe catching on the floor. Without thinking, I fling my arms wide and try to catch myself, but only succeed in knocking a photo from the wall.

It hits the ground hard and shatters, the glass fragments scattering.

"Crap." My wrists hurt, and I roll my hands in circles to get the feeling back into them, but as much as I'd love to crouch here and pick up every piece of glass, I need to move.

When I glance at my watch to see if I have enough time to reset the cameras, fear eats at me.

One minute. I'd try if I wasn't worried about a second reset immediately notifying the police.

I scramble to my feet, leaving the photo, the frame, the glass. It crunches under my shoes as I fly out the back door, only pausing long enough to lock it behind me. My lungs burn as I race across the backyard. It's a full moon, and I feel exposed, sure that anyone looking out their window will see me and call the cops.

But I'm past the pool, then into the woods. The security fence is rough under my hands, and I almost drop the folder, but I get over the fence with it clamped tightly between my teeth.

When I hit the ground, I don't pause to catch my breath. I still have to make it through this neighborhood, then across the street to the gas station.

Someone honks at me as I run across the road, but I don't slow down. I have the folder gripped tightly in my right hand, and I'm already digging for my keys with my left when I slow to a walk to approach where I left my car.

But it isn't here.

Sweat breaks out on my palms, and my head starts to

pound. I finger my keys in my pocket, panic rising in the back of my throat. At least I have the folder I took from Mitch's closet, but what good is that going to do me if I can't get back to my motel?

A Honda pulls up to the pump closest to me, and three teenagers pile out. They're laughing and carrying on, and I watch as they enter the gas station, then turn back to look at their car.

They left the keys in it. I can see them hanging in the ignition, and I actually take a step closer to the vehicle. All I need is to get back to the motel. I wouldn't trash the car. I wouldn't—

I catch myself as I'm reaching for the door and shake my head. What am I doing? This isn't me. Someone had to have towed my car, and all that means is that I need to ask the clerk where they took it. I can call an Uber, get a ride to the impound lot, pay the fee...

My head spins, but it's not like I have a choice in the matter, is it?

I roll my shoulders back and head for the building, but before I reach the door, someone's hand claps down on my shoulder.

THIRTY-THREE

HANNAH

"You're supposed to be dead," I say.

Jo whips around to face me, and even though I had a sneaking suspicion I was right about who was poking around in my brother's house, it still shocks me to come face-to-face with her.

"Hannah," she breathes, and I close my eyes for a moment, trying to understand how we ended up here. How she can be here.

How she's alive.

This doesn't make sense. It's some terrible dream I'm having, but even as I wish that to be true, I know I'm wrong.

Jo's here. She's alive. And I don't have any idea how that can be possible.

The door opens, and some teens exit. They're laughing and carrying on, each holding a bottle of soda and a bag of chips. One of them stares at us as he passes, but he doesn't speak, and I don't move until they're gone.

"What do you want?" Jo's voice is a whisper. She glances from left to right, her eyes wide, and I wonder what she's more afraid of.

My brother?

Or the police?

I open my mouth to tell her I saw her on my brother's security system, then pause. The last thing I need is to give her any ammunition she can use against me, and I have no doubt that she'd love to tell Mitch that I've been spying on him and his precious little wife if push came to shove.

"I pulled in to get gas," I lie. "And saw you walking across the parking lot. Really, for a moment, it felt like I'd seen a ghost, but here you are. Flesh and blood."

Her shoulders sag, and she seems to sink in on herself. "We can go somewhere and talk."

"Oh, you better believe it." I loop my arm through hers and snug her close to my body. "How long has it been since I last saw you? Two years? Just barely, I guess. How does it feel to be resurrected from the dead?"

She swallows hard. It's almost funny to me how terrified she is, and with good reason.

"We had a funeral for you," I hiss as I shove her towards my car. "Get in there and start figuring out how you're going to talk me out of calling the cops."

She's silent. We buckle in, and I start the car, then lay rubber as I tear out of the gas station. I'm afraid to take her back to my house in case Mitch is watching me the same way I'm watching him.

But that's me being paranoid, right?

The diner down the road is open all night long, and I pull in without asking Jo if she's okay with going here. What she wants doesn't matter. Besides that, there's no way in hell Mitch would ever be caught dead here, so he'll never catch us talking.

The smell of fried eggs and buttered toast envelops the two of us as I follow Jo into the diner. Sharr's has been here for years and become quite the fixture in town for anyone needing some carbs to soak up all the beer they drank at a dive bar down the road.

"A booth, please," I say to the server before she opens her mouth. Her eyebrows fly up at my tone, but she wisely doesn't say anything. Instead, she leads us to the back. Pushing Jo out of the way, I slide into the far side of the booth so I can keep an eye on the door.

"Would you like to hear our specials?" the server begins, but I cut her off.

"Two all-star plates with bacon and coffee." I hand the huge plastic-coated trifold menus back to her and wait until she's hurried off to the kitchen to turn my attention on Jo.

My sister-in-law.

"We cremated you," I tell her. "How in the world are you sitting here right now? And, better yet, why? What would possess you to come back to Vermont?"

"I came back because I saw the happy news." She keeps her hands folded in her lap. Before I can respond, the server appears and puts our coffees down. "Thanks," Jo tells her, then dumps in a packet of sugar and takes a sip.

That's how she's always taken it.

My first thought when I saw a glimpse of her face on the security camera was that she had to be an imposter. It doesn't make any sense that my sister-in-law could actually be here, right in front of me, alive.

Then I thought maybe she had a twin, but I didn't remember her ever saying anything about that. There's only one person who would know their way around the house like she did though.

It was luck that I saw her running across the road to the gas station on my way to Mitch's house. Luckier that I was able to catch her before she got in her car and drove off.

"You mean Mitch getting married?" I keep my eyes on my coffee as I pour in some milk and creamer and wait for her response. It's been a long time since I saw Jo, but I always remember her being flighty, and I don't want to push her or scare her any more than I probably already have.

"That's the news." She puts her mug down and pushes it out of the way. "Tell me, did he kill his friend so he could marry Aimee?"

"Is that why you're here?" I sit back in the booth; the cheap vinyl sticks to the backs of my arms. "Did you come here so you could protect her from her new husband?"

She doesn't respond, but she doesn't need to.

"You did," I say, understanding dawning on me. "Let me guess, you saw the news, you had some PTSD of being married to him, and you came back. But before we get into that, I want you to answer this question: how are you not dead?"

"I had some help from a friend."

"Must be a really good friend to pretend that you got burned up into a pile of ash." I consider her. She's put on some weight, which would have sent Mitch into a fit when they were married, but she's carrying it surprisingly well.

"They were."

"You paid them, didn't you?"

"No." She shakes her head to drive the point home. "Some people are there to help you even if you don't have anything to offer them. I know you don't understand what that's like."

Her claws are out, but they're not very sharp. I ignore her sass.

"So you pretended to be dead with the help of your friend. You moved away, started a new life. You still go by Jo?"

"Nope." She doesn't offer her new name.

"And then you decided to be the savior of women and come back here to help save Aimee from your husband." My mind races as I think about how I can use this to my advantage.

It's obvious Mitch doesn't know she's here or she wouldn't be sitting across the table from me. Jo isn't stupid, although she did royally screw up when I caught her in my brother's house. Still, even though she dropped the ball on that, there's no way she would come here without having a plan of action.

And that means I need my own plan.

"Tell me about the folder," I say, and this gets a reaction. Jo shifts a bit, obviously uncomfortable. She has the folder on the seat next to her like that's going to be enough to keep me from thinking about it. "You stole it from my brother."

"I took it," she admits. "But you don't need to worry about it."

My mind races as I work through what might be in the folder. I don't have to think for long before it hits me—a copy of the contract.

Fine. Let her figure out exactly how messed up this situation is. Heck, I'll even tell her everything I know if that's what it takes to get her to let her guard down. She'll want someone to chat to about what Mitch is doing to Aimee, I'm sure of it, and I'm willing to allow her to feel like she's in on the secret.

Jo's a wild card, showing up like this. She knows a lot about my brother and what he's capable of. The problem with me killing Mitch to get his money is now I know she could pop out of the woodwork and take it for herself, since she technically is still married to my brother.

Which means she has to disappear too. For real this time, not to whatever Podunk town she's been hiding in. She needs to disappear for good.

Or she's going to ruin everything.

THIRTY-FOUR

JACKIE

Hannah didn't just pay for my meal; she also took me to get my car out of impound and paid the fee for me to drive it away. My cheeks burn with embarrassment when I think about the smug expression on her face as she swiped her credit card so I could get my car back.

Was she always this insufferable? When I first married Mitch, I didn't think she was this awful, but maybe I blocked it out because I was so happy to have his ring on my finger.

Mitch was larger than life when I met him. I never wanted to marry a doctor, not when they had such a bad reputation for working long hours and being difficult to be married to, but he was different. We met when he was in med school and I was working at a veterinary clinic. He'd found a dog that had been hit by a car and brought it in, and even though we weren't able to save the dog, something sparked between us. It was a fairy tale of epic proportions... until we walked down the aisle and a switch flicked in him.

Gone was the man who stopped on his way to work and picked up a bleeding dog to get it help. He was replaced with someone who pressured me to quit my job and cared more about what I looked like than who I was on the inside. The change broke my heart, but I wasn't willing to give up on our marriage.

Not right away.

My eyes flick to my motel-room door, and I get up to double-check that it's locked. It is, and I pull the curtain to the side to make sure nobody's watching my room. I didn't tell Hannah where I'm staying, for obvious reasons, but she's sneaky, and I wouldn't put it past her to loop back around after leaving me and follow me to see where I am.

Maybe I should change motels.

Spinning away from the window, I eyeball my suitcase. It's spilled open, clothes bursting out of it. I didn't know how long I was going to be here and certainly didn't know what to expect to be doing, so I packed a bit of everything. Even though it's a mess in here right now, there's no reason why I couldn't pack up and get out of here in the next half hour.

Back to the window. As I watch, a large black SUV pulls into the parking lot, and I feel my heart kick up a notch. I hold my breath as it parks. The headlights go off. A moment later, the doors open and a young couple gets out. The woman goes to the backseat and pulls out a car seat.

I exhale.

"You're being paranoid," I mutter to myself, then let the curtain drop back into place. It's one thing to worry that she might follow me or try to get me on my own, but another entirely to stand at the window like a scaredy-cat.

I force myself to sit back on the bed. The first thing I did after getting back and locking the door was pull out my phone. Now I turn it over in my hands, thinking through what to do next. I can't lose sight of what I came here to do. Maybe I can get Hannah on my side?

Yeah, I'm not sure about that. I don't believe for a second that she happened to be driving by and it was coincidence that she saw me. It was like she knew I was in his house before she ran into me, before she saw Mitch's folder in my hands.

I was careful to turn off the security system while I was there. There's no way I'm on any of the cameras.

Unless...

I close my eyes and try to put myself back in the house. I saw the obvious cameras, the ones I know Mitch would have had installed, not just so he can make sure his house is safe and protected when he's gone, but so he can monitor his new wife.

But what if there were more? It's no coincidence that Hannah drove by at the perfect time and then recognized me, no matter what she said. The only way she could have known that I was the person breaking into Mitch's house is if she saw me on the screen and recognized me. Then it was sheer luck she saw me on the road.

Does she have her own security system in Mitch's house? The thought is as thrilling as it is terrifying. The possibility that Hannah is spying on her brother tells me something is going on there.

And I want to know what it is.

Maybe she's also worried about Aimee. Warmth flows through me at the thought. If I had someone on my side, this would be so much easier. Facing Mitch is scary, but with Hannah there to help me, I know I can do it.

I put down my phone and pick up the folder I took from Mitch's closet. Hannah knows I stole it from her brother, but she didn't seem to care.

If she didn't know what was in it, I'm sure she would have asked to see it, but... it hits me. She didn't care that I took it because she already knows what's in it, which means she has to know how bad it is for Aimee.

Thinking through all of this makes my head hurt, and I drop to my knees by my suitcase and pull out a small bottle of gin. I hate gin. It tastes like floor cleaner. But when I really need something to take the edge off, it's the perfect option. I won't drink it because I like it. I'll drink it because I need it.

I take a swig, then immediately start coughing. After forcing myself to drink a little more, I cap the bottle and stick it back in my suitcase.

There. Something to take the edge off is all I need. Just something to cut through the terrible static in my head that's making it difficult for me to think.

Back to the bed, and this time I open the folder and start reading. It's all in legalese, and I take a while to get through it all.

After an hour, I sit back. The food I ate at the diner combined with the bit of gin I drank sits heavy in my stomach. It feels like a rock, and I flop back on my bed, my mind racing.

Mitch was a terrible husband. He was controlling and overbearing and wanted everyone to know not only how much money he had, but to think that he was the most powerful and important man in the room. The way he treated his staff? Abhorrent. How he talked to me? Disgusting.

And from what I've read in the contract, things have gotten worse.

Originally, I'd hoped that Aimee was as crazy as him. Because at least then she'd be able to handle herself around him, but now I'm not so sure that's the case.

There has to be some reason he'd be able to get her to agree to everything she did, some blackmail he has on her. Why else would she be willing to sign this horrible contract?

When I ran from Mitch, I left her in the past too. Can I trust her?

My phone is heavy in my hand when I pick it up, but

instead of texting Hannah, I dial in a number I know from heart.

It's dangerous reaching out to her, but I don't feel like I have a choice in the matter.

I have to hope she picks up.

THIRTY-FIVE

AIMEE

Saturday

Hannah hasn't told me her plan for getting rid of Mitch, and I'm getting antsy.

The more I poke around in the house, the more I want to hurry this up and move on with the plan. Hannah acts like she has it all under control, and I'm willing to do whatever it takes to get out of this situation.

Even if it means killing Mitch.

The thought terrifies me, but if that's what it takes, then that's what it takes.

And what about giving her money? She can have it all. I don't care about how much is in the bank accounts—I want my freedom.

The house? I'll sell it to her in a heartbeat. I won't even be greedy—a dollar is all I'll ask, just so we have something for the paperwork. No way will I want to stay in this house when all is said and done. I want out.

If I can make it out.

"I think something I ate for lunch is disagreeing with me."

It's almost four, which means Hannah and her date should be here soon for dinner. What I can't understand is why she's bringing some guy around the house when she knows that the two of us have to get a move on with our plan. Why introduce another person? Why make things more complicated than they already are?

Unless...

Unless she has her own plan, that is. There's no way for her to know that I don't really trust her, not when I'm going along with everything she says and lying to her face.

But what if she's doing the same to me? Is it possible that she'd screw me over at the last second, or is that a fear I have because I don't trust her?

My stomach twists.

"You really don't feel good? We had the same thing." My husband turns to me, a glass of whiskey in his hand, one perfect eyebrow cocked. He's dressed like we're going out to a five-star restaurant, not like we're hosting in our own home.

"It's that time of the month," I lie. "I don't always feel great."

"You'll be fine. I want you at dinner."

"I'll do my best, but if I feel worse, I'm going to have to go to bed early." I'm not normally this argumentative with him, but I'm feeling on edge. I need to get Hannah on her own so we can discuss our plan. Why isn't she moving ahead with it faster? It feels like she's dragging her feet or avoiding it, but maybe that's me being paranoid about what we're going to do.

"Aimee," he says, my name a warning.

"Fine. I'll be there. I'll play the perfect, doting wife, just like I'm sure Jo did before she died."

His inhale is sharp. "I asked you—"

"Not to bring up your dead wife, I know. But she's a ghost in our marriage, Mitch! If you would tell me about her, I could get over it. Move on."

"Not an option."

I want to hit him. If I thought I could get away with it without making my life worse, I probably would. But the role I'm playing—that of a loving wife who's not only easy-going but also gets along with everyone in her husband's life—certainly wouldn't dream of smacking her spouse on the cheek.

Even when he deserves it.

"Fine. I'll be the perfect wife you want," I spit at him. "Don't you think I play the role well?" I turn in the dress I'm wearing so it flares out a bit and he can get a good look at it. It's one Hannah and I bought together, and I already know he loves it.

"You look incredible," he begins, but then cuts himself off. "I'm sorry, is that a *tattoo* on your thigh?" Before I can move, he grabs the hem of my dress and yanks it up.

"Sure is." I take a step away from him, already smiling at his expression. "You like it?"

"Do I like it?" His grip turns into a fist, crumpling the fabric of my dress. "No, I don't like it. Tattoos are trashy. When did you do this?"

I shrug. "This week. And it's not trashy. I love it."

"It's a band logo. For..." He frowns, staring at my leg.

"Green Day," I tell him, then yank my dress from him and let it fall back over my thigh. "I have an appointment booked in a month for a half-sleeve." I pause, thinking. "And a septum piercing."

"No. You don't. You will cancel both." He's staring at me like he's never seen me before. "What has gotten into you? I give you an inch of freedom and you... what? Decide to go get tattooed and pierced? No way. Not my wife."

"Well, then maybe I shouldn't be your wife." My heart pounds. For years I've been Aimee. I've been afraid of conflict. Afraid of upsetting people.

It feels good to be Steph again.

"You and I are going to discuss this," he tells me. "Don't think for one moment that this is over. You will get that lasered off, and you will stop this nonsense." He opens his mouth to continue his tirade, but the doorbell rings, and he releases me. "Do not show anyone that piece of trash on your thigh."

I don't nod. I don't react. He stares at me a moment longer, then hurries to open the door, leaving me waiting in the hall. As I stand here, my mind races.

I'm getting to him. This is good. He's off-balance, and now I only have to worry about Hannah keeping up her side of the deal.

But before I can worry about her turning on me, her voice rips me from my thoughts.

"Aimee, look at you! You're wearing one of the new dresses we got you. And don't you look nice?" She rushes up to me and air-kisses my cheeks, a bottle of wine in one hand.

I force a smile. "I was thinking the same thing about your dress! We clean up so well."

She grins at me. The two of us have a secret, we're playing a game, and nobody else knows what we're doing.

Heck, I'm not sure I even know what we're doing.

Before I can think of something else to say, a man slips his arm around her waist and pulls her to his side. I glance up at him, surprised. Mitch had said his sister was dating someone, but I didn't think they'd be this touchy-feely already. But what do I know? I'm the one who has a contract telling me exactly how often I have to sleep with my new husband.

"I'm Patrick," he says, extending a hand. "I've heard so much about you... Aimee."

Did he pause before he said my name? Maybe I'm being paranoid, but I'd swear there was a slight pause. There's a possibility he forgot it and had to dig deep in his gray matter to remember my name.

Or there's always the possibility that Hannah told him the

truth. Would she do that? Only if she were going to turn on me, I guess. We need to be on the same team, at least for a bit longer —but I'm overanalyzing everything with her. It's possible she's lying to my face and working against me, isn't it?

Ice trickles down my spine when I consider that.

"Come into the living room!" Mitch appears at my side, as jovial and pleasant as if we hadn't just had an argument. He links our fingers together and lifts my hand to his mouth to press a kiss against it. My skin crawls.

Do I love my husband? No, I don't.

And I never will.

I pushed him hard just now, but he'll never let Hannah and Patrick know that there's trouble in paradise. He loves me. He's obsessed with me. He chose me and won't let anyone say a bad word against me.

But what if Hannah became a threat? What if she turned on me? Would he kill his own flesh and blood for me? I need to talk to her about the plan she promised she'd come up with, but if I don't trust her? If I need someone to save me from her, would Mitch do it?

I'm not sure.

I need to be prepared to save myself from both of them.

My body moves on autopilot as I follow the three of them down the hall. But with every step I take, my mind races more.

Mitch is obsessed with me.

Can I use that to my advantage?

THIRTY-SIX

HANNAH

The fact that Aimee is going along with my plan without knowing all the details excites me, even though I know she's going to want to talk about it eventually, probably even tonight. Until then, I can change it on a whim without worrying about her catching on. I have complete control right now, at least in regard to her. Patrick on the other hand...

I push that thought away. An idea struck me last night when I was with Jo. If she had stayed dead, she wouldn't need to be involved in this messy business, but now that she's back... well, I know who Mitch's money will go to when we kill him.

Aimee doesn't though, and I might be able to use that to my advantage.

But not tonight. Tonight, I need to keep my head in the game. Patrick is pulling strings and making me stay close to him so he can be sure I won't take the money and run. It's an annoyance, nothing more. As soon as he gets his money, he'll be out of my life.

Right?

I'm staring at a bookcase groaning with leather-bound

books. Has Mitch ever even read any of them? Or are they all for show? It's hard to know with my brother. He's brilliant, I won't ever argue against that, but there's a lot about him that feels fake.

Like these books that I don't think he reads. The gorgeous paintings on the walls that I'm pretty sure he hired someone else to pick out for him. What about the fact that I don't think he actually goes shopping, hiring someone to manage his wardrobe for him instead?

Everything about Mitch is perfectly curated. It's designed to make people think he's incredible, that he's flawless.

But it's all a lie.

"So, Patrick," Aimee says, and her voice yanks me out of my thoughts, "how did you and Hannah meet?"

"Oh, we've known each other for years, haven't we?" He leans back and puts his arm around my shoulders. "Hannah's the one who got away and I never thought I'd get back. Joke's on me, I guess. I shouldn't have waited so long."

"And Patrick just came to our house to install our security cameras. Normally, I wouldn't want the help to come to dinner, but here we are," Mitch tells his wife, and my heart drops. That's not something I wanted brought up tonight. Mitch does a great job making connections when I don't want him to, and the last thing I need is for him to figure out what's really going on here. "What a coincidence."

"Really?" Aimee looks interested. "That's got to be a fascinating job. I bet you get to see into so many people's homes and lives."

"It really is." Patrick's voice is warming up like he's enjoying the direction this conversation is taking. "I'm so lucky—"

It's my cue to say something. "I'm the lucky one," I tell him. The words feel fake and forced, but as long as Aimee and Mitch believe them, it doesn't matter. "To have you? You might think you're lucky in your job, but I'm lucky in love."

"So sweet," Aimee says, then turns to my brother. "Aren't they darling?"

"Incredible. But not nearly as romantic as our story," he responds.

"What's your story?" Patrick leans forward a bit. It feels like he's too eager, and I want to tell him to relax, but the truth is that I want to know what lie my brother is going to spin as well.

"I was there to pick up all the pieces when Aimee's fiancé died," Mitch lies. "He and I were really good friends, and it made sense for her to fall into my arms after their relationship ended."

"How long ago did this happen?" Patrick looks back and forth between the two of them like he's really worried about Aimee's mental health. "It sounds like a horrible experience to have gone through."

"It's been a while," Mitch begins, right as Aimee cuts him off.

"Just a few weeks. Mitch was the first to fall, of course. He pursued me relentlessly, even when I told him I didn't think I was quite ready for a relationship."

My brother stiffens, but Aimee isn't finished.

"That's the thing about Mitch, I guess," she says with a laugh. "He can talk you into anything if he wants it bad enough. The man could have been a politician, the way he knows how to get what he wants. Anyway, we're married now, and who really cares what people say about us moving so quickly?"

Patrick clears his throat. "What a story," he begins, but again Aimee keeps running her mouth.

"Really, though, I don't know that I would have been so willing to get into a long-term relationship that quickly if it hadn't been for Hannah."

Frustration surges through me. What is she trying to pull?

"What did Hannah do?" Patrick asks.

"Nothing," I say, probably a little too loudly to keep the two of them from continuing this conversation. I didn't do anything. I just—

"Oh, she slept with my fiancé before he died." Aimee's beaming at me like she won the lottery.

"Aimee." Mitch's voice is a low warning, but she doesn't look at him.

"Wow," Patrick says, but this time I'm prepared to keep the conversation from going back off the rails.

"Luckily," I say, shooting daggers at my brother, "none of us are here to dredge up the past. I'm sure everyone has some skeletons in the closet they'd prefer stayed hidden."

"Not all of us," Patrick brags. "Some of us are totally cool with our past."

Will he shut up?

I clear my throat.

"You two keep up with throat clearing and I'm going to ask you to leave," Aimee says with a laugh. "If you're sick, I don't really want to break bread with you."

"We're fine," I snap. "What time is dinner anyway?"

"Five." My brother sounds frustrated. Normally, I'd like the idea that I'm exhausting him, but right now I want to end this evening. "I told you that when I invited you."

"Right. But no appetizers? No pre-dinner drinks? I thought you considered yourself the ultimate host, brother."

Mitch stills, a flash of anger on his face, but he gets up. "Let me get your drinks," he says before striding from the room. "We'll see who forgot to bring them to us."

"Go with him," I say, elbowing Patrick in the side. "Help him."

To his credit, he hops right up and hurries after my brother. I'm finally alone with Aimee, and I lean forward to ensure nobody accidentally overhears the two of us. "We need to talk about the plan."

"Good." Her voice is a whisper, and I can barely hear her. "I want this over with. As soon as he's..." Her voice trails off, and she refuses to say the word.

"Dead. As soon as he's dead, you can give me my money." .

"Yes. So what's the plan?" She glances past me to make sure the men haven't returned. "Are we doing something tonight?"

Tonight?

"Not with Patrick here."

She nods, then leans closer. Even though there's a coffee table separating the two of us, it feels like our noses are about to touch. Everything around us has disappeared. She's the only thing I can see.

"Then why did you bring him? I want—" She stops herself and takes a deep breath. There's a flush creeping up her chest. "I want out of this. This marriage, this house, this town."

No way can I tell her that I brought Patrick because I made a deal with the devil and he wasn't about to let me handle things on my own. I'm frustrated with myself for not having the money to pay him outright for the camera installation, but it's not my fault.

None of this is my fault. It's all Mitch's.

"I have a plan," I tell her, even though that's not totally the truth. I had... well, the beginning of a plan, then Jo showed up and I knew I had to consider what her being alive could mean, and how I could use that to my advantage.

"Tell me your plan."

"You have to count on me right now, okay? Tonight is not the night. We have to—"

"Hannah. Stop. If you don't know how you want to handle this, then say that. I can help you come up with a plan."

I shake my head. "No, I've got this under control. Not a thing goes on that I don't see, and I—"

"What does that mean? *Not a thing goes on that I don't see.*" She frowns, and I see her brain working. "Are you watching us?"

Crap. "What? No."

"Yes. You are." She leans back a bit, her mouth falling open as she stares at me. "You kept texting me, and I wondered how you knew what I was doing."

"Aimee—"

"And now this whole *not a thing goes on that I don't see*, like you're some kind of magician, but you're not a magician. But you are dating the guy who installed the security cameras here." She pauses. "What did you do?"

THIRTY-SEVEN

HANNAH

"Someone was in our house last night," Mitch announces out of the blue, and the rest of us look up at him. We're on the third course, some delicious steak that I want to hate but can't because it's perfectly cooked, and this is the first he's mentioned anything about suspecting someone was in his house.

Patrick frowns. "That's scary. What did the police say?"

"Funny thing," Mitch says, and he pauses long enough to make sure we're all watching him. "They never came. And I checked the cameras, but there's no footage of anyone in the house."

Aimee glances at me, but I ignore her. I know she's dying to finish our conversation about the security cameras in this house, but we were interrupted by Mitch and Patrick and haven't had the chance.

Thank goodness.

"So how do you know they were here?" Patrick puts his fork down and leans back in his chair. "The police weren't notified; there isn't any footage of them. It sounds like—"

"They broke a picture on the wall and left it on the floor." Mitch's voice is quiet, but there's anger simmering under his words. "Glass was scattered all over the floor. It took forever to clean up all the shards."

"Isn't that why you have a cleaning person?" I ask, and he glares at me.

"Aimee and I had just gotten home from a lovely dinner. The last thing I was going to do was leave the glass overnight and make someone else clean it up in the morning. What if she'd stepped on it?"

"That's weird." Patrick genuinely looks concerned, and I fight to keep a smile off my face. "Did you reach out to the company at all today to let them know what was going on?"

"I *am* reaching out to the company. I'm talking to you." Mitch rolls his eyes. "I want you to look at it after dinner. See what went wrong and fix it."

"Of course." Patrick takes another bite, but my appetite is gone.

As much as I love seeing my brother upset, the last thing I need is for him to grow wise to the fact that Jo was sneaking around in his house and that I know about it.

"I still think the house was settling," Aimee announces with the confidence of someone who isn't aware they're going to make things worse. "I've lived in houses before that creak and moan. Haven't you ever seen cracks on the drywall up near the ceiling? It's not a bad thing; it's—"

"Houses like this don't settle, darling," Mitch snaps. "They're built to withstand anything, and besides, a little shifting will not make a single framed photo jump off the wall."

"Right." Aimee's smile is tight.

"Well, maybe it was a ghost," I say, trying to lighten the mood. The last thing I need is for Patrick and Mitch to go digging together. I trust Patrick would keep his mouth shut if he were to find anything out of the ordinary on his own, but if Mitch were there... Well, he'd be forced to tell the truth about what he saw, wouldn't he?

"A ghost. Sure, Hannah. Anyway, the rest of us who aren't completely delusional can deal with this after dinner. You, me, and my office." Mitch looks pleased with himself, and I kick Patrick to make him look at me.

He does, and I widen my eyes, then slowly shake my head.

"I don't know if I can do that right after dinner," Patrick says, obviously picking up on my cues. "But tomorrow could work. I can call you in the morning and—"

"I pay enough money to have someone deal with this tonight. Either you do it with me, or I will make it so nobody wants to hire you and will destroy your company. Do you understand me?"

"Perfectly," Patrick replies.

"Honey," Aimee says to Mitch, "do you think you could not threaten our dinner guests? I thought tonight was going to be a lovely night and here it's turning—"

"You know what?" Abruptly, Mitch stands, the legs of his chair scraping against the floor. "Why don't we go look right now? No time like the present, right? Let's not drag our feet." He balls up his napkin and tosses it on the table.

I stand with Patrick, but Mitch holds out his hand to stop me. "Not you. Not Aimee. This is something for the two of us to handle."

"Mitch, you can't be serious right now. We're in the middle of dinner and you two are acting like children."

Aimee's got balls, I'll give her that much. Her eyebrows are knitted together, and she's staring at her husband like she hates him.

"I've never been more serious. Stay here, Aimee. For once, do what I tell you."

And with that, they leave. Patrick follows Mitch, the two of them rushing out of the dining room like the house itself is on fire and they're the only ones in the world who can stop it from burning down.

I sink back into my seat and drain my drink. Patrick hasn't finished his, so I reach over and take it. Once I've finished it, I put the glass back on the table and look at Aimee.

"Ghosts?" she asks, and I shrug.

"It is weird, when you think about it. One picture frame knocked off the wall, but nothing else was touched?" I don't want to sit here and chit-chat with her, but this is the perfect opportunity for me to dig for information and find out how much she knows. "Nothing else was out of place? Nothing was missing?"

Jo had come out of Mitch's bedroom with the folder, so I know she had to have grabbed it from in there. But where? He's not the type of guy to leave things like that lying around, so it must have been locked up somewhere. What else did he have locked up?

"You seem a little eager about this." Aimee tilts her head to the side and stares at me. "I can't help but think maybe you know more than you're letting on."

"What, you think I snuck into your house, poked around, then broke a picture frame before I left? Please. You're reaching."

"Maybe." She shrugs and takes a sip of water. "But maybe you were here looking for a way to handle our Mitch problem."

"It wasn't me."

"Fine." She levels her gaze at me. "But we still need to figure out a plan." She leans forward, her voice lower. "And you need to come clean with me. It seems too perfect that you're dating the guy who installed cameras over here and you suddenly have the uncanny ability to text right when I'm doing something, doesn't it?"

I smile at her, but inside I'm raging. Aimee's smarter than I thought she was. "Way to change the subject while I'm trying to help you figure out who might have broken into your house. And as for the cameras? You can't prove anything."

"Not yet I can't." She chews her lower lip. "So what's your plan? If you're really serious about doing this, why not take Mitch out tonight?"

"I already told you. Because Patrick is here." I stare at her, giving her a moment to think through what I said.

"Right, because he's such a Boy Scout. I don't think you have a plan. I think you're scared and looking for a way out of this."

I ignore her sass. "I have a plan." My voice is low to match hers. The men aren't close enough to hear us talking, but it's not worth the risk. When I whisper to her what I want to do, her eyes widen.

THIRTY-EIGHT

AIMEE

Sunday

Melinda stands in front of me, her dusting rag in her hand, but she doesn't answer my question.

"Melinda," I say before glancing at the window to make sure Mitch is still by the pool where I left him, "you were employed here when Jo was alive, right?"

She takes a deep breath before glancing in the same direction I did. "I was."

"And can you tell me—"

"Mrs. Ellis, I don't want to be rude, but Peter talked to you and Dr. Ellis fired him."

I close my eyes, my mind racing. She's right. If Mitch gets a whiff of what I want to talk to her about, he'll sack her before she has a chance to ask what she did wrong. Still, I can't help but think that maybe she'd get a better job than this one.

Who wants to clean on a Sunday? She wouldn't normally be here on the weekend, but she missed her usual shift Friday because her son was sick. So magnanimous of Mitch, to give her the option to come in over the weekend, which meant she had to get emergency childcare today.

"Here." I move quickly, taking my sapphire earrings out before either one of us has a chance to consider what I'm doing. "Take these and tell me what you know. Please."

"Oh no, you're not making it look like I stole," she says, backing up and pressing her hand to her chest. "Dr. Ellis would—"

"Right. You're right." I silently berate myself as I slip them back into my pocket. *That was stupid of me.* "Just answer one question and I promise I'll back off, okay?"

Her nod is stiff. Her eyes cut to the window before she looks back at me. "One question."

"Did my husband kill his first wife?"

Melinda goes pale. She takes a step closer to me before leaning forward. "Just be careful. That's all I can say." Before I can respond, she whips around and hurries out of the room.

It feels like the air has been knocked out of my lungs. I reach out and grab the back of the sofa for support, then walk into the kitchen and pour myself a shot of vodka. The first one goes down smooth, so I follow it with another.

Steph wouldn't think twice about day drinking. Right as I'm about to pour a third shot, a sound from outside draws my attention, and I glance out the window to see Mitch on the phone.

He's storming back and forth, his movements jerky and rigid. The day is gorgeous, with a cloudless sky and birds chirping, but he's walking around like something terrible has happened.

He looks livid. Slowly, like he's going to know what I'm doing, I put the vodka away. Rinse out the shot glass. There's a bag of chips the new chef keeps stashed in the back of the cupboard for her snack, and I remove the clip and eat a handful. The entire time, I'm keeping half an eye on him.

Still pacing. Still gesturing wildly.

I take a deep breath to prepare myself to go back outside, but Mitch bursts through the front door before I leave the kitchen. He's still on the phone, and I watch as he walks past me, his head turning back and forth like he's looking for me.

I freeze.

He didn't see me, and I don't know that I want him to.

"No, you listen. Last night, you acted like I was an idiot, but believe me, someone was in this house. You can't—"

I lean forward. Why did he stop talking? He's in the hall by the front door, and I watch as he hangs up his phone and shoves it into his pocket, then reaches out and takes a photo off the wall.

It's hanging right where the one fell Friday night. He turns it over in his hands like he's going to find an answer regarding how it got on the wall written on the back, and as he does, I know why he's so angry as he looks at what's in his hand.

It's his wedding photo.

But I'm not the bride.

THIRTY-NINE

JACKIE

Hannah has a baseball cap pulled low on her head when she finally ducks into the diner to meet me.

"Here," I call, waving my arm so she can see me. Instantly, I feel foolish and drop my hand back into my lap. Hannah has a way of making me feel a bit like a wreck. Even when I made an effort, she managed to look more put-together, more in control.

And now my clothes are all from thrift stores, and she still looks like a million bucks.

"Did you order for us?" she asks, sliding into the booth across from me. "I'm starving."

"Two burgers and fries." I point as the server approaches. He gives us our food, tells us to call him if we need anything, then disappears.

"Good. Thanks." Without preamble, Hannah takes a huge bite of her burger. "I have to be honest with you—I think you're right to be worried about Aimee."

"You do?" I twist my napkin. "Why do you say that?"

"I was there for dinner last night and Mitch has her completely under control. She's terrified of him."

I knew it.

No way can that monster of a man ever have a healthy relationship with anyone. I knew it from the moment I found out he was married—he's only going to choose someone weaker than he is so he can prey on them and bend them to his will.

It's what he did with me, after all, and tigers can't change their stripes.

"What happened? Did he hurt her?"

"No, he's not stupid." She pops a fry in her mouth and waits to speak until she's chewed and swallowed it. "But you can tell. *I* can tell. Remember how he used to lock the food up so you couldn't eat outside of pre-approved times?"

"He does that to her?"

Hannah nods. "Sure does. And he didn't let her have a phone until I bought her one and convinced him she needed to have contact with someone outside of their marriage. But it's not like he lets her spend time with her friends."

"Because they would see the problem and try to get her to leave him."

"Exactly." She takes a sip of her water and watches me over the top of her cup. "You thought he was a control freak when you two were married? He's worse now. You read the agreement she signed, but that's not all of it. I think he's going to kill her."

My breath catches in my throat. I don't know what to say. When I managed to get away from him, I never thought I'd willingly put myself near the man again. And even though I need Hannah on my side if I'm going to help Aimee, the thought of Mitch figuring out I'm around is terrifying.

But there is no justice in the world if even one woman is being abused. And even though there are systems set up to help women when they're in trouble, many don't have the strength to reach out. Or they know reaching out will put victims in more danger.

I got lucky, but only because there was one person willing to stick her neck out for me. Speaking of... as surreptitiously as possible, I pull my phone from my purse and check it to see if I've gotten a call back.

Not yet, and worry gives me a headache. If Mitch ever found out how this person helped me, what steps were taken to ensure I could get away from him... Well, it wouldn't be good.

"Hey, earth to Jo." Hannah snaps her fingers near my face to get my attention. "I know you and I weren't super close when you were married to Mitch, but we need to work together to save Aimee."

I take in the expression on her face, and it terrifies me. "You're scared for her, aren't you?"

"I am," she tells me, her words earnest. "Aimee doesn't deserve this. Neither did you. I couldn't see it. I was so wrapped up in my own world and the life I wanted to have that I wasn't able to see how you were suffering."

I exhale slowly. The agreement I read was worrisome, but I didn't think... well, I didn't think Mitch would kill Aimee so quickly. I was married to him a lot longer before he tried to get rid of me, but if Hannah is telling the truth, we need to hurry to save her.

I was right to come here.

I clear my throat, my mind racing. "Okay. You obviously have a plan about how you want to take care of this. All we have to do is get Aimee out of there, move her to a new place, and not let Mitch find out where she went. It should be easy, really, especially if the two of us work—"

"Is that really good enough?" Her question cuts through my thoughts, and I level my gaze at her. "Think about it. We get Aimee out of there, and then what? He finds another woman to take her place. You know as well as I do how charming he can be when he wants to. At the beginning, before he showed his true colors, did you have any idea what you were getting into?"

I shake my head, and she smiles, satisfied.

"So you can agree—we need to do more than simply get Aimee out of there."

"What are you saying?" My heart beats faster as I wait for her to say the one thing I'm sure she's going to.

Sure enough, she pushes her plate out of the way and leans on the table, getting as close to me as she can. "We kill him."

FORTY

AIMEE

"Someone's messing with me," Mitch says. He's pacing back and forth in the living room dressed to the nines because we're supposed to leave the house for a dinner invite. Instead of grabbing his keys and ushering me to the car, however, he can't stop worrying about the photo on the wall.

Suddenly he spins on me, jabbing his finger through the air. "Did you do it?"

"Me?" My mouth drops open in shock, and I shake my head. "What are you talking about? Are you really asking if I found a photo of your first wedding, found a frame, then hung it on the wall? Why in the world would I do that?"

He doesn't respond at first, and I get the feeling he's weighing each of my words, looking for the lie.

"To mess with me." He's coming closer to me now, his eyes locked on me like he's waiting for me to make a wrong move. "You thought it would be funny."

"Please." I'm sweating, but I don't want him to know how terrified I am of him right now. His expression? Yeah, it's the same one he wore in Florida when he was pointing his gun at his sister. "I don't think anything about that is funny. I'm married to you. I love you. Why would I want to ruin that?"

I don't know how I say that with a straight face, but I do, and he buys it.

For now at least.

"You're right." He seems to deflate a bit, his shoulders rounding forward. There's a crystal decanter with whiskey on the sideboard, and he pours himself an inch. Then a second. It isn't until he's had his third that he speaks again. "You're absolutely right, Aimee. I'm so sorry. I love you so much, and you wouldn't want to hurt me like that."

If it meant I got my freedom? I'd hurt you any way I had to.

"Definitely not," I tell him and force myself to hug him. He relaxes against me as I do. "It had to be someone else. One of the staff maybe?" I feel bad pointing him in Melinda's direction, but there's other staff as well.

"Not a chance." He kisses me, then pulls back. "Hannah."

"Hannah? She wouldn't," I say, but my mind is already slotting the pieces into place, and you know what? I can see why he made that leap. She says she's on my side, that we're working together, then she watches me on cameras. I know she does.

"Yes, she would." He yanks his phone from his pocket and stabs his screen. "I'm handling this now."

"Hey, don't you think we need to get going?"

The look he gives me is dark. "You're cool with my sister messing with our marriage?"

"I didn't say that," I tell him, and my mind flicks back to the paper I found tucked behind his baseboard. I want him to stay happy. I'll say whatever I have to as long as it keeps him happy with me, because he's dangerous, and I know the truth about what he did to his first wife.

And I don't want to die.

"We might not make it to dinner," he says and presses his phone against his cheek. When Hannah answers, he spins away from me, and I wonder if he wants privacy so I can't hear what the two of them are saying or if he's so angry he can't stand still.

"What kind of joke is this, Hannah?" he bellows, and I slowly lower myself back to the sofa. "What do you mean *what do you mean?* You thought it would be cute to hang up a photoshopped wedding photo in our hall."

He pauses, listening, his free hand clenching into a fist as he does. Boy, I'm glad I'm not on the receiving end of this call.

"No, she didn't." He glances at me. "She wouldn't."

I hate him and he terrifies me, but it's nice to hear him take my side. *For now.*

"Well, of course the security system wasn't on when we were in the house. The cameras only activate when the system is turned on and we're out and about."

Good to know.

"Sleepwalking? Where would she even get the photo in the first place?"

I sit quietly, my hands tucked in my lap. It's terrible of me to say, but I'm rather enjoying this. As long as his rage is pointed at someone else, it isn't pointed at me.

"Whatever. Stay away from us. I don't want you to call, don't want you to show up. Do you understand?" He pauses, and I think he's about to hang up the phone, but then he falls silent and listens.

What is she saying?

"Of course, if you really needed us, we'd be there for you. But you can't do this to me." He stabs the phone to hang it up and angrily shoves it back in his pocket. Before turning around to face me, he reaches up and carefully pushes his hair back into place. It already looks perfect, but someone like Mitch will not let a single errant strand mess up his night.

When he finally turns back to me, I stand up. "Did she admit she did it?"

"No."

Of course she didn't.

"Do you believe her?"

"I don't. My sister has problems."

"If she did it, do you think that maybe her heart was in the right place and then you called and were angry and she got scared?"

"Aimee." He walks over to me and takes my hands in his. "Believe me when I tell you, my sister is not a good human. She's crazy, and the fact that she did this and won't come clean about it scares me."

Two peas in a pod, the Ellis siblings.

"Right. Well, I'm so sorry this happened. I hope we can still have a good night."

He brushes my cheek, and I fight to keep from pulling away. "We will."

A wave of bravery washes over me. "Tell me about her," I say. My voice is neutral. Level.

He stiffens, and his hand falls to my shoulder. "Who?"

"Jo. She was beautiful. I had no idea." It's dangerous to push him when I know he doesn't want to talk about Jo, but I'm hoping the whiskey will loosen his tongue and calm his temper.

His fingers tighten. "She was."

I suck in a breath. His hand is so close to my neck. Is he strong enough to choke me? Is that how he killed her? "I'm so sorry," I say, and I'm encouraged when his grip relaxes a little. "Losing her had to be so difficult."

"It was a nightmare. I loved her." He drops his hand from my shoulder and scrubs it down his cheeks.

The man is good. Not as great an actor as I am but still good. If anyone were watching, they might actually think he was sad over his wife's death.

I glance down at the photo on the coffee table next to us. Really, it's a hack job, and I'm shocked that Mitch hasn't noticed the photo is actually from our wedding, not his and Jo's.

Unless he has noticed and hasn't reacted, which is a terrifying thought.

It was tricky getting her photo out from behind his baseboard without him noticing, trickier still to get to the local pharmacy so I could copy the photo, cut out her face, and impose it on my body.

Her original photo is back up where it belongs in his bedroom, so I doubt he'll ever realize what happened or even that it went missing.

And yeah, it was dangerous to go shopping right after I finally convinced him to give me a credit card, but I hid the purchase among a ton of others, including Midol and tampons, so he wouldn't question what I needed or what I was buying. I had to do something to get him off-balance and see if I could get him to admit killing his wife.

Hannah keeps claiming that she has everything under control, but I can't fully depend on her. I'm caught in a web between the two of them, and I'm doing everything possible to survive this, but to ensure I do, I want to make sure I have a way out.

Everything right now is a risk, and Aimee has never been a huge risk-taker.

But Steph is.

FORTY-ONE

HANNAH

Mitch thinks he can make me stay away from him and his precious wife?

No way.

I've been through too much—done too much—to back down now. It's been hard, but that's fine. I can do hard.

And even though the plan has changed, my determination hasn't. My drive hasn't.

There's only one thing that can make everything I've been through worth it, and that's Mitch's money. To get it, I have to get closer. I have to be the danger my brother never saw coming.

But as I hold the lit match in my fingers and look around my house, dropping it and walking away is still more difficult than I thought it would be.

FORTY-TWO

AIMEE

Monday

Mitch's phone wakes me up.

Even though we don't share a bedroom, I can hear his ringtone as clearly as if he were in the bed next to me, and I roll over, grab a pillow, and press it down on my head to block out the sound.

He doesn't normally get calls in the middle of the night, but when he does, it's the hospital. Someone must be having a terrible night for him to get called, and even though it's horrible to think, I'm thankful it's not me. I glance at my watch.

Two in the morning.

A few minutes later, right when I'm dozing off, my bedroom door flies open. My heart pounding, I sit up, pulling my blankets with me and holding them tight to my chest.

"What's going on?" I ask, then reach to the side to turn on my bedside lamp. "Is everything okay? Do you have to head in to the hospital?"

Even when he does, he doesn't tell me. He'll leave me a note downstairs or text my phone to let me know what time he thinks he'll be back, but he never wakes me up. Not like this. And as the light clicks on and I see his face, my stomach drops.

Something bad is happening.

"There's been a fire," he says, and that makes me throw back the covers. But I stumble slightly when I get up, disoriented from the back and forth between sleep and waking over the last few minutes, and I reach out to the mattress to steady myself.

He's at my side in an instant, his strong arm banded around my waist. I give my head a moment to clear, then gently tug away from him.

"Is the fire here? Are we okay?" My eyes flick around the room as I think about what I would take if this place were about to go up in flames. Nothing here is personal, not since he went through my closet and threw things away. It's all replaceable, and as long as I get out, I don't care about the clothes, the purses, the jewelry.

"We're fine. Our house is fine."

Sighing, I sit down on the edge of the bed. "Okay then, what's going on?"

"It's Hannah," he says, and his voice sounds strangled.

Immediately, I'm back at the night when I lost my twin. The terrible thing about losing a sibling is that nobody understands how painful it really is unless they've gone through it themselves. Sure, there are doctors and therapists who want to help you process your grief, but the one person you want to help you through it is gone and not coming back.

"Hannah's dead?" Shock rolls over me like a heavy wave, and I suddenly feel like I can't breathe. Reaching up, I grab for him, not because I love him and want him to feel my support, but because I need something sturdy to ensure I don't drown in the grief of my own memories.

"She's not dead," he tells me, but before he can say anything else, he's cut off.

"My house burned down, but I'm fine." Hannah swoops

into the room, an overnight bag over her arm, a huge grin on her face. "Thank you so much for letting me move in!" She throws herself at her brother, the bag falling to the ground. I watch as he hugs her, then I realize what feels strange about this.

How does she have an overnight bag if her house burned down?

My heart beats hard, and I recoil away from Mitch. Being dragged out of a good sleep is bad enough, but then seeing Hannah waltz into my bedroom like she owns the place is too difficult for me to understand.

"She's moving in?" I ask Mitch, dragging my eyes from the overnight bag up to his face to see what he thinks about this whole thing.

His body is stiff as he hugs his sister then gently pushes her away from him. She's crying, tears streaming down her cheeks, and when he pushes her back, she glances at me for a moment. Was that a smile? No. Surely not. Her lips are pulled back into a grimace.

Mitch's pajama pants are slung low on his hips, his torso on full display, and while I'm sure there are plenty of women in the world who would murder to be this close to a half-naked man who looks like him, I can't focus on anything but the fear growing in the back of my mind.

This is exactly like Florida.

Did Hannah burn down her house to get close to Mitch so we can kill him? That would explain how she had time to prepare an overnight bag before arriving here.

No. No way. She wouldn't, right? Not without telling me the plan.

But what part of the plan has she shared with me at all? Not much. Nothing, really, besides the fact that she wants to poison him and has already got what she needs.

"She's moving in until she can find her own place to stay,

but I couldn't very well expect her to do that at two in the morning, could I?" he says.

His words are cold and sharp, and I wince away from him as I stare at his sister.

Her chin is lifted, her eyes bright. It's the middle of the night and her house just burned down, but she's dressed to the nines, with her hair perfectly pulled back in a bun. She doesn't look like someone who just woke in fear as her house and all her possessions went up in flames.

"How did you get out?" I manage, scooting to the side so I can better see her while she answers.

"Pure luck. Patrick had been over, and we'd watched a movie. I'd actually seen him out the door and was getting ready for my shower when I smelled smoke."

"You can't stay with Patrick?" I ask.

The look she gives me is lethal. "I'm not interested in shacking up with some guy I'm dating, Aimee. Maybe you're cool with that kind of behavior, but I have a reputation to live up to."

I look at Mitch. "Honey," I say, my voice imploring, trying to sound as desperate as possible. Surely he'll turn her away. He was pissed off at her over the whole photo debacle, and I can't believe he'd change his mind that quickly.

But he gives my shoulder a squeeze before he speaks, and as he does, my heart drops. "We take care of family, Aimes. You know that. And Hannah made it clear that she needs me." He swallows hard, and I can almost imagine everything he wants to say but can't.

She has dirt on me.

She's crazy.

She probably started the fire herself.

"You won't even notice I'm here," Hannah announces. "I'll be in the room right next door, but I promise I don't snore." She throws me a wink, then turns to Mitch. "I can't thank you enough for opening your home to me. Why don't you get back to bed and Aimee and I can have a minute to talk?"

"Mitch, no—" I reach for his hand, but he leans down, kisses me on the forehead, and walks out of the room without a backwards glance.

I whip around to face her.

"It's going to be a sleepover," she tells me as she sits down on the edge of my bed. "Doesn't that sound great?"

"Remind me why you don't get a hotel? I know you're short on cash, but Mitch would cover it, I know he would."

Her eyes narrow. "I'm not going anywhere. You photoshopped that photo, didn't you? Where did you get the picture of her? He erased her from his life after she died."

"I didn't," I lie.

"You did. What, you think pushing his buttons is the best way to deal with him? No way. It's time to move things along. Why else do you think I'm here? This is the next stage in the plan. I called him crying, and he had to let me move in with him."

"You burned your own house down," I tell her.

"Aimee." She gasps and presses her hand against her chest. "What an accusation. Really, do you think I'd do something that crazy to move in here?"

Yeah, I do.

"Well," she tells me, continuing like she didn't ask me a question, "that's not an accusation I want you throwing about in front of your husband, okay? This is good. It's going to allow us to carry out our plan."

She burned down her own house. I know it.

I want to move away from her, but I'm terrified that any movement will set her off. You always hear about people having crazy eyes, but I'd never actually seen it in person. Now that I have, I want to get away from her. Sure, I was going to team up with her to take care of Mitch, but this is a step too far. An action this extreme tells me she's not playing with a full deck. Best to not let her know how much she scares me.

"Well, I guess now you can put your money where your mouth is," I tell her. "If you're really willing to go through with the plan that is."

"You wound me." Her tongue flicks out and licks her lower lip before she continues. "You're going to keep on like nothing is different, like you couldn't be happier to be married to him, okay? Everything is prepared. We need the right moment."

"How will I know when that is?"

She grins at me, and my heart sinks. "You have to trust me."

Mitch is on one side of me. Hannah on the other. I already know that he killed one wife.

And I know she promised me we'd work together to both get something out of this, but I don't trust her.

FORTY-THREE

HANNAH

I don't care what anyone says, I'm not moving out of this house.

Aimee has pulled up a few hotels in the area on her phone and has been showing my options to me for the past half an hour after breakfast, obviously desperate to do whatever it takes to get me out of her house.

Why? Why is she getting cold feet about helping me? She promised me she'd help me kill Mitch, but kicking me out of the house will make that harder. I burned down my house to have a better chance at handling Mitch and to keep an eye on her, and now I'm glad I did.

Does she have her own plan? Is she after my money? Just because she said she didn't want it doesn't mean a thing.

She could be lying to me.

"Aimee," I finally say, reaching out and lightly touching her hand so that she puts her phone down on the table, "while I really appreciate the hard work you've put into helping me, I think the best thing for me right now is to stay here with you and Mitch."

She takes a deep breath. "I know, but we just got married,

and I don't want you to feel uncomfortable when we... you know."

"Every other day, according to the agreement," I tell her, and her face falls.

"Mitch?" She turns to her husband, but my brother is currently grabbing his keys and phone from the table, and he barely glances at her. "Mitch, please, you know how much I value my alone time, and it doesn't really seem fair to take that from me."

"She's my sister!" He slams his hand down on the table directly in front of me, and Aimee shrinks back from the sound. "*And you are my wife*. Honor me. Do you understand? You've been pushing my buttons, Aimee, acting like... someone I don't know! The makeup? The clothing? The tattoo? I don't know what you're trying to do, but it's time you put a stop to it and remember what I've done for you. You made a vow to honor me and do whatever I want you to do. And even if you don't take our wedding vows seriously, you better not forget the contract you signed."

I don't move.

I don't breathe.

Neither does Aimee.

He bends over her, his eyes searching her face. She's as still as me, obviously waiting for the storm to pass. "Where did you get that eyeliner? I told you to stop wearing it."

Aimee blinks at him. "I had it in my makeup bag."

"No, you didn't. I would have thrown it away. Dig out any others you have hiding from me and throw them away too. And take it off before I get home."

Aimee reaches up slowly, one finger extended. My heart is in my throat as she rubs her finger across each eyelid, smudging it out. "Better?" she asks. Her words are a dare.

"You look like a gutter rat."

"I like black eyeliner. I'm happier like this."

What is she doing? She's going to get herself killed, and everything I'm working towards will fall apart.

"My wife—"

"Should have some freedoms, don't you think?" Her voice is quiet, but there's more strength to it than I would have thought possible. I hold my breath as I wait to see what's going to happen.

Finally, he huffs. Straightens up. Stalks out of the kitchen without saying goodbye.

Aimee and I sit silently until we hear the door to the garage slam, then it's like that snaps us out of our reverie.

I exhale slowly. My phone buzzes, and I check the text. When I see it's from Jo, I turn the screen so Aimee has no chance to see what's on it.

You need to come talk to me. Now.

Yeah, that's not happening right this second.

Aimee turns to me, her face pale. She looks confused, but her eyes narrow when I slowly clap.

"Well done, Aimee. Well freaking done. You've poked the bear, and now he's going to go to work and try to save people's lives. How are you going to feel if he kills someone, and it's all because you pissed him off?"

She doesn't respond. Instead, she drains her coffee and pushes back from the table. Before she can escape the dining room, however, I reach out, grabbing her wrist.

"Was your stupid eyeliner really worth it?" I stare at her. "Your tattoo? Is this really a hill you want to die on? Because I guarantee you, Jo died on a much smaller, more insignificant hill. What, you think you're some tough girl who can stand up to him or something?"

She stares at me, and it hits me what she did.

"Oh, you're channeling yourself, aren't you? Okay, *Steph*, where are you darting off to so quickly?"

"I'm going to my room." Her voice is cold. It's wild—I can almost see her internal struggle as she tries to keep her temper under control.

"I thought we were in this together. Don't you see? Me being in the house makes taking care of him that much easier, so stop trying to kick me out. Now, be honest with me about something, okay?" I lean closer to her. "You hung up that photo, didn't you? Admit it."

"No." She tries to jerk her arm away, but I keep my grip tight.

"No?" I can't help but laugh. She's doing everything she can to mess with Mitch and throw me under the bus, but she's clueless when it comes to one very important detail. "Then who do you think hung it up?"

"You probably." She juts her chin out at me.

"Mmm, interesting theory, but wrong. I prefer to not make him incredibly angry."

She lifts her chin. "If I remember correctly, killing him was *your* idea. Just so I have things clear, you're cool with that but not ticking him off?"

"That's right," I tell her. "Now I'm going to put my neck on the line *for you*, and us being in the same house will make final planning a lot easier, don't you think?"

"Probably."

I'm surprised she admitted it, but I refuse to let my shock show on my face. "Good. Then no more secrets. No more lies," I tell her as I let her go. She takes one step away from me, then another. She pauses in the doorway, then turns and races out of the room. I have to leave soon too so I can figure out what's going on with Jo, but I wait until I hear Aimee upstairs in her bedroom.

My theory? That she got scared I was going to turn on her

and photoshopped that wedding photo to throw Mitch for a loop and throw me under the bus. The only mistake she made?

The woman she included isn't Jo.

FORTY-FOUR

JACKIE

Hannah sits on the edge of my bed while I pace back and forth from the motel-room door to the bathroom. She looks calm, unflustered, but I can't sit still. Not when I know how much danger Aimee is in. Not when I know we have to do something about Mitch.

"Would you sit down?" Hannah pats the bed next to her. "You're making me dizzy and haven't told me why in the world it was such a big deal for me to come over here."

I whirl on her. That's Hannah for you, calm and collected, well aware that she has more money than most people and she's not afraid to use it to get what she wants. I don't have that luxury.

"You told me we were going to kill Mitch, but then you left me hanging." I hold my phone up and wave it at her. "Ignoring my texts? Come on, Hannah—you can't tell me you'll help me and then not loop me in."

Her mouth tightens. "For your information, my house burned down. I've been in crisis."

"Oh my gosh." I finally stop pacing and lean against the wall, my mind racing. What does this mean for our plan? Will she still be able and willing to go through with it? Hannah thinks on her toes, I know she does, but I don't know what this will do to our alliance. "Are you okay? What happened?"

"I'm fine. I'm living with Mitch since I lost everything."

I take her in. Her hair? Perfectly sleek and pulled back. Her clothes look neat, clean, but they're from a few seasons ago. "Did you have to go shopping today? Because I never would have guessed that you lost everything."

"I was able to save a few things," she sniffs. "I got lucky."

Lucky. Right. This was planned, and a chill races up my spine at the thought.

"I'm glad you're okay," I tell her, then take a step closer to her. "But now that you're here, let's come up with a plan. Does he have a gun? We could—"

"You tell me. *Does* he have a gun?"

Her turning the question around to me makes me blink in surprise. "Um, I don't know. I don't think so." There wasn't one in the safe when I found his contract, and I can't think of where else he would have hidden one.

"Great, so a gun is out." She crosses her arms and stares at me like she's enjoying this. "Any other ideas?"

We need something foolproof. Hannah and I can't mess this up. We'll make sure we get the dosage right, and we'll make sure we stick around long enough to see the job through, unlike when he tried to kill me.

"Poison," I tell her.

She nods. "Exactly what I was thinking."

"But I don't know where—"

"I do. You leave that part to me." She rubs her hands together like she's a cartoon villain, then gives me a huge smile. "I'm glad you're here to help me take care of this."

I nod, but there's something about the way she's looking at me that's concerning. Hannah and I were never really close, not really, no matter how much I tried to reach her. She kept me at arm's length, both literally and figuratively. "It's nice to have a plan."

"Yeah, you came in hot without direction, didn't you?" She's still grinning at me. But right as she opens her mouth to say something else, her phone beeps three times in a row.

The smile slides right off her face.

She yanks her phone from her purse and angrily taps on her screen.

Then, before I can ask her what's going on and if everything is okay, she races out the door to her car.

FORTY-FIVE

AIMEE

Hannah didn't tell me where she was going, but after she's been gone half an hour and there's no sign of her returning, I make a run for it.

I can get out of here and handle what I need to before she or Mitch catch on that I've left the house.

I hope.

If he's in surgery, then I'm golden because he'll be busy and won't know I'm missing for a while. If he's sitting around in his office hanging out, then my time is limited, and I really need to hurry before he checks in or wonders where I am.

And as for my sister-in-law? I have no idea where she is, but I'm not looking the gift horse of some time away from her in the mouth. Any goodwill she built with me she lost when she kept being cagey. I'll pretend I'm still working with her, but I have to take care of myself as well.

Pulling into the parking lot, I glance over my shoulder, terrified that Hannah might have caught on to where I went and followed me.

But although there are plenty of cars in the lot, her vehicle isn't one of them. I exhale and get out, taking a moment to consider what I'm doing before I go inside.

This is where she bought my burner phone. And if I'm lucky, the guy will have something I can use to protect myself. A gun, maybe. That would be great. Sure, there are plenty of knives in the house, but I can't rely on being able to stab Mitch if he comes for me. And what about Hannah? Do I really think she's on my side?

I mull it over. No, I don't. I want to believe that she'll help me kill Mitch and go away when I give her his money, but I'm terrified she'll turn on me too.

It's early morning, but the sun is bright, and I slip on my sunglasses before looking around the parking lot again.

When Hannah doesn't pull in, I exhale hard and hurry to the building. There's a bell over the door, and it jingles merrily as I yank the door open and step inside. The store is dimly lit, with long shelves of packaged food.

I don't have to look closely at them to see they're all covered in a fine layer of dust. While this place puts on a front of being a convenience store, I have a very good feeling that the only people who come in here are people like me.

Desperate people. People looking for something you can't get delivered from Amazon.

"I'm coming!" a voice yells from the back. "Hang out by the counter!"

I nod even though the person who called to me can't see me and make my way over to the grimy glass counter. When I look through it, I see old packs of gum, Zippo lighters, and cigarettes.

Soft rap plays from a stereo behind the counter, and I glance out the window to make sure I haven't been followed.

Still no sign of Hannah.

Sure, she could have parked down the street and walked here so I couldn't see her, but the longer she doesn't appear, the better I'm feeling about the possibility that she's returned home.

The idea of her wandering around the house looking for me makes me grin.

Unless she looks on the cameras and sees I've left.

The grin slides off my face at the thought.

"Hey, sorry about that. I appreciate you waiting. I had something to take care of in the back." A man brushes aside a dingy red curtain that doubles as a door to the back room and steps into the dull light of the main room. He's thin, tall, and pasty white like he hasn't seen the light of day in a while. His hair is slicked back with grease, and his clothes are all one size too big for him.

My mouth drops open when I see him. "Greg?"

His head snaps up to stare at me. "Do I know you?"

"You sold me a roofie," I tell him, planting my hands on the counter and leaning over it to get a bit closer to him. No way would I ever forget this guy. I met him in a dark alley when I bought the pills from him. It felt so stupid, so cliché, but that's the truth.

And now to find out he's the one who Hannah has been working with?

My mind races.

"You a cop?"

"No."

He pauses. "I sell a lot of people a lot of things. What are you doing here? What do you want?"

I take a deep breath. "I need protection."

"From?"

"My husband and his sister."

It's his turn to pause and take a deep breath. "They out to kill you or something?"

I nod. "Yeah, I think so."

"Leave town."

"It's not that easy."

His eyes flick up and down my body, obviously taking in the

nice clothing I'm wearing. They snag on my wedding band, and I have the sudden desire to shove my hand into my pocket so he can't see my ring, but I stay perfectly still.

"You have money. With money, everything is easy."

"My husband has money," I correct. "I'm along for the ride."

This gets a nod, like I'm finally speaking his language. "Alright, so you want protection. What were you thinking?"

"A gun."

"I don't deal in guns."

"I know you do because you sold a friend of mine a gun."

His eyebrow arches, and once again he looks me up and down. "Hannah."

"Right."

"She's the reason I no longer deal in guns. Taking it across state lines and then shooting it off when the police were nearby? What an idiot."

That's not exactly what happened, but if I tell him the truth, not only will he know I was there, but he might be even less inclined to help me.

"She's a loose cannon, but I'm not. Please."

"No guns." He crosses his skinny arms and stares at me. Terrible tattoos peek out from his sleeves. They look like an elementary school kid drew them.

"So you're cool with me being thrown to the wolves?" I ask. I'm desperate, and I look out the window again, but nobody is coming towards the building.

"No, I'm cool with saving my hide." He pauses, chewing on his lower lip, then speaks again. "I'll give you a taser. It won't kill them, but it will keep them off you long enough to make a run for it."

A taser is something at least. It's not powerful enough for me to really feel safe, but it should be enough for me to sleep easily at night. Truth be told, I should be happy with that, but I'm not.

"I can buy a taser at Walmart. Give me a gun, or I'll make sure you don't have any more clients."

His entire demeanor changes. He seemed a little unsure of himself at first, and I erroneously thought that meant I could take control. But now he straightens up and plants his hands on the counter in front of mine.

Sure, he's skinny, but he seems wiry. He looks scrappy, like the kind of guy who can definitely hold his own in a fight.

"Listen here," he tells me. "If you want a taser, you'll take it. But if you threaten me one more time, I will rain so much hell down on you that you won't be able to survive the storm."

I blink in surprise and lean back from him. "I need a gun," I say, and I know I sound whiny, but I can't help myself. He opens his mouth to respond, but whatever he's going to say is cut off by the sound of the bell over the door tinkling as someone enters behind me.

FORTY-SIX

JACKIE

Hannah tore out of the parking lot so fast I thought she was going to hit a curb and roll her car. She was hardly here for a few minutes before her phone chimed and she ran back to her car without saying goodbye. Without knowing what bee is in her bonnet, I don't know how long she'll be gone, but I should have some time to get into Mitch and Aimee's house.

I want to speak to Aimee face to face, and I have to hope she's home. Hannah promised me she had things under control and would get the ball rolling on getting rid of Mitch, but she didn't stay long enough to tell me her plan, and I don't want to sit around and wait for her. I'm seeing a side to Hannah I never knew, and it scares me. Is she really going to help when push comes to shove, or does she have her own agenda?

And what about Mitch? He's smart. Cunning. I'm terrified he's going to see an attack coming from a mile away. It's probably crazy to try to talk to Aimee, but I don't know what else to do.

I park down the road from Mitch's house, unwilling to be too close in case Hannah hurries back before I can escape.

There's a part of me that wants to go over the back fence like I did the last time I was here, but my chances of getting caught doing that are too high.

Mitch hires staff who he knows will be extremely loyal to him and fires anyone who dares cross him. This is great if you're him, but if you're his wife, there's no way you can let your guard down around any of them. I wonder if Aimee has learned that lesson yet or if she still thinks that she's safe here.

The wig I have on is itchy, and I feel like I'm going trick-or-treating, but I adjust it anyway, pull on an ugly bucket hat I grabbed from the free box at the closest thrift store, adjust my overalls, and pick up a clipboard. Only when I'm sure I look the part do I walk up to the house.

If anyone were to pay close attention, I'm sure they'd see my heart hammering away in my chest. I feel like it has to be lifting my shirt with every beat, but I don't have time to try to calm down.

I ring the doorbell.

Going in through the front door is risky, but I think it's smartest for me to let the staff in the house see me. They won't recognize me, not dressed like this. I'm sure of it. If I can get in the house, then I can not only snoop around but maybe get to talk to Aimee.

"Hello?" The chef is at the door. She's new, not someone I recognize. It's silly, but I was expecting the chef who was here when I lived here. Peter... that was his name. He always looked bored, and I remember how much free time he actually had in between meals. The one time I'd tried to bond with him over reading trashy sci-fi novels, he'd shot me down. Mitch didn't allow fraternization between the staff and me.

But this woman doesn't look bored. Her keen eyes drill into me like she can read my mind.

"Hi, I'm Linda Burnett from the United Methodist Church right down the road. We have a group of individuals going door to door offering any kind of help around the house that home-owners might need."

"We're fine, thank you." She starts to close the door, and I stick my foot out to stop her.

"Are you the homeowner?"

She closes her eyes for a moment. "I'm not."

"Okay, can I speak to the homeowner?"

"He's not home."

"And his wife?"

"Unavailable."

"I can wait for her," I tell her.

"No. She's unavailable." She straightens up a bit and stares down at me. My mouth drops open to argue, but she continues. "You are not welcome to come inside." She seems to grow, filling the doorway so I can't scoot past her.

I should have considered this as a possibility. If I escalate this, I risk her deciding to call the police.

Or worse, Mitch.

"Okay, I'll come back later." I pull my clipboard closer to my body. "I hope you have a great day, and—"

"Wonderful. Have a nice day." Pointedly, she looks at my foot, which is still blocking the door. I move it, stepping back, and let her close it in my face.

That was a disaster.

I want to get to know the woman Mitch married. I want to look her in the eyes and know for sure that she needs my help. Because as much as I wish I could trust Hannah, how much does she know about what's going on with Mitch's new wife?

Although, if I'm being honest, I'm still Mitch's wife, aren't I?

That thought hits me as I get into my car and drive away. Both on my way to Vermont and my entire time here, I've been thinking about saving Aimee and making sure that her husband doesn't hurt her.

I still want to do that. It's still the goal, but I have to make sure we're going about it the right way.

Hannah thinks the only way to save Aimee is to kill Mitch, but even though I agreed with her, I'm not so sure. I still think we can get her away from him and save her that way without getting any blood on our hands.

But what if she's right?

My life in Texas is fine. I love how simple it is, how I've created a routine that works for me, but I'd be lying if I said I didn't miss the money that came with being married to Mitch.

If he were gone...

I shake my head to clear the thought, but it springs right back up, unbidden, an itch I can't quite get rid of.

If he were gone, Aimee would be safe. That's the main reason I'm here.

But if he were gone, not only would she be safe, but I'd be his beneficiary. We never divorced. Everyone thinks I died, and that would be tricky enough to explain, but I think I could.

What if I came back from the dead? What then?

"Then I'd be rich," I mutter to myself as I drive back to the motel. "I'd have everything I needed and wouldn't want for a single thing."

A smile curls my lips.

Think of all the good I could do. I wouldn't be a dragon like Mitch is, sitting on a hoard of gold, unwilling to help others. No, I could make sure the public library had funding, pay off lunch debts for kids, even work with the local food bank to ensure the homeless had enough to eat.

And, sure, I'd upgrade my living quarters a bit and buy a car that doesn't sound like it's about to explode every time I stop. It would be amazing, and I wonder if Hannah has had the same thought. Is that why she's dragging her feet? Is she trying to figure out a way to get her money?

The thought that she might be more worried about her money than protecting Aimee gives me pause.

The light turns green right as I pull up to it, and I gas it through the intersection.

I'm so focused on getting back to my motel that I don't see the car coming.

FORTY-SEVEN

HANNAH

Greg's eyes widen as he recognizes me, and I like the power that shoots through me when I realize I scare him.

"Hannah," he says, and I kick myself for ever telling him my real first name. "What are you doing here?"

"I came to check up on my sister-in-law," I tell him, looping my arm around Aimee's shoulders. To her credit, she doesn't wince or pull away, even though I'm sure her skin is crawling from the contact.

"Sister-in-law?" Greg's always been pale, but right now he looks like a ghost. If he doesn't have a heart attack right here from putting all the pieces together, I'll be shocked.

"She sure is, Greggy boy," I tell him, then yank Aimee with me away from the counter. She stumbles against me, and I catch her. "You didn't see us," I tell him, then turn Aimee so we're facing the door.

"I only came in about—" Aimee begins, but I cut her off.

"You. Outside. Now." I push her forward, then follow behind her as quickly as possible to shove her outside. Once we're on the pavement and the door has closed behind us, I turn to her. "What were you doing chatting with Greg?"

She's quiet for a moment, then the words spill out. "I wanted a gun."

"Are you serious right now? Why?"

"Just in case you need help—

"Killing my brother?"

She nods. Her hands are clenched into fists, and she glances around like she's worried someone will be watching.

"Well, if you would have talked to me instead of doing something stupid, I would have told you that I have it under control, remember?" I pause, enjoying her watching me. "I've got everything I need to poison him."

"Great. Your buddy Greg wouldn't sell me a gun anyway, so if that's the plan, we need to move on with it. I don't know why you're dragging your feet."

I exhale slowly. As long as I can calm her down and get her out of here without her making a scene, it'll all work out.

Thank goodness for the tracker on her phone, or I never would have known she was here. It's little things like that, like my planning ahead, that put me in a better position than her. "I'm not dragging my feet," I tell her. "I'm planning. We get one shot at this."

She nods, then abruptly changes the subject. "How did you know I was here?" she asks. "Or were you coming to buy something else illegal?"

"Sheer luck," I tell her, but she's still talking.

"You got here right after me, even though I was looking behind me to make sure I wasn't being followed. I'm sure you could check the house cameras to see that I left, but how did you know where I was going?" She pauses. "Did Greg call you and let you know I was here?"

"You're paranoid," I scoff, but she isn't finished.

"There's a tracker on my car, isn't there?" She sounds confident, and I blink at her, my mind racing.

"You're right. You caught me. Although it was Mitch's idea, so don't blame me."

That stops her in her tracks. Her mouth hangs open, and I can see her mind racing to try to decide if she believes me or not. If she figures out that I'm the one who was tracking her, no way will she continue to think that we're working together. Besides, it's believable that Mitch would put a tracker on her.

No way will she question that, right? And it's not like she can ask him.

My phone buzzes in my purse, and I glance at my smart-watch to see who's calling.

The hospital. Mitch.

I tap the red icon to send him to voicemail. Whatever he wants, I'll deal with it later.

"Tonight," I tell her. "Your chef will make dinner, as always, but when it's plated and on the table, you'll distract Mitch. I don't care if you go outside to look at the flowers in the garden or if you seduce him, you will get him out of the way. Understand?"

She nods. "And then you'll—"

"Put the poison in his food." My plan doesn't end with that, but she can't know what else I'm hoping to accomplish.

"He's ruthless. If you don't put enough in his food—"

"I've got it under control." I grin at her, but before I can think of anything else to say, her phone rings.

She almost drops her bag digging it out. "Hi, Mitch," she says, her shoulders sagging with relief. "Oh, hanging out with Hannah."

Great. Now he'll know I dodged his call on purpose and wonder what's going on. Still, it is weird that he called me from the hospital and not from his personal cell. While she talks to my brother, I pull out my phone and listen to my voicemail.

Oh no.

It wasn't Mitch calling at all.

FORTY-EIGHT

JACKIE

The doctor standing at the foot of my bed is blurry.

I blink hard, and he snaps into focus.

"There you are." The smile he gives me is relaxing. "We've got you bandaged up, but I thought I lost you for a minute there. How are you feeling?"

"Everything hurts," I tell him, and that admission makes the pain wash over me. I fight against it and surface in time to hear him speaking.

"—you'll be better. Of course, that depends on if you're willing to take it easy."

Easy. Like not helping Hannah kill Mitch.

"I can do that," I lie.

"Great. You're pretty bruised up, especially on your ribs, but you lucked out and didn't break anything. I'm not sure how you got off that easy—most people wouldn't walk away from an accident like that."

"Old Corollas are built different," I manage, earning a smile.

"That's the truth. Unfortunately, even your old Corolla couldn't completely protect you when you were T-boned. You sound coherent, but I want to keep you here a bit longer for observation."

My head swims as I try to focus on what he's saying. I hear his words, and they do make sense, but there's part of me struggling to string them all together into a coherent thought. Answering him? That seems completely impossible.

Wait. Observation? No. Absolutely not. I shake my head, but my vision swims when I do, and I close my eyes, breathing deeply to try not to throw up.

"I know you want to leave, but—"

"No." The word bursts from me, and he looks surprised. No, please don't make me wait. I can't sit around here. I have... things to do."

"Everyone feels that way when I'm standing here telling them they need to sit tight. You're in good company, but you can't leave. Not yet." He pats my foot under the hospital blanket. "Hang out here for a bit and I'll get some more tests ordered, okay?" He starts to turn away, and I'm hit with the realization that I can't let him leave. Not yet. Not until I know how in trouble I really am.

"Will I be okay if I leave?"

He turns back with a sigh. "Probably, but I can't say for sure. Remember I said there's substantial bruising on your ribs, and I want to do a CT scan and ultrasound to make sure you don't have any internal bleeding."

Internal bleeding? I'm not a doctor, but even I know that's bad. Still, I think I'm fine. Yes, I'm fine. My thoughts are coming clearer, and wouldn't it be the opposite if I had internal bleeding? I'm feeling better, and I know one thing: I have to get out of here.

"And then I'll be free to go?" It's difficult, but I manage to look as much like a rule-follower as possible. I'm brown-nosing the doctor, but the hospital is the last place I can be long-term. It's not safe.

What if Mitch found out I was here? He'd want to finish the job—I know he would.

My heart beats faster.

"Yes, as soon as we've determined that you are safe, we'll discharge you."

Now that the thought of Mitch has entered my mind, I can't get it out of my head. I can picture him walking down the hall, his steps purposeful as he turned into my room.

And then he'd kill me.

"I want to be discharged now," I announce, and I'm grateful that my voice doesn't break. "I can't be here."

He frowns. "I can't recommend that. You were in a bad accident, and—"

"I have someone who can pick me up," I say, mentally crossing my fingers that she'll help me. Hannah will be upset that I don't reach out to her, but I don't like the way she drove away from the motel without telling me where she was going. I know she wants me to believe she's helping me, and I was...

But something's telling me to be careful.

He sighs, closing his eyes and looking up to the ceiling as if in prayer. When he finally looks at me again, I'm terrified he won't let me leave, but then—

"I can't hold you here, but I don't agree with this."

I'm already flipping back the blanket. Dizziness makes me sit still for a moment, but I don't want him to be able to tell that I'm struggling.

"—if you would wait, we can make sure you're okay and—"

"I can't wait." Mitch has become a specter, and I'm terrified that he's going to realize I'm here. No matter what, I have to get out of here. "Believe me, I just can't. I have to leave!"

I don't realize I'm screaming until I see him hold his hands up between us to get me to calm down. My breathing is erratic, my bangs stuck to my forehead. I must look a mess, and if I'm not careful, he might not let me leave. Instead, he might escort me right up to the mental health ward, and I'd be a sitting duck there waiting for Mitch to come finish the job.

"You will be leaving against medical advice, but I can't stop you. Call your ride and we'll get you out of here, okay? I hope you feel better."

"I'll be fine." I force myself to stand and fight the urge to reach out and brace myself on the wall. If he sees me acting that weak, he might change his mind and try to keep me here. "I have one thing to do, and I'll be fine. This will be over."

He doesn't respond, but it doesn't matter. He can't help me.

Only one person can.

FORTY-NINE

HANNAH

I toss my keys to the valet and race to the front doors of the hospital. They whoosh open, and I'm immediately engulfed in the scent of antiseptic. Someone calls for Dr. Albers over the loudspeaker. A nurse rushes past with her hands full. A small child stands by the wall, eyes wide, a bouquet of flowers in their hand.

I hate the hospital. It's not an uncommon reaction to entering one, I know, but my stomach still tightens, and I force myself to keep breathing as I rush to the women at the front desk.

"I'm Hannah Ellis," I say as soon as one of them looks up at me. "I missed a call from the hospital saying that a patient had been brought in from an accident and I was one of her emergency contacts." I still can't wrap my mind around Jo willingly putting me down as an emergency contact, but the knowledge gives me relief: she must really trust me.

"Okay, and what was the patient's name?" The woman is older and wrinkled, and she turns to her computer with the speed and grace of a DMV employee. "I can look them up for you."

"Jo," I say, then pause. Wait. That's her real name, but it's not what she's going by now. "Actually, she goes by a few different names, so I'm not sure which one she'd be using now."

"Which one is her driver's license under?" She removes her hands from the keyboard and rests them in her lap while she looks at me. "You must know that."

I take a deep breath. "I'm sorry, she's—can't you look up who was brought in after a car accident? Surely there has to be that information on your computer." I reach out and tap the top of her monitor, earning myself a glare.

Slowly, she turns from me. "Wanda, can you come help this woman? I don't know what to do for her."

Wanda. Great. With my luck, I'm going to have two of the Golden Girls trying and failing to help me. I might as well go room by room, patient by patient, trying to locate Jo.

To my surprise, Wanda is about my age, with bold winged eyeliner and a sharp fringe. "Who are you looking for?" she asks, already leaning over the older woman so she can look at the computer.

"My friend was in a car accident—" I explain, but I'm cut off.

"This woman doesn't know her friend's name," the older woman says, and I roll my eyes.

"I know her name. She changes it and goes by different ones from time to time. That's why I'm struggling here."

"Oh." Wanda frowns at me, but after a moment, she looks back at the keyboard. "That makes it tricky, but I can narrow it down. I don't know if I can tell you the patient's name, however. Do you know who called you?"

"They left a voicemail," I explain, then mentally kick myself. "And I deleted it."

"Then you're out of luck," the older woman begins, but Wanda cuts her off.

"I'm sorry, I wish I could help you more. Give me a minute and I'll see..." Her fingers fly across the keyboard.

It takes all my self-control not to launch myself over the desk and look at the screen.

"Okay," Wanda says, then glances at the woman in the seat. "Christine, why don't you take your break? I know your ankles swell when you sit for too long, so you go walk around and I'll handle it."

Christine doesn't need to be told twice. She shoots me a reproachful look before she gets up and skedaddles away, allowing Wanda to sit down in her seat.

"Okay, I can't tell you much because I'll lose my job, but I can tell you that a woman was brought in after a car accident and released."

"Released? How? Did she drive away?" My mind races. If that's the case, all I have to do is swing by Jo's motel and check on her. She's a vital part of my plan now, and I need to keep her uninjured.

For now.

"Um..." Wanda lowers her voice. "Maybe someone picked her up? A friend? Her guardian angel?"

"What? No. Who?" I plant my hands on the desk and lean over it, trying to catch a glimpse of her screen, but she's fast and closes the window she was looking at. "Oh, come on. You have to know."

"If there's nothing else I can help you with, then I'm going to need you to step out of the line so I can help the next person." The smile on her face is fake and annoying.

"Fine. Fine." I move out of the way, already pulling my phone from my pocket.

Patrick picks up before I even make it outside.

"How's my favorite fake girlfriend?"

"I need a favor," I tell him, stepping back so I'm standing

against the hospital wall. "Jo got picked up at the hospital, and I need to know who helped her out."

He barks out a laugh. "Alright, let me rub my magic lamp here and ask the genie to break into the hospital's security system for me."

"I don't need your sarcasm."

"Yeah, well, you can't ask the impossible and expect me to deliver. There are limits to my power, Hannah."

"That's not how you acted before. You were all high and mighty like you could do anything, so don't pretend like you can't now."

"I appreciate your faith in me, but—"

"It's misplaced. I see that now." Without thinking through the repercussions, I hang up on him. Then, for good measure, I silence my phone and drop it back into my purse.

I have to hope that Jo is at her motel. If not, then she's gone rogue, and I have no idea who might be helping her. Her sneaking around with a guardian angel isn't part of my plan. I have to find her before she rears her head in front of Mitch or Aimee. If this is all going to work, there's only one place I need her.

In the morgue.

FIFTY

AIMEE

I see the dark expression that crosses my husband's face when I shy away from his touch.

We're next to each other at the dining room table, Hannah across from us. Dinner is salmon over a bed of greens, and while I'm sure it's delicious, every bite tastes like sand. I upheld my part of the plan and got Mitch out of the house for a few minutes before dinner, but was it long enough for Hannah to put the poison in his food? There wasn't a good way to ask her, and I'm terrified of either outcome. He could die right in front of my eyes, or dinner finishes without anything happening to him.

Either way, I feel like I'm on stage in a play and I've never read the script.

"Patrick didn't want to join us for dinner tonight?" I ask, daring to break the silence growing at the table.

"We're on the rocks," Hannah tells me. She holds my gaze while she spears a bite of lettuce. "I guess not every relationship is as perfect as yours."

Is she trying to tell me something when she looks at me like that? Or am I reading into things? My hands are sweaty, and I wipe them on the napkin in my lap. It's not like I can ask her if she managed to get the poison in Mitch's food.

If I'd been able to buy a gun, I'd feel better right now, but it's best if I don't rely on anyone at this table.

"He wasn't good for you," Mitch announces. "You can do better than someone like that."

"What's that supposed to mean?" She hasn't taken the bite of lettuce yet, and she pokes her fork at him. "*Do better* than him."

"Just that. He's lower class."

"I guess maybe if you hadn't stripped me of my portion of our parents' estate, I wouldn't feel the need to go slumming."

Listening to them is like watching a tennis game, but I keep my eyes studiously on my plate. They've got to stop arguing if he's ever going to take a bite of his dinner.

"They didn't think you would make good financial decisions," Mitch tells her. He sounds tired, bored with the conversation, like the two of them have had it multiple times already. "You know this."

"Right." She stabs another piece of lettuce, then puts her fork down. "I'm going to my room."

"Dinner isn't over." Mitch reaches out and rests his hand on my thigh. I tense at the contact but force myself to relax so he can't tell how uncomfortable I am.

"Oh, it is." She tosses her napkin onto her plate and stands up, her chair legs scraping across the floor as she does. "It's been over." With that, she turns and stomps her way out of the dining room.

To my surprise, Mitch lets her go. I thought he'd try to stop her, that he'd at least call to her and make her come back to apologize, but we sit in silence as she hurries up the stairs and down the hall to her room. When she slams the door, I wince, but Mitch doesn't respond.

"Well, she's in a delightful mood," he tells me, letting go of my thigh and taking a bite of his salmon. "You two hung out today, didn't you? Did she have this crappy attitude the entire time?" A smile plays on the corners of his mouth, and I'm immediately reminded of when we met in Florida.

As much as I don't want to admit it, especially while I'm living in his house and under his rules, Mitch is addictive. You *want* him to like you. It's clear why people are drawn to him, and Mitch has a lot of people around him who love his personality and sense of humor. I haven't seen that side of him in a while, but he's always down for a laugh and can even let Hannah's theatrics roll off his shoulders when he's in a good mood.

But when he's not? Then you better buckle up, buttercup, because it's about to get hairy. Now that I've seen both sides of his personality, I'm even more convinced of the fact that I don't want to piss him off.

It's not just that I'll upset him. I've never been one to worry about upsetting men. The problem isn't his feelings, it's what he might do when he feels pushed to the edge. He has all the control in our relationship, and that means I can never predict what he might do.

"I mean, her house burned down, but other than that? Not really." I pause, considering how far I'm willing to go. "I was planning to be by myself, but she bumped into me in town." I take a bite of my dinner and gesture at his place. "How's your meal?"

He ignores my question. "She bumped into you."

I swallow hard. Did I say the wrong thing? "Yeah, is that okay? I thought we were cool to hang out, but if it's a problem, I need to know. I—"

"Get your purse," Mitch announces, dropping his fork to his plate with a clatter.

I have a bite of food halfway to my mouth, and I stare at him. "What?"

"Get. Your. Purse." He stares at me. "Now."

"Don't you want to finish dinner? It's so good."

He doesn't respond, and a question spills from my lips. "Did I do something wrong?" I'm already on my feet as I ask the question, already stepping away from the table, but I pause in the doorway, unwilling to commit to doing what he told me to do until I know for sure that I don't have a choice.

Why won't he finish his food?

"I don't want to eat. What I want is to see your purse. I bought it for you, and I want to see it. So go get it."

I don't want to argue with him, not when I can see the look on his face. Instead, I turn and race upstairs.

Outside Hannah's room, I pause, my ears pricked to hear what's going on behind her closed door. There's nothing, and even though I want to stand here for a while longer to see what she might be up to, I dart into my room.

My bag is in my closet, and I grab it, then hurry back to the stairs. At the top, I pause.

Is Hannah in Mitch's bedroom?

My hand trembles as I reach out and carefully turn the knob. I'm fully expecting to push his door open, but it doesn't open. I drop to my knees, tilt my head to the floor, and try to look underneath.

There's a crack of light, but nothing else that I can see. Mitch isn't the kind of guy to leave a light on in his room, but it's not like I'm going to go downstairs and tell my husband that I'm trying to look into his room because I think his sister has broken into it.

Instead of worrying about it, I go back downstairs and hand my Kelly to Mitch. He doesn't pause before digging into it.

ChapStick. A pack of Kleenex. Tampons. Breath mints. My wallet. Nothing looks out of the ordinary, and I have no idea what he might be looking for.

"Mitch—"

"Give me a minute." He turns my bag upside down and shakes it. Finally, he sighs, then looks at me. "Has Hannah given you anything else?"

"What is this about?" I ask. My mind is racing, but I'm not following him.

"Did she give you anything else? Answer the question, Aimee."

"My phone, I guess." I reach down to my pocket, where I have it stashed, but he holds his hand out for me to hand it over, so I dig it out. "Okay, here."

"Unlock it," he tells me, and I do. Nervous, I watch as he taps into my phone, his finger flicking across the screen as he looks through my apps. Not that I've downloaded any—the last thing I wanted was this exact scenario. Finally, he sighs and hands it back.

"What was that about?" I ask, sliding it into my pocket. He doesn't immediately respond, and I shove my belongings back in my bag. "Mitch? Why the sudden interest in my stuff?"

"She's following you," he tells me, and a chill races up my spine. *I knew it.*

"What do you mean?"

"Just that. I checked in on the cameras today at work and you left the house well before she did. You two ended up at the same place?"

I nod.

"And you didn't tell her where you were going?" When I pause, his voice drops. "Tell me the truth, Aimes. I'm serious right now."

"I didn't tell her." My mind races. "She just showed up."

"She probably installed something on your car. You can buy trackers and attach them without much problem, and I bet you that's what she did." Abruptly, he stands, pushing back from the table. "I'm taking your car to get checked for a tracker."

I freeze, Hannah's words from earlier circling through my

mind. Was she telling the truth? Or was she lying to me to keep me from turning on her? "You're the one who put a tracker on it," I manage.

"Me?" He frowns as he stares at me. "What are you talking about? Why would you say that?"

"Hannah said—"

"*Hannah said.*" Each word has a sharp edge, and I wince away from them. "I bet she did. I'll be back after I find the tracker, and then I'll deal with her."

Back? You might not even survive driving down the driveway. My mind races as I try to remember how much he's had to eat. Did he eat enough poison? I glance at his plate.

Did Hannah even put it in his food?

I swallow hard. "You know how to do that?"

"I know someone who does. Stay home."

"But dinner—" I begin, but he's already whirled away from me.

He grabs my keys from by the door and stomps out into the garage. I sink into my seat, my appetite gone, and look up at the ceiling.

Hannah is up there, and if she's been tracking me the way Mitch thinks she has, then I need to be more careful. Has she been lying to me this entire time? Worry eats at me, but there's nothing I can do about her following me right now.

I take a deep breath and exhale slowly, then it hits me that now's the perfect time to see if she's in his room. If she's lying to me, I need to know.

If I have to protect myself, now is the time to find out.

FIFTY-ONE

HANNAH

I'm sure Mitch didn't eat enough of his poisoned dinner to kill him, which means I'm going to have to do this the old-fashioned way.

I need a gun. It's reliable and my best option for finishing this.

There's a safe in his closet, and while that's probably my best bet, I've tried a few codes and nothing will unlock it, so I let his clothes fall back into place and hurried out of his closet.

Speaking of Jo...

Her phone goes to voicemail, and I hang up. *Where is she?* Someone had to have gotten her out of the hospital, but who? *A guardian angel.* There's a limited number of people Jo would tell she's in town, much less let take her from the hospital.

Everything is falling apart.

I stop and press my hands into the sides of my head. This night is getting away from me. I have to get it back under control —and fast—if I'm going to get the one thing I want.

Jo's not dead, that much I'm sure of, because I think the hospital would have told me if she'd died. They'd have no reason to lie about her being picked up. Unfortunately for me, I need her to die so my plan will work. I can't kill her if I don't know where she is, and right now I'm spinning my wheels trying to figure out what to do.

Downstairs, there's a loud slam, and I jerk to attention. I hurry to the door and listen, going so far as to lean against it so I can hear as much as possible.

Nothing.

Then someone starts running up the stairs.

Panic grips me, and I step back from the door, my hand out and flailing for the light. I hit it on my third try, the click sounding louder than I thought it would.

Footsteps stop right outside the bedroom door. My heart is in my throat, and my spit sours in the back of my mouth.

Aimee? Or Mitch?

One would be problematic. One would be dangerous.

The person is standing right outside the door, and I step closer to it, swallowing hard as I try to get my heart rate under control. I need it to slow down so I can hear what's going on. My mind races, and I'm having trouble thinking.

"Hannah. What are you doing in there?"

Aimee's voice makes me recoil from the door. I don't respond. I don't even breathe.

"I know you're in there, and if you don't open the door right now, I'm telling Mitch everything. That you wanted to poison him. That you're crazy for your money."

I think she's bluffing. I heard a slam downstairs, and I'd bet anything that Mitch left the house in a hurry. She's here by herself, and she has no way of getting backup.

Confident that she didn't catch me doing anything I'm not supposed to, I throw the door open. "You promised me you'd help me kill Mitch."

"Yeah, and then you made him so angry at dinner he didn't eat but two bites. Super helpful, Hannah."

"I'm not the one who drove him out of the house." She pauses, and I know I'm right. He's gone.

"What are you doing in my husband's bedroom?"

"Doesn't matter," I tell her. I take a step towards her, expecting her to move out of the way, but she seems to dig in her heels. "Move."

She raises her hand, and I see what she's holding. "Smile for the camera, Hannah."

"Are you recording me?" I reach for her phone, fully intending to grab it and throw it down the stairs, but she jerks back. "What are you doing? You think you're gonna record me and turn me in to Mitch? You think he'd let you walk away from the fallout in one piece? Not when I tell him we were planning on killing him together until you got cold feet."

"He'd never believe you. He knows about you following me out of the house earlier today. You put the tracker on me, and he knows it. Is it on my car? In my purse?"

I have to fight to keep from glancing at her phone.

Mitch doesn't realize the phone is the problem. And him leaving the house right now at such a pivotal moment tells me one thing—he has no idea how much danger he's in. He's not running away; he's still trying to fix things, but why? Does he love her that much? Whatever the reason, the man is clueless as to what's about to happen to him.

Good.

"No tracker on your car," I finally tell her. "Scout's honor. You're a crap driver, like an old grandma with a pot of chili in the back, taking turns at ten miles an hour. If you drove like a normal human, then it wouldn't be so easy to follow you."

She doesn't respond. Just keeps her phone pointed at me. Annoying.

"What, you gonna show Mitch I was in his room? Is that your idea of a good time? Wow, sounds fun." I wave at the camera. "Hey, Mitch! I was in your room!" I'm frustrated and getting even more so the longer she stands there staring at me like a cow.

To think I hunted her down for years, and I could push her down the stairs right now. That wouldn't end it, would it? But I no longer dream about her dead. I dream about the money Mitch stole from me. It does burn me that she told me she'd be on my team and now is turning on me, so really... she'd deserve what was coming to her. But not yet.

I refuse to put this much time and energy into something just to lose everything. No, as great as pushing her would feel, all it would do is cause Mitch to rain his anger down on me. I know the security cameras here have a great shot of where the two of us are standing right now, so either he'd kill me or turn me in to the cops.

Still. When I close my eyes, only for a second, I see myself reaching out. I see my hands on her shoulders, the way her eyes light up with fear. It's delightful, the mental image of how her lips purse together like she's going to puzzle her way out of this, then how her head snaps back as I push her.

I can hear the sound of her body tumbling, head over heels, until she finally smacks the first floor and is still.

And it's thrilling. I take a deep breath, smelling my perfume and her fear. She's a prey animal, and she hasn't looked away from me since I came out of Mitch's room. Knowing that I scare her, that I have that much power of her, is intoxicating.

I take a step towards her to see what she'll do, and I'm delighted when she moves away from me. She might act like she has all the power, but the reality is that she's scared of what I might do.

"Admit it. You photoshopped Mitch's wedding photo." It's driving me nuts that she keeps lying about this. With everything drawing to an end, I want to know the truth. She doesn't confirm, but I don't need her to. "Yeah, I knew it, even when you acted like you were innocent before. Where did you find the photo you used?"

Aimee swallows hard. It's clear she's not sure whether she should answer, but she finally clears her throat. "It was in Mitch's things."

I frown. "Where?"

"Hidden in the top drawer of his dresser. Why?"

That explains why I didn't know it existed. I'm nosy but not really one to dig through my brother's underwear.

"Just curious. He didn't eat enough of his food. We'll have to try poisoning him again another night because when he's upset like this, he won't want anything to eat. We've lost our chance."

Her shoulders fall. "No. No, no, no, there has to be something we can do, some way we can get this night back on track! He's upset, and we can use that against him."

I take a deep breath to try to calm down. "He's been upset since your Photoshop stunt." Aimee has no idea that was a terrible thing for her to do. It tipped her hand to Mitch, even if he won't let himself believe that his precious wife is the one who put up the photo.

"I thought it would get him off-balance. I thought he'd start to question himself, and we'd have the upper hand." She pauses. "I can see why he married her."

I stare at her. "Why he... what?"

"Married her." Aimee's still holding the phone between the two of us, but her hand has dropped, so she's no longer filming my face. She doesn't seem to notice. "Jo. His first wife was pretty."

A laugh bubbles out of me. "That wasn't Jo."

FIFTY-TWO

AIMEE

Who was the woman in the photo?

I ask Hannah, but instead of responding, she grins at me and shakes her head. My stomach drops, and I rush into Mitch's bedroom, turn on the light, drop to my knees, and pull the moveable piece of baseboard out of the way.

This time I don't hesitate putting my hand inside to pull out the papers, but I brush empty air.

"No," I whisper, angling my body so I can reach deeper into the space without my hand cramping. My fingers brush the back of the hole, the sides, the floor. I turn my hand and reach up to feel if he somehow stashed them higher, but there's nothing.

My heart pounds, and my cheeks feel flushed. Slowly, like I'm in a daze, I put the missing piece of baseboard back and sit back on my heels. My body moves on its own as I stand and open the drawer in Mitch's dresser where I found the woman's photo. I used it to photoshop the wedding photo, then slipped the original back in here.

It's gone.

As my head spins, I lean against the dresser for support, my eyes locked on my feet. Slowly, I look around me, trying to wrap my mind around what's happening. My phone is on the floor. Glancing at it, I see it's still recording.

A lot of good that did me. I don't know what I was thinking —it's not like I can show the video to Mitch to prove... what? That Hannah is messing with me? The only thing it shows is that I'm the one who altered his photo to freak him out.

It didn't work. Is that why he moved the photo? Because he knew someone was messing with him? It disappearing only raises more questions than it answers, and now I'm left wondering who this woman was. I close my eyes and think about what she looked like. Pretty, with thick hair and a huge smile on her face. It was clear that whoever took the photo of her loved her, and I naturally assumed it was his wife.

Why else would he have the photo hidden away?

My fingers tremble as I open the browser on my phone. It's never crossed my mind to google his first wife, and why would it? Not only does he check my phone every day to make sure I haven't done something I wasn't supposed to, but I assumed the photo I found was of her, and why wouldn't I? It's the only photo in the house of anyone but Mitch and me. I'm an idiot.

Jo Ellis.

The first link is for her obituary, and I click it, a sour taste in my mouth. Even though I don't want to know what happened to her, my eyes still skim the words until they land on her photo.

She was gorgeous, and vaguely familiar, as if I've run into her before, but I don't know where or when. A perky little nose and freckles that made her look like the girl next door, but hair that had to cost a fortune and lips people would pay to have. My gut twists knowing that she's dead, and it makes me sick knowing Mitch had something to do with it.

But she's definitely not the woman in the photo.

"You gotta get it together," I mutter, pushing myself off the floor. I shove my phone into my pocket, then let myself out of

Mitch's room. Hannah's standing at the top of the stairs where I left her, obviously waiting for me.

She wanted to push me down the stairs, I'm sure of it. I saw the desire burning in her eyes. But she didn't. Because we're still a team.

"Aimee? You okay?" She steps out of the way as I push past her to go downstairs. My body moves on autopilot, and I can't seem to stop my feet.

Downstairs, I pace. I can't stand still, and I don't know what to do with myself. What a mess I've made of things. There are so many mistakes I've made, and they've all brought me here— married to a murderer, scheming against him with his sister, but unable to do anything useful because I keep screwing up.

I turn at the bottom of the stairs and loop back through the main part of the house. My mind is on overdrive, and I barely register the furniture, the art, the gorgeous paintings on the walls. I cross over to where I hung up the photo of Mitch and some random woman thinking I could surprise him and throw him for a loop.

And what did I do? Nothing, apparently. All I did was show him my hand and let him know that I'd been sneaking around. This entire time I thought I was channeling my old self, channeling Steph, and all I was doing was acting a fool.

He didn't call me out though, which is strange. Either he still believes Hannah is the one who photoshopped the photo or he's keeping his cards close to his chest.

Why wouldn't he confront me? He could have called me out, but he didn't, and I can't wrap my mind around it.

"Think," I mutter. I have my hands planted on my hips as I stare at the photos on the wall. The one I photoshopped is missing, and I wonder what he did with it. Probably threw it away.

And I thought I was so tough. What a joke.

Tears burn my eyes, and I angrily wipe them away. I married Mitch because I didn't have a choice, but I honestly thought I'd find a way out of this. Now, though, I'm seeing that there isn't one.

I screwed up.

There are footsteps behind me, but I don't bother moving. There's nothing Hannah can do or say that will make me feel better. I told her I would work with her, but then I doubted her behind her back. If I hadn't done that, if I'd been all in on getting rid of him like she is, maybe our plan would have worked.

But I kept running my mouth about her to Mitch and drove him away from dinner, and now I'm going to be the reason our plan doesn't work.

A sob tears from my throat, and I sink to the floor. I miss my friends. I want them in my life. I need their arms around me and to hear them talk me through what's going to happen. They'd fix this, I know they would, but as much as I'd love to call them, I can't. Mitch made it clear I wasn't allowed to have them in my life, and for all I know, they've moved on. They didn't need me.

Nobody needs me.

Now the tears fall, and I can't stop them. I'm sniffling and wiping them away with the back of my hand, my mind still racing as I think through what options I might have to fix this.

And then I remember one person who said they would be there for me if I needed them.

FIFTY-THREE

JACKIE

Every part of my body hurts, but at least I'm not dead.

That's what I keep telling myself anyway. The truth of the matter is that I feel like I could die and, if my luck continues the way it has been, I wouldn't be surprised if that's what happens.

Just up and die. Survive Mitch, survive a car accident, survive all the crap that has led me to being the person I am today and kick it right here on one of the most comfortable sofas I think I've ever stretched out on.

"Can I get you anything else? I can't believe the doctors let you leave the hospital." The woman hovering near me is worried. She hasn't said anything about her concerns, but she doesn't need to. I can see the way she's frowning, how her smile hasn't reached her eyes since she picked me up at the hospital.

Her voice is tight, exactly like it was when I called her. I want to tell her I'm okay, that she can relax, but the truth of the matter is that I don't know if I am.

I survived this, and from what the police are saying, it was some freak accident. A kid on his phone, texting. Of course. But better than it being planned, better than it being a hit, and I have to believe them because the alternative is that my mind runs away in fear.

"I'm fine." Shifting, I push myself so that I'm sitting up. It makes the room spin a bit, but I'm not keen on telling her that. She'd only grow more worried, hover more, try to get me to go back to the hospital, but there's no way I'm doing that. "Really, I appreciate you letting me come here. I didn't know who else to call. And I appreciate you swinging by the motel and getting all of my things."

She sits down next to me, lowering herself slowly, so she doesn't rock me with too much movement. "I'm glad you called. But I thought you had left town forever. It would have been the smart thing to do." Her tone takes on an edge, and I wince.

"I know, but I had to come back when I saw the news."

"I helped you, Jo. You put me at risk when you showed back up, you know that?"

Her tone makes me glance at her in surprise. One of the things I appreciate about her is how even keeled she always is, but that's not true right now.

"I'm sorry," I tell her, and while I am sorry I upset her, I'm not sorry for what I've done. I have to help Aimee, and I'm not leaving until I do.

She sighs and presses her fingers into her temple as if to get rid of a headache. "I know, I know. You went through it, and you don't want anyone else to go through it."

"Exactly—"

"But it was stupid of you to come back here. You have to stay here—do you understand me? No leaving the house until you leave the state. I'm not going down with you."

I stare at her, frustration making it difficult for me to speak. "You want me to—"

"Hibernate here. What, did you actually have a plan, or were you going to come in with guns blazing?"

I stiffen. She doesn't have to call me out like this. "More of a general idea with a bit of planning thrown in."

"What planning?"

My mind races.

"Yeah, you don't have a plan, do you? Luckily, I have a way to get rid of Mitch once and for all."

FIFTY-FOUR

HANNAH

Of course Aimee would assume that the woman in the photo was Jo. It's easy to follow her line of thinking. I'm surprised Mitch had the photo tucked away for safekeeping. Unfortunately for her, that means that she clued him in to the fact that she doesn't trust him.

Which begs the question: how long will he let her survive after she showed him she isn't on his side? If only he'd eaten more of his dinner, this night would be drawing to a different conclusion. But while getting rid of him is part of my plan, it's only one thing I have to tick off my to-do list before my big payday.

I need to find Jo. My entire plan hinges on getting her here and killing her so I can frame Aimee, but if she's off licking her wounds under a rock somewhere, then I won't be able to put my plan into action.

If Mitch dies and Jo comes forward, she gets all his money.

If Mitch and Jo both die, however, Aimee's marriage will be invalid. She'll take the fall, and I'll get my cash. I can see the headline now.

Married for Money and Willing to Kill for It

It'll be easy to spin: Aimee married Mitch because he was rich but then had to off him and his actual wife to get his money. Jo showing up caused a wrinkle in my plan, that's for sure, but killing her will iron everything out.

Thinking about her spurs me to action, and I whip out my phone, call her, and wait. It rings a few times and clicks over to voicemail. Frustration courses through me, and I hang up, then drop my phone back on the bed next to me.

Change of plans.

I can't hunt her down, not when she's not in the one place I know to look: the motel. I've already swung by there and banged on her door, but no matter how much I tried to bribe the guy at the front, he wouldn't tell me if she'd checked out. The possibility of running into her randomly? Slim to none. Closer to none, I'd say. I was able to convince her it was luck that I saw her crossing the road that first night she broke into this house, but no way I actually have that kind of luck.

So wandering around town looking for her is out. I can keep calling her, but she has my number and she'll see my missed calls. If she wants to get in touch with me, she's perfectly capable of doing that.

The more I think about it, the more I realize one unfortunate truth: I don't have any way of getting to her. No way of finding her. And while that sucks, I'm happy that I've reached that realization now because it means I can focus on the one way I'm going to be able to find her.

I have to drive her out. Get her to come to me.

FIFTY-FIVE

AIMEE

Mitch doesn't come home for three hours, and I spend every single minute of them in the living room waiting for him.

Every once in a while I hear Hannah moving around upstairs, but she doesn't come down to talk to me, and I have no interest in approaching her. Glee was written all over her face when she told me that the woman I photoshopped into the photo with Mitch wasn't Jo. She didn't elaborate though, and that means I'm still clueless.

Of course, I was going to assume that woman was his wife. It's the only thing that makes sense, that he had a photo of Jo stashed away where only he could find it, but according to Hannah, I was wrong.

So who is she?

I sit perfectly still, my hands on my knees, staring at the wall. My mind races the entire time, and when the door from the garage swings open, I snap to attention, my pulse already kicking into high gear.

"Your car is clean," Mitch tells me, tossing me my keys. I grab them and push them into my pocket without thinking. "No tracker. No bug. I don't know what game she's playing, but I'm going to find out right now."

I stand. "She's in her room, but..." My voice trails off as I debate whether to tell him that Hannah was in his room before she disappeared into hers. The words came out without me having the chance to think about them, but I'm not sure if I want to have that conversation with him.

He'll blow up. I know he will. And then he'll confront Hannah, which is the right thing to do, but what if she tells him I was the one behind the fake wedding photo?

"But what?" He towers over me, and I take a deep breath.

"But maybe there isn't a tracker. If you can't find one and you didn't put one on my car... Anyway, I haven't seen her since she went up there. She's been really quiet, and I've been down here."

He stares at me, and I have the distinct feeling he's cataloging me, looking for any sign of lying, any sign that he shouldn't believe what I'm saying. I must pass the test, however, because he takes a step back from me, exhaling hard as he runs his hand through his hair.

"This is over," he finally says, but he mutters it to himself. I stare at him, trying to sort through what he might mean, but before I can ask him what's going on, he spins away from me and stalks towards the stairs.

FIFTY-SIX

JACKIE

"I need your keys." My entire body aches, and I'd love nothing more than to lie down and take a nap, but I can't do that, not when I know time is running out for Aimee.

Hannah won't be able to keep her mouth closed for long. I remember having her as a sister-in-law, and the woman couldn't keep a secret to save her life. Either she's going to let on to Mitch that I'm alive and here, or she'll try to help Aimee on her own and screw everything up.

I can't let either of those things happen.

She told me she wanted us to work together, but right now I'm not feeling like I can trust anyone.

My friend stares at me from the doorway. She's been watching me as I work through what I'm going to do, but now that I've finally spoken, she shakes her head. "No way. You got in an accident, and you need to rest. Stay calm. Besides, I told you I'd take care of things."

"Oh, I am calm," I lie. When I stand, my head hurts, but other than that, I really feel okay. "I'm calm enough to tell you I need your keys, I need to go over there, I need—"

"Were you not listening to me? I risked everything for you, and I can fix this! I just need to plan it all out."

The guilt trip works. My stomach twists, and I swallow hard. This is why I didn't immediately call her when I got to town. Sure, falling in with Hannah was stupid, but I knew exactly where I stood with her. Besides, I didn't feel like I had a choice, not when she could blow up my plan simply by telling her brother that I'm still alive.

And not when she told me she'd help me get rid of Mitch so he couldn't ever hurt anyone again. I believed her, and now I'm feeling stupid for that. Whose side is Hannah really on?

"I could have lost it all," she continues. "In fact, if I'm being honest, I could *still* lose it all. Do you know what would happen to me if people found out what I did for you? I'd be run out of town."

"Nobody is going to find out," I tell her, trying to sound more confident than I feel. "I need to go over there and check on Aimee."

"And what if Hannah and Mitch are in the house as well?" She hasn't moved from the doorway, but I swear she seems to grow. She fills it, staring at me like she thinks I've lost my mind.

Really though, I probably have.

"Then I guess I'll have to deal with them," I tell her.

This causes her to shake her head, and she rushes across the room to take my hands.

"Jo, listen to me. You survived him. That's amazing! It's something to be celebrated. Are you really willing to walk back into that den of vipers? You have a life now, and—"

"I'm in hiding," I tell her, and I mean it. The entire time I've been in Texas, I haven't considered the fact that I've been hiding not only from my past life, but from any future I might have. "Do you know what it's like to have a new name, a new life? To never be truly honest with your friends because your past might catch up with you?"

"And do you know what would have happened to you if I hadn't got involved when I did? If Mitch had called someone—anyone—else?"

"I'd be dead," I tell her, and she nods, the movement sharp and jerky like she's glad that she's finally getting through to me.

"Exactly. You'd be dead, and if Aimee is really in trouble—"

"She is."

"I think so too, okay? But who would be able to help her out? Nobody. Let me stop him."

She could stop him.

She could, I really think so. She knows he tried to kill me, so why couldn't she get involved and save Aimee? Why wait? She said she has a way to get rid of him once and for all. So why drag her feet? Maybe because she's scared. Maybe because she wants me to do it but is afraid to admit it.

And maybe I've already lost everything, so what else is there for me to lose? She risked losing everything for me once. No way is she going to risk it all again for Aimee.

"So you think I should wait here? Let you do your plan?" I ask, watching as her shoulders loosen. She's tight. Terrified of what I might do.

"Yes. You get it, thank goodness. You need to stay here, stay out of sight. The best thing for you to do is to keep quiet and hidden, and then we can come up with a plan, okay? Does Mitch deserve to die for what he's done? Yes, he does." Her face twists, and I see something there, some hidden pain I don't know about.

But before I can ask her, before she elaborates, the expression is gone, and she looks as neutral as she did a moment ago.

"You're thinking something," I say to her, and she nods.

"Yes, it will take a few days to put into motion, but I can protect Aimee, protect you, protect any other women he might try to hurt. You have to let me handle it. I'll go about it legally, and while it will take time, it'll be worth it."

We don't have a few days.

"I can do that," I tell her, and while I feel bad lying to her face, I don't have a choice. If she thinks I'm listening to her, she's going to help me out. But if she suspects that I'm going to handle things on my own, then I lose everything.

"Good. I know this is hard, Jo, and I'm sorry you're going through it. But you're not in any shape to confront Mitch or Hannah right now. Stay here and rest up. Let me handle the planning and take care of everything."

I nod, and she exhales with relief.

"Okay. Good. We're on the same page. Now I'm going to step outside to grab the mail. You need anything?"

"No." I force myself to smile at her.

Then I force myself to wait until she's outside, the front door closed behind her.

I force myself to count to ten, then I race to the front door and peek out the window to make sure I still have time for what I'm about to do. She's at the mailbox but must feel my eyes on her because she looks up.

I jump back, then reach out and lock the door. She's running up the path to the house now, yelling something I can't make out. I step back from the door, then turn, racing into the kitchen. Her purse is on the counter, and I lunge for it, already digging my hand inside when I hear her reach the front door.

Her pounding on it makes me wince and makes my head hurt even worse, but I don't stop what I'm doing until I have her keys in my hand. Triumph and fear shoot through me, and I step back from the counter, then turn for her garage.

She's ringing the doorbell now, pressing it over and over, the sound flooding the house. I reach up with one hand and clap it over my ear, but I can't cover both, not with the keys, not when I'm already reaching out to open the door to her garage.

"Jo!" she screams, and I freeze, then remember that she can't get me, that she can scream all she wants, but I'm untouchable, and I hurry into the garage. With the door closed behind me, she's cut off, but I can still hear the dull thud of her ramming her shoulder into the door.

I have to hurry. When she hears the garage door go up, she'll realize that I'm making a run for it. I buckle in. Adjust the mirrors. Start the engine.

Taking a deep breath, I mash the door opener and press down on the gas, already reversing as the door goes up.

I'm halfway out of the garage, ready to gun it and get out of here before she stops me by slamming into my window. I scream, then turn to look at her, ready to apologize, to tell her I'm sorry even though I'm sure she doesn't understand that I don't have a choice, and then I see what she has in her hand.

I hit the brakes.

FIFTY-SEVEN

HANNAH

Mitch pounds on my door.

Even without seeing who's standing in the hall, I know it's him. How? Because he's my brother, and I grew up with him practically breaking down my bedroom door when he was mad at me.

"Come on in," I call, but the door is already swinging open. Rude. Why even knock if you're going to let yourself in without waiting for an invite?

"You need to leave," Mitch announces with the finality and aggression of someone who is more than used to getting their way.

"Leave?" I'm still stretched out on the bed, but I sit up now so I can get a better look at him. I want to see him so I can tell if he's joking or not, but he doesn't sound like he is. "Like leave your house? No."

"Hannah." His voice is a warning, and I choose to ignore it.

"Mitch. Do you really want to piss me off when I know what skeletons you have in your closet?" I let that sink in and hope he believes me. If he doesn't think I'm telling the truth—if he's not scared of me—this will never work. "Because you have more in there than even I thought, don't you?"

"What does that mean?"

I swing my legs off the bed and stand up. Mitch loves towering over people like his height is enough of a reason for him to be respected. It's annoying and ridiculous, and I want to be standing so I feel like we're on even ground.

"It means that I know enough to have you put in jail. Stealing my money from Mom and Dad? And I know you make bank at the hospital, but how many of your investments are above board? And what about that gorgeous brunette you dated who went missing a few years ago?"

"I didn't hurt—"

"You can't prove you didn't."

"Bold of you to threaten me when I could kill you. You have skeletons too, Hannah—don't forget that."

Yeah, there is that. But there's one thing I know to be true about Mitch, and it's that he doesn't do anything without thinking it through for an excessively long time. It always drove me nuts when we were kids, how I was ready to jump in without looking, and he organized and planned and made pros and cons lists and debated with himself about whether he should take the plunge.

So yeah, he might be pissed off at me right now, but he's not going to kill me tonight. I have a little time.

"Listen. I know you think you have everything under control because that's how it's always been, but what would you say if I told you that not everyone in your past has stayed dead?"

"What?" he snaps, and I almost wince away from him, but suddenly I have the upper hand. It's dangerous, what I'm doing, but I've never been afraid of throwing someone else under the bus to protect myself.

"You have a lot of skeletons in your closet, but one of those skeletons is back."

A crease appears between his brows as he tries to suss out what I'm saying. I can imagine him thinking back through the women he's hurt, the ones he's charmed and left for dead, trying to work out who I mean.

"What are you talking about?" He pauses, his eyes flicking back and forth like the answer is going to appear in front of him. "*Who* are you talking about?"

I open my mouth to tell him, but before I can say anything, the doorbell rings.

FIFTY-EIGHT

AIMEE

I spring off the sofa and rush to answer the door when I hear the doorbell. I have to see who's at the house before Mitch makes his way down the stairs to check for himself.

The woman standing on the front porch is breathing hard. She has one hand braced on the house itself like she's too tired to stand up without its support. When I open the door, however, her eyes snap to mine, and there's a spark of recognition there.

I've seen her before. I narrow my eyes at her, trying to figure out who she might be.

Someone from the party Mitch threw for me? That's incredibly likely. There were so many people here at the house and I hadn't met most of them before that night. All the faces seemed to blur together, and who's to say this woman wasn't here?

But that doesn't feel quite right.

"Aimee?" Her voice is tight, and I feel something shift in me.

"Do I know you?"

"No, but..."

"You were at the park," I say. It hits me: how strange she acted at the park when we ran into each other, how intense she was. And now she's followed me here, to the house, and she knows my name?

I move to close the door, but her foot snaps out, and she blocks it with a dirty sneaker.

"Yes, and you need to come with me." Her eyes flick past me, and she reaches out to grab my arm, but I step back. "Please, don't let him know I'm here."

"*Him?* You mean Mitch? Who are you? Why are you here?"

Before she can get a word out in response, there are heavy footsteps behind me.

"Get away from her!" That's Hannah, her voice thick with anger. She pushes past me, shoving me out of the way. When she slams the door, she does it with such force that the woman on the porch cries out and moves her foot.

She turns the top lock, then the bottom. It's only when the door is locked up tight that she looks back at me. Before she can say anything, however, Mitch pounds down the stairs and ends up at her side.

"Who's out there?" He practically growls the question.

"She—"

The woman knocks on the door. Soft, like I'm the only one she wants to hear it.

"Aimee! Are you okay? Who was that?" Mitch grabs me by the shoulders and gives me a little shake. Terror makes my skin feel tight; my blood feels cold. My teeth slam together, and pain shoots through my head.

"She's—" I begin, but the woman is still quietly knocking, and Mitch is still shaking me. "I don't know who that is, I really don't!"

He lets go of me, and I stumble back, my mind racing as I

try to work through what's going on. That woman on the front porch knows me, or followed me here, or something.

"Everyone calm down." Hannah grabs Mitch's arm. "Let me handle everything, okay? I got this."

"She looked like Jo." Mitch's voice is soft, like he's confused, but his words have the weight of a boulder, and I shift uncomfortably as I feel them land in my gut.

"Jo? Your first wife?" My mind is reeling. "But she's dead. You said she's dead." I take a deep breath to slow down. "You killed her. Hannah said you—"

"Hannah told you *what*?" Anger drips from every word.

I take a step back from him. The fury etched across his face right now? Yeah, I have a pretty good feeling that's what Jo saw right before he killed her.

"Aimee, what did you say?" He doesn't let me get away from him. Each step I take backwards is met with him taking one towards me to close the gap. "That I *killed* her?"

My mouth is dry. It feels stuffed full of cotton, and I force myself to nod at him. I'm horribly, terribly aware that I've screwed up, that I've signed my death warrant, that there's no way I'm ever walking out of this house again.

"Jo can't be alive. She—" He cuts off and whips around to look at his sister.

Hannah's face matches mine. Pale. Wide eyes. Obviously aware that everything is going south and there isn't a single thing she can do to stop this terrible train wreck we're all on.

"Hannah." I can't see Mitch's face, but I hear him swallow hard. "You told Aimee that I killed Jo?"

"She's obviously alive," Hannah begins, but Mitch holds up a hand, stopping her.

"She's..." He turns and grabs the door, ripping it open. "Jo!" When he screams his wife's name, I take a step back, then another.

I have to get out of here.

"Jo, where are you?" He's on the porch now, screaming for his wife. A shiver races down my spine at the raw emotion in his voice, but I can't focus too much on that.

His first wife isn't dead. He didn't kill her, no matter what Hannah told me. I should be relieved by that, but all that's happening is I have more questions.

I'm moving to flee, to run upstairs and get out of here, when Hannah stops me. She grabs me by the arm, her fingers sinking into my flesh, and leans close to me, her face directly in mine.

"Jo's alive," I gasp out. "He didn't kill her. Oh my gosh, what's going on?" I shouldn't look for comfort in this woman, shouldn't trust that she might help me, but I have nobody else to turn to, nobody else who might understand what I'm going through.

"Jo!" Mitch is still on the porch, but the next time he calls her name, it sounds further away, like he's hunting her down.

Was he... happy when he realized she was the person on the porch? That's insane, but for a moment I thought I saw an expression on his face like he was excited. Not upset. *Happy.*

But no. He killed her—or he tried to—so there's no reason he'd be happy to see her on his porch. I must have read him wrong.

Unless he's happy he gets to finish the job.

"What's he going to do when he finds her?" I jerk back from Hannah. My arm stings from where she was gripping me, but I barely notice the discomfort. "We have to go out there and help her!"

"Don't you worry about Jo," Hannah tells me. "She's scrappy and she'll be fine. You're the one I'm worried about."

"Why? What's going on?" I ask her, but the words are automatic, ones I've said a dozen times before without giving them any thought. They flow easily from my lips. My brain feels like it's on high focus. I notice my goosebumps, the tightness in my stomach. I notice everything, especially how close Hannah is standing to me, but I can't think through what I need to do next.

"You'll be fine. Mitch will handle Jo," she tells me, but there's a bite in her voice. As she speaks, she reaches up and brushes her hair back from her forehead. My eyes fall on her wrist and the bangle she's wearing.

It's the one from the hidey-hole in Mitch's room. That's where I found the photo with the hair clippings as well as Jo's death certificate. It made sense to me for Mitch to have put the bangle there as a trophy from killing his wife. I have no reason to believe that Hannah knew about the hidey-hole except for the possibility that—

It hits me.

That hidey-hole? It's not Mitch's.

It's Hannah's.

FIFTY-NINE

JACKIE

I'm running as fast as I can, but then I trip.

It's a root from a tree growing up through the yard, one I swear I asked Mitch to deal with when I still lived here, one he promised me the landscaping crew would take care of.

My body already hurts from my accident, but that pain is nothing compared to what shoots through me when I hit the ground.

Knees and wrists hit first, then I roll to the right, my shoulder slamming into the hard dirt. The air isn't knocked out of my lungs, but I exhale hard, my vision swimming even though I try to blink it clear again.

"Jo!" That's Mitch. His voice wraps around me like a blanket, but instead of being comforting and making me feel safe, I feel like I'm being choked. Smothered.

I force myself to roll to my knees. I brace my hands on the ground, and a shooting pain ricochets up my left arm into my elbow. A gasp tears from my lips, and I shift my weight to the right.

When my vision clears, I get my feet under me, then stand,

forcing myself to stay upright even though everything feels wobbly.

One step. Then another. I'm moving as fast as I can towards the backyard because I know I can't loop around him to my friend's car. He'll catch me, stop me, kill me.

Now he knows I'm alive, and I'm screwed.

It's dark outside, which means there are plenty of shadowy places for me to hide. I stumble towards the closest one, a dark smudge behind the grill.

Ten feet to go.

Eight.

Five.

I'm almost there, and while that doesn't mean I'm going to be safe, it will give me respite. I need a few minutes to get my head on straight, to breathe through the pain, to figure out a way out of this.

Two.

One.

I drop to my knees, ignoring the biting pain that shoots up my legs, then crawl forward, a gasp escaping my lips as I settle down behind the grill, my hurt arm tucked against my body to protect it.

My eyes scan the darkness. There's no sound. No movement.

I take a deep breath and hold it, then force myself to let it out slowly in a stream. If I'm panting, he'll hear me and find me. If I keep breathing slowly, little amounts of air at a time, I can get out of this in one piece.

Right?

Right.

My lungs scream for me to exhale, so I do, small wisps leaving my lips. A bit at a time, so quietly I can't hear it, so I'm confident there's no way Mitch will ever hear me. I don't know how I'm going to get out of this, but I'll cross that bridge in a minute. Maybe he'll go inside to get a flashlight or to turn on the outside light. No matter what he does, I need a few minutes to—

There's a creak to my right, and I gasp, whipping around to see what might have caused it.

Mitch.

He's staring down at me, breathing hard. His hands open and close at his sides until he reaches up and runs his hand along his chin, the stubble grating against his skin.

I freeze, the perfect prey, hoping against hope that this is a bad dream, that I'm going to wake up in my home in Texas, but before I can convince myself that I'm making this all up, he speaks.

"You're supposed to be dead."

SIXTY

HANNAH

Try as I might, I can't focus on any one way this is all going to play out. There's no way to pretend like Jo isn't back from the dead, no time to figure out how Aimee and I are going to explain everything before we kill Mitch.

Because we have to kill Mitch or all of this falls apart.

But then what else do I do? Do I kill them all and end up the executor of his estate? Is that the only way I can finally get the money I deserve? Jo showing up put a wrench in my plan, but Mitch seeing her? Yeah, that turned the entire evening on its head.

My mind races as I think through what to do.

Mitch has to die for me to get any money. Jo does too, or everything will go to her because Aimee's marriage isn't valid. Not only does Jo have to die—I need her body to disappear because then the money will go to Aimee.

Or Jo's body is found, and Aimee takes the fall for both murders, but then there would have to be an explanation of how she came back from the dead.

My head hurts trying to work through everything that might

happen, and while I know I need to make a decision about what to do soon, I can't settle on a final plan.

Aimee is the wild card now. Alive or dead, she could ruin everything. Does she walk away from this with me? Will she give me the money if I kill Jo to ensure she still has access to it? She promised me she'd work with me as long as I helped her get free from my brother, but I can see her drawing the line at killing someone else, someone innocent.

I need some plan that I'm sure will work. Something she won't be able to squirm her way out of.

"You told me Mitch killed his wife," Aimee says, rudely yanking me out of my daydream about how to kill everyone. "How is she here? Is that really her?"

"That's Jo," I tell her, tugging her arm to get her to follow me. I'm not sure what to do with her yet, but I don't want her near the front door in case Mitch bursts back in. "In the flesh."

"How is she not dead?"

Good question.

That's something I'd love to know myself, since I'm the one who got the drugs and fed them to her. I'm the one who calculated the dose to kill her. I'm the one who was going to identify her body after she was found and taken to the hospital, so Mitch didn't have to see his precious wife dead on a slab.

And I was happy to do it too. Happy to see her dead, the woman who was taking so much of my inheritance. I didn't get the chance to because—

Because someone else went in my place.

Because Jo wasn't really dead.

I miscalculated what I gave her.

I stumble to a stop, my hand slipping from Aimee's bicep. I don't have all the pieces figured out yet, but they're slotting into place.

Someone saved Jo, then they hid her from me. From *us.* They moved her out of town, helped her start a new life; they went out on a limb for this woman, and now she's back, and I didn't realize her being alive meant that someone was working against me because I was too focused on Aimee.

"Hannah?" Aimee's calling me, but she's backing up as she does. "Hannah, are you okay?"

I blink at her, unable to make sense of what I'm finally understanding. All this time I thought Jo was dead. And yes, her showing up made it clear that the ball was dropped somewhere along the way, but I had no idea who was working against me.

"I messed everything up," I choke out, but Aimee's no longer looking at me. Her gaze is locked on someone behind me. Her eyebrows crash together in confusion.

"What are you doing here?" she asks.

SIXTY-ONE

AIMEE

Hannah whips around faster than I would have thought possible, but she's not fast enough to stop what's coming.

The person who snuck into our house lowers their gun until it's pointing directly in her face.

"Hello, Hannah."

Hannah freezes, but if she's afraid, she doesn't show it. "What are you doing here? And why do you have that gun? Put it away."

"No." The person chuckles. "You're not the one calling the shots any longer, are you? It's my turn to shine."

"Yeah?" Hannah crosses her arms. "And what do you want from me?"

"Justice."

"Justice," Hannah scoffs. "If that's the case, you and I want the same thing, and you should go find Mitch." She swings her arm out, gesturing at the backyard, and I don't move.

Neither does the person holding her at gunpoint.

"Justice for my sister."

"Oh yeah? I don't know who your sister is, or *was*, or what you want me to do about them being dead, but I don't give a crap—"

She's still prattling on, probably trying to distract the person to keep them from shooting her, but I can't focus on what she's saying.

Then it hits me who this person is. She looks familiar but not because I've seen her before. It's in the glint in her eye, the way she cocks her upper lip.

I know who she is.

Just like I knew that bangle Hannah took from behind the baseboard in her brother's room looked familiar.

This woman wants justice for her sister.

The woman in the photo.

SIXTY-TWO

JACKIE

"Get away from me!" My body screams for me to lie down and rest, but I lurch to my feet, away from Mitch, already throwing one hand up between the two of us to protect myself. "Get away!" I take a deep breath, then scream, "Help!"

"Stop running!" He's closing in on me.

I stumble away from him, and the backs of my knees hit a chair. Even before I know what's happening, I'm sitting down, leaning back as far as I can without falling.

"Jo! Don't move!" He's bearing down on me, and I scream as loud as I possibly can.

Instead of stopping in his tracks, which is what I thought he might do, he keeps coming, his arms out in front of him. I can't see his face, but it doesn't matter what he looks like right now, does it?

Not when I know he's going to finish the job.

"Jo." Mitch drops to his knees in front of me, his fingers dancing over my arms, my knees, like he's too afraid to actually touch me. "Jo, hey, listen. Are you okay? What are you doing here?" He exhales hard. "You're alive."

My heart feels like it's skipping beats. It's thudding around like a wild animal, banging at my ribs in an uncomfortable rhythm. He sounds... not as angry as I thought he would be.

But I have to keep my armor up. I know all too well how easily he can twist things around so I feel like the bad guy. Just because he's acting nice and caring right now doesn't mean he is.

He did try to kill me, after all.

"Please don't hurt me," I whisper. Now that I'm not trying to run from him, I feel every ache and pain in my body. "Please don't hurt me. I'm sorry, I—"

"Hurt you?" He reaches out for me but drops his hand when I recoil. "Hurt you? Jo, you're alive! Why would I try to hurt you?"

Tears stream down my face. I can already feel my nose stuffing up. "To finish the job."

He's toying with me like he always does. I don't know what he's hoping to get out of making me feel terrible, but I'm sure he's enjoying his little roleplay. Mitch loves making other people uncomfortable, and I know this is funny to him. I'm stupid, coming back here, thinking I could help Aimee. Mitch has the upper hand as usual. He always wins.

"Finish the job—what? Jo, they told me you died. Hannah told me you died. She—" He cuts off abruptly, frowning.

Yeah, she thought I died because you tried to kill me.

"Please don't hurt me," I whisper.

"Someone saved you." A switch has flipped in him. Anger seeps out of every pore. "Someone viewed your body. Told us you died. Brought us ashes. Is she the reason you're still alive?"

I swallow hard, unsure of why he's switching topics so quickly but grateful to have some of the heat off me. "Yes. She saved me."

Mitch closes his eyes. "Norma."

SIXTY-THREE

HANNAH

"You killed the woman in the photo?" Aimee shrieks. It's clear she wants to attack me, but she's smart enough to stay out of the way of the gun that's still pointed at my face.

"I didn't," I tell her, but the woman with the gun cuts me off.

"Stop with the lies, Hannah. You killed Fiona, and you sat back and watched as your brother tried to kill Jo. You're evil, you know that?"

Evil?

"What is this, a Disney movie? And I'm some evil villain? I didn't do anything to Fiona, and I certainly didn't do anything to Jo! I—"

"You hated her from the moment she married your brother. What, the money your parents left you wasn't enough?"

"Well, since you're asking—" I begin, but now it's Aimee's turn to cut me off.

"Hannah was going to kill me," she says, and the woman's eyes darken. "She said she wasn't going to, but no way do I believe her."

I swear, I don't know who this woman is. I recognize her,

but only in that vague way when you're sure you've seen someone before but can't quite place them. She's familiar, but not pretty enough to make anyone stand up and take notice.

It hits me. She's one of Mitch's lawyer friends. A chill grips me when I think about what information she's been privy to. Was she one of the ones who helped him come up with his contract?

"You're Norma," I tell her, and she nods.

My eyes flick to Aimee. She's far enough away from me now that I'd have to lunge for her to take her down, and I have a very good feeling that Norma here would put a bullet in me before I could move.

"I didn't kill your sister," I tell Norma, who scoffs.

Of course that didn't work.

My lips are dry, and I lick them as I try to think through what to do next. Mitch chased after Jo. There's no way of knowing what he'll do when he finds her, but I can't count on him coming to my rescue anytime soon.

Think.

"Mitch did." Tears stream down my face. "I know this is hard to believe, but it was Mitch. He's... out of control. He's aggressive and violent and terrifying. I've been afraid of him for years. He controls our inheritance. He tried to kill Jo. He killed our parents..."

"He killed your parents?" Norma asks, and I nod.

"He did." I wipe my tears and suck in a breath. I have to sell this. "You have no idea what it's like living under his shadow—"

"Yeah, except you wanted to kill me," Aimee says, cutting off my monologue.

"I wanted to kill the woman who murdered my boyfriend, and that isn't you!" I whip around to face her. "Don't you see? We had a plan to work together. You got your freedom, and I got my inheritance. Don't you think, if I wanted to kill you, I would have already done it? I want to be left alone, but he won't leave me be! I wouldn't hurt a fly! I've been trying to help you. Why else would I get you a phone?"

There's a flash of doubt on Aimee's face, and it spurs me on.

"He kills people," I whisper. "And he keeps trophies from his kills. It isn't me. It wasn't ever me." Her eyes flick to the bangle on my wrist, and she presses her lips together.

Okay, fair. Maybe I shouldn't have put it on, but I'd forgotten how much I liked it. Mitch never knew what happened to it, never realized where I had it hidden. Keeping my trophies in his room was a stroke of brilliance. He never knew they were there. I only kept one thing from each person I killed, so it wasn't like I was greedy. From Fiona, the bangle. From Jo, her death certificate. And from our parents?

Well, the locks of hair obviously.

"The woman in the photograph," Aimee says, speaking slowly. "Who was she?"

"Tell your friend here to put her gun down," I say. In response, Norma takes a step closer to me. "You still don't believe me that I'm not dangerous?" Norma doesn't respond, so I answer Aimee's question. "She and Mitch dated before he married Jo. She and I were friends, but I didn't know she was your sister." I turn to the woman with the gun and press my fingers into my lips. "I promise you—I didn't know. He killed her, and then he killed Jo, and I thought I could save Aimee."

Norma's gun wavers a little. I don't think she realizes it, and Aimee certainly doesn't notice, but I do, and it gives me a flash of hope. Without knowing where Mitch and Jo are, I can't be too confident, but maybe I can turn this around. If there's one thing I'm good at, it's thinking on my feet.

"And you were going to go along with killing him?" the woman asks.

Aimee nods. "He's controlling and demanding. I never thought I'd marry someone like him, someone so—"

I clear my throat. "Jo's back from the dead, which means you're not married to Mitch."

She freezes, and realization dawns on her face. "I'm not married to Mitch." Her words are slow, like she can't quite understand them. "His first wife is still alive, and I'm not married to him." There's hope in her voice now. "I can run." She wipes her hands on her pants and turns to Norma. "Will you help me? Please?"

Um, hello? Is she forgetting that she promised to get me my inheritance? I knew she was going to backstab me the first chance she got. My hands clench into fists when I think about what I'd like to do to her.

"What about Jo?" I ask, and both Norma and Aimee turn to look at me. "She's out there with Mitch, the man who tried to kill her once. Do you really think he's going to let her get away this time?" I wave my arm to make my point.

Norma speaks. "Where did you get that bangle?"

It's Fiona's. "Mitch gave it to me for Christmas." It's a dangerous game, this lying, but I'm hoping Aimee is off-kilter enough to not call me out.

Aimee opens her mouth, and I'm sure she's dying to tell Norma that's a lie, but I don't give her the chance to speak.

"Please," I say, twisting my face so I look as scared as possible. "Mitch is out there with Jo. He's going to finish the job like he did with Fiona." My voice is tight. "You have a gun—you have to save her!"

Norma hesitates. I hold my breath, waiting to see how this is going to go. Either she rushes out the door to save Jo, or she stays here to protect Aimee.

But she can't protect both of his wives.

"Lock yourselves in a room," she finally says to Aimee. "I'm going after Jo."

"No! Please!" Aimee claws at her, but Norma pulls away,

twisting so Aimee's hands fall from her arm. "Don't leave me. You said you would help me!"

"Hide," Norma tells her, then her eyes flick to me. "Both of you stay safe, okay?"

"We will," I say, and even I'm impressed with how scared, yet so brave, I sound.

Norma races for the front door, leaving me alone with Aimee.

Finally.

SIXTY-FOUR

AIMEE

The last thing in the world that I want is to be left alone with Hannah right now.

Her plan has changed, I'm sure of it. It doesn't matter that she's told me over and over again that the two of us are a team, that we're working together, that she doesn't want to hurt me. I don't believe her.

"You tried to kill Jo, didn't you?" Asking this question is stupid, but I can't help myself. I have to know the truth. "Mitch seemed really happy to see Jo, but you—"

"Jo was supposed to be dead." Hannah's eyes are sharp as she stares at me.

"Yeah, but she's not!" My mind races. There have been so many lies, so many secrets, and they're all starting to make sense. I don't want to tell her what I fear to be true, but I have to know if I'm right. "The bangle. The hidey-hole. Those were trophies, weren't they? And they're yours." My breath catches in my throat. "It was all you, wasn't it?"

She doesn't answer my question, but I don't need her to. I know the truth.

"You and me, Aimee. It was always going to be this way."

Hannah grins at me, reaching out like she's going to touch me, but I take a step away from her. I'm afraid to turn my back and run, but as long as I keep some distance between the two of us, I should be okay.

Right?

"You always wanted to kill me. All this time when you were pretending to be my friend, it was all a lie, wasn't it?"

She sighs. "No. It wasn't all a lie. I needed you! Or I thought I did, but now you know the truth, don't you? I can't let you walk away, not when I can still fix this."

"You mean get your money? You'd really kill all of us to get your money?"

"I'd burn this entire place down with all of you in it if that's what it took."

My mind barely has time to understand what she said before my body reacts. I turn on my heel and run through the house, down the hall, past the living room, to the stairs.

I'm halfway up them before she catches up with me.

"You can't run from me!" She lunges forward, catching me by the ankle.

I pitch forward, throwing my hands out to brace myself for the fall. The stairs are hard, and pain splinters up my arms upon impact. Twisting, I roll over so I'm on my back and kick out, planting a foot right in Hannah's stomach.

She cries out, and I roll back over, crawling now in my effort to get up the stairs.

Once I'm up there, I'll... what? Run to my room? Barricade myself in there? I haven't gotten that far with my plan, but I know I have to get away from her. I need to call the police, need to get Mitch to protect me, need to do something.

I'm in the hall. My room is so close, and I push myself to my feet. Only a few more steps and I'll make it. My breathing is hard, and my vision narrows. This is what it feels like to be hunted, to know that you have no way of surviving. I force myself to move as fast as I can and refuse to look over my shoulder to see where Hannah is.

In my room now.

I turn, slam the door.

Throw the lock.

Tears stream down my face as I step back from it, my hands out in front of me as if that's going to be enough to stop her if she tries to break down my door.

The sound of her slamming into my door never comes.

But there are gunshots.

One.

Two.

Three.

SIXTY-FIVE

NORMA

I stare down at the gun in my hand, then slowly look up at Mitch.

Three shots to the chest. He slumps on the deck, his mouth and eyes open, his face staring up at the sky.

He'll never kill anyone again, but—

Panic courses through me as I whip around to see who else is out here with us because there has to be someone. The gun in my hand? It was for show, to make a point.

It wasn't loaded.

SIXTY-SIX

HANNAH

The sound of gunshots makes me freeze.

I'm halfway down the hall to Aimee's room and even though I'm not entirely sure what my plan is, I do know she will not make it out of here alive. Part of me relishes the thought of sitting on her chest, my hands wrapped around her neck, squeezing until she gasps her final breath.

Did I really get over her being involved in Brian's death? I thought I had, although that's not something you can casually bring up at therapy. But now that she's running from me—*now that she knows the truth*—I need her gone.

But before I can deal with Aimee, I have to deal with those gunshots.

Norma. That's who had to have helped Jo, and she's still helping her. She's the reason Mitch's first wife is still alive, the reason she's here to haunt me.

I have to stop her.

The hairs on the back of my neck stand up. I swallow hard, then whip around, the feeling of someone watching me too much for me to handle. At the top of the stairs, I press up against the wall, then turn and peek down to the first floor.

Nobody's coming.

My mind races as I sort through what I should do. Handle Aimee? But what if Norma interrupts us? I can't very well turn my back on the front door.

Fear propels me down the stairs. I burst out the front door, my eyes scanning the dark. I have to make sure Norma stays on my side. That she believes me when I tell her Mitch is the killer.

Maybe she shot him.

That thought hits me, filling me with excitement. *Maybe she shot him and she wants to save us.* If that's the case, I'll come up with a new plan. I'm patient.

I've already been waiting for my money for years. This small setback won't ruin anything. I'll adapt. I have to.

"Norma!" I cup my hands around my mouth and scream her name. "Norma, where are you?"

There's movement by the front path, and I lean back into the house and flick on the outdoor light. It mostly illuminates the porch, but some light extends onto the walkway.

Jo?

Norma?

Mitch?

Surely not Mitch, surely not him when he's obviously the bad guy in the situation and I'm sure Norma will have taken care of him. She'll kill him to protect Jo, I'm sure of it, but—

The person walking up to the house is a man.

I gasp and take a step back, my hand fluttering to my throat.

SIXTY-SEVEN

AIMEE

Mitch is dead.

I should be happy about that, but my mind can't concentrate on what's going on. I don't know the truth of anything anymore. I'd been afraid of Hannah when she crashed our beach vacation, but after marrying Mitch, she seemed to have turned over a new leaf. Or, at least, she pretended to. Now that I know she'll stop at nothing to get her money, I don't want to be anywhere near her.

And what about his first wife? Jo was never dead, which is something I'm struggling to wrap my mind around. She was alive this whole time, which means he was married to her.

I can walk away from this. If only they'll let me.

If only *Hannah* will let me.

Patrick sits at the head of the dining room table where Mitch usually sits. He's tapping away on his phone.

Deleting things.

"There," he finally says and puts the phone down on the table. "According to my security company, tonight is gone. Wiped off the map. Well, except for some copies of certain clips I'm keeping. But nobody will know I was here." He points at

Norma. "You. You weren't here. Neither were you." He gestures at Jo.

I turn to look at Jo, but she won't look at me. Tears well up in her eyes, but she doesn't make a sound.

"What? Why the long faces?" He laughs and leans back in his chair. "Did you guys really think I'd see what was going on here and *not* want to come join the party? Please. You couldn't pay me to miss this. Besides, I wanted to come and protect my investment." He grins at us, then reaches out and takes Hannah's hand.

She stiffens but doesn't pull away.

"So here's the plan," he continues, as if we're talking about brunch and deciding where to go for bottomless mimosas. "Our company will call the police and report an intruder, which will explain away what happened to Mitch."

"The cameras don't show anyone on the property," Hannah says. "Won't the police think it a little strange that he died out of nowhere?"

"Luckily for our mystery shooter, they were standing in a blind spot," Patrick counters. "The police will look for who it might be, but come on. Some people at this table have already gotten away with murder already. Now, are you going to keep interrupting, or can I continue?"

She sits silent, and he takes it as a cue to keep speaking.

"Great. Mitch is dead, may he rest in peace. That means you," he says, pointing at Jo, "are rich."

She shakes her head. "I'm dead. I can't come back—"

"Probably not. Maybe with the help of a great lawyer, you can. Or maybe Aimee gives you the money you deserve. I have no idea, but you'll figure it out. You," he says, turning from her and pointing at me, "are nobody."

I exhale slowly. I'm not a huge fan of people telling me what to do, but right now I don't mind the fact that he's taking control. I don't want to be the one to figure out what's going to happen or how we're going to get out of this.

Not that I did anything wrong exactly, but I'm sure the police would frown at me being involved in three murders, even if my involvement comprised of simply existing in the vicinity.

"We already knew that she's nobody," Hannah quips, pulling her hand away from Patrick. Unfortunately for her, he tightens his grip on her fingers.

"I'm not finished." Patrick looks around the table. "Norma, right?" The woman nods, and Patrick speaks again. "Like I said, you were never here. You and I are going to leave, and nobody will be the wiser. But I'll be watching. Does everyone understand?"

Hannah and Norma nod. Jo and I do as well, when he turns to look at each of us.

Acting. It's acting, what I have to do. It's pretending like I don't know anything, like we were surprised, like—

"How are we supposed to explain that she's still alive?" Hannah asks. She's staring at Jo, and I see in this moment how much she hates her sister-in-law. Her eyes narrow when she looks at Jo, but Jo seems unbothered. "We had a funeral for her, in case people aren't following along."

"Only because you and your brother tried to kill me," Jo says, so offhand, so cavalier, that I think for a moment Hannah is going to flip. Her eyes narrow, and she opens her mouth to speak, but Jo continues, cutting her off. "If you hadn't tried to kill me, none of this would have happened."

"If you weren't stealing my inheritance—"

"Enough." Patrick slams his hand on the table, and all of us snap to attention. "This is my plan, and we're sticking to it."

I nod without thinking about what I'm doing. The reality is that I'm busy thinking about what my life is going to look like. After this, I'm free to leave.

Free to move out of Vermont like I thought about before. I

settle back in my seat, a smile playing on my lips, but then I catch Hannah's eye.

She's glaring at me, her mouth tight. Every muscle in her body is tense, and she looks like she could launch herself across the table at me if she had the chance.

"Everyone out. I'm calling the cops in five minutes," Patrick says.

Self-conscious, I stand, pushing back from the table as quietly as possible, but Hannah doesn't look away from me.

I clear my throat. "Were you ever on my side?"

My question makes her blink in surprise.

"Yes, I was," she tells me. "Mitch is a jerk. *Was* a jerk. To his wives. To me. You weren't in my crosshairs until I thought you were going to turn on me."

"So as long as I helped you get you what you wanted..."

"You would have been fine."

I don't believe her.

She doesn't move, not even when Patrick pulls her hand to get her to follow him.

"Babe, come on," he says. "Everyone's leaving, and you and Aimee need to get into position."

"Stay," I say, dragging my eyes away from Hannah and staring at him. "Stay with us. You and Hannah are dating, and the cops wouldn't think anything of—"

He's already shaking his head. "Not a chance. You think I want to be around when they come sniffing? No way. It's only you two here. Got it?"

I feel cold, but I nod in response. Patrick gives me a tight smile, then turns to Hannah.

"Listen to me," he tells her, but when she doesn't look at him, he grabs her chin and forces her to. "I'm leaving the house, but I will be watching every single thing that goes on in here. You are going to play nice. Do you understand me?"

Hannah doesn't respond.

"I asked if you understood. Your brother's body is cooling out there on the deck, and we need to call the cops, but I will not do that until I know for sure that you will not do something stupid as soon as I leave this house. You still owe me my money, and I'm sticking to your side until I get it. Although," he says, drawing out the word, "we make a good couple, don't we?"

She ignores his last sentence. "If by *something stupid* you mean hurting Aimee, I won't do it," she says, jerking her chin out of his grip. "Tonight."

SIXTY-EIGHT

JACKIE

Three Months Later

"She's booked a trip to Mexico," Norma says.

Aimee glances at me, but I don't make eye contact with her. Norma's great and has been really helpful in... well, everything after Mitch died, but she's still a lawyer.

Sure, she came to the hospital when Hannah tried to kill me. She procured ashes and forged a cremation certificate to prove that I was dead. She stuck her neck out for me, and while I'll never forget what she did for me, that was her saving someone, and I'm asking her to help kill someone.

She's a life-saver, not a life-taker.

"Mexico," Aimee says, as if she has no clue exactly what Norma is saying. "Just for fun?"

"Looks like it." Norma shrugs. "Listen, I know I told you two I'd help you stay abreast of what Hannah is up to, but she and Patrick aren't coming for you, not when you gave them as much money as you did. You two can move on and not look over your shoulders any longer."

Yeah, right. I don't know about Aimee, but until Hannah is cold and in the ground, I'll always be looking over my shoulder. Anyone who could point a finger at me is a danger. The only person I really trust is Norma.

Even Aimee thinks she's in my inner circle, but she's not. Not really. We're relying on each other right now because neither of us has a choice in the matter.

"Thank you," Aimee tells her. "I know you've been put in a difficult position as her lawyer but still reporting to us."

"Well, the paycheck helps," Norma says, glancing at me. "And what you told me about the trophies you found in Mitch's room... I thought he killed Fiona. Why wouldn't I?"

I reach out and touch her hand, but she isn't finished.

"It was always Hannah, wasn't it? She was upset about her inheritance, so she killed her parents. She thought my sister was going to take her money if she married Mitch, so she killed her. And then you." She looks at me, and I force myself to nod.

"That's what we think," I tell her.

Aimee doesn't speak.

Norma clears her throat. "Neither of you deserved what happened to you. What I don't understand, Jo, is why you don't want to go to the police. Hannah tried to kill you, and that's a great defense for you faking your own death. We could—"

"That's not what she deserves, and you know it. There's not enough evidence against her," I tell her. "Besides, they think I'm dead. It's been tricky enough getting as many of my assets as possible moved into an account in my new name without raising suspicion." That had been difficult, I'll admit it. Relying on Aimee to give me what was rightfully mine was infuriating because I didn't want the police to find out I'd faked my death.

It's involved a lot of trusting people, but that's almost come to an end. Good thing Norma was willing to help me and was willing to tell Aimee she didn't have a choice but to give me my money.

Sure, she still has the house. Huge accounts. She has

enough money that she'll never have to work. Her kids, if she has any, won't have to work. Her grandkids... yeah, they're all set for life.

I know this was hard, but I did what I came to do—save her.

And soon I'll never have to see her again.

But first? We're going to Mexico. There's one more thing to do there.

EPILOGUE
AIMEE

I'll admit it: Hannah looks great in her bikini.

She may have only started going to the box so she could screw my fiancé, but she obviously kept up the hard work, as evidenced by her abs. What's the saying? You could bounce a quarter off them?

Or maybe that saying is about her butt. Either way, she looks amazing.

Too bad she's about to die.

I watch from a distance as she accepts a drink from the bartender. She's going to think he gave it to her for free because of how she looks and not because I already paid for the drink.

And I didn't only pay for it. I paid enough to match his salary for the next two years. It was worth it to get him to add the tiny vial I brought to her drink.

Rosary peas work quickly, especially when ground up. I've been planning this trip and had the peas soaking for a while before straining the mixture into the vial and giving it to the bartender. It'll be painful and scary, and then, before she has time to get help, Hannah will be gone.

She takes a sip of her drink, then throws her head back and

laughs at whatever the bartender is saying. By the time she finishes it, he'll have disappeared.

There. He's taking off his apron. Turning and walking out of the bar, exactly like we discussed. She meanders over to a seat by the pool and settles in.

The man next to her reaches over and takes her hand. Even from here, I can see the way she pulls away from him, but she doesn't have a choice in the matter. *Patrick.*

He made good on his threat on sticking around Hannah as much as possible. He wants money from her, and while she must have paid him off with some of the cash we gave her, he's clearly not interested in going anywhere.

I'd have loved to poison him too, but the man doesn't drink, and he's incredibly careful about his food. He did end up saving my life in his own twisted way, so I can give him a pass, as long as he stays away from me.

But I can't give Hannah one. Not if I ever want to live without looking over my shoulder in fear.

The two of them talk for a moment, then she takes a few more sips. My palms are sweaty with excitement, and I wipe them on my towel before glancing back at the bar. By now, the bartender should be getting in his car. Driving away.

I exhale slowly and turn to look at the person next to me. After today, I'll never see her again.

"To a job well done," Jo says, holding up her glass for me to cheers. I do, then take a tiny sip.

Man, I love rum and Cokes. You know what I don't love?

Being this close to the woman who wanted to kill me. Hannah might not be a threat right now, but I still can't wait to put her in my rearview mirror. She lied to me to get me on her side when she was the killer.

It's horrifying. She's the ultimate gaslighter, and I fell for it hook, line, and sinker.

But here's the thing about Hannah: yes, she kept trophies

from the people she killed, but she did a great job covering her tracks. I've looked. Jo has looked. Norma has looked. If I didn't *know* Hannah had killed Fiona and her parents, and tried to kill Jo, I'd never know.

She can't be allowed to live. A woman like that is too dangerous. No, she doesn't want to come after me now because she's placated with money, but what happens when the money runs out? What happens when Patrick pushes her or says something that sets her off?

She decides to come for me, that's what happens.

Mitch and Fiona only dated for a short period of time before Hannah killed her. It's not that she hated her brother's girlfriend—she couldn't stand the thought that anyone would get the money she thought she deserved.

We had to take care of her, and we chose poison. Just like she did to Jo and Fiona. Just like she was going to do to Mitch. I'm not a betting woman, but I imagine that's how she took out her parents as well.

Only fitting that's how she's going to go.

Jo exhales hard, yanking me back to the present.

"It's finally over." I drain my glass before putting it down on the sand. After a moment, I stretch before bending over to get my bag. Hers falls over in the process. "Don't worry, I've got it," I tell her as I right it. Jo's on her feet before I finish my sentence.

"I'm glad I'm never going to see you again," she says, extending her hand.

"Same." Her grip is firm, her skin cool. I know my palm is sweaty, but I still frown when she wipes her hand on her shorts.

"You going back to Vermont?" She grabs her bag and slides it onto her shoulder as she waits for my response.

"For a while." I know I need to be careful sticking around so Hannah and Patrick don't recognize me, but I'm not making the same mistake Hannah did when she tried to kill Jo. No way am

I walking away from this until I know she's good and dead. "You? Texas again?"

She chews her lip. "Not Texas. I don't want to say."

I don't blame her. I wouldn't come for her, and Hannah will be dead soon, but she'll enjoy peace of mind by covering her tracks. "I hope you settle down somewhere nice," I tell her, and I mean it.

After all, would I have survived Mitch and Hannah without Jo? Probably. *Maybe.* And while Jo suddenly coming back to life did make things a little tricky, I've never had anyone stick their neck out for me like that. It was nice.

"Take care of yourself, Aimee." Jo gives me a mock salute, then she's gone, hurrying back to the resort, her mind probably already on the plane flying away from here.

I wish I could walk away, I really do, but I refuse to leave until I see this through. I have to know that—

Hannah stands, her movements jerky. Like it's a dance, Patrick stands too, his arms held out from his body like he wants to grab her but is afraid to touch her. She grabs her throat, then claws at it, her eyes wide.

It's happening.

I want to look away, but I won't let myself. I'm not a monster, not someone who daydreams about watching people die, not even people who would willingly kill me, but I have to see this through. If I don't, every creak in the night, every car following me for more than three blocks, every time I think someone knows my secret, will be terrifying.

Hannah turns with a jerk. She's looking for me, I know she is. Her head swivels left and right, but after a moment, she sinks back down to the sand. I cover my mouth with my hand as I watch, excitement making me lightheaded.

I should leave. Sticking around to watch the aftermath is dangerous, but I'm having a hard time dragging myself away from the show. Patrick leans over, then he stands and calls for help.

A waiter rushes over, one I don't recognize, but it doesn't matter how many people rush to her aid. She's too far gone.

Still, I wait.

Just a few more minutes.

Just until I know for sure that she's dead.

Now there's a crowd of people around her, all of them bending over her, one man fanning her face like that could possibly be enough to bring her back. Someone motions for everyone to move, then starts CPR.

I find myself breathing faster and faster as he presses down on her chest, then gives her rescue breaths. My heart hammers away, and I lean forward on my chair to get a better view.

This goes on for a few minutes, then the man stops. He wipes his hand across his forehead and looks up at Patrick. I can't hear what's being said, but I see the way Patrick's shoulders slump forward, how pale he suddenly is under his tan.

And... scene.

It's time for me to leave, so I stand, scooping up my bag in the process. I'm halfway to the resort when I feel someone staring at me. Against my better judgement, I pause, then turn to look back.

There's still a crowd of people around Hannah's body, so it's difficult at first for me to pick him out.

Patrick.

Staring at me, his hands clenched into fists, his eyes locked on mine.

A LETTER FROM EMILY

Dear reader,

Thank you so much for reading *Unmarried*! If you enjoyed it, and want to keep up to date with all my latest releases, just sign up at the following link. Your email address will never be shared, and you can unsubscribe at any time.

www.bookouture.com/emily-shiner

I told myself two days ago that I would *finally* sit down and write this letter to y'all, my wonderful readers, and then what happened? Laundry. The garden. Some dry fall leaves fell, and I just had to take the dogs for a long walk.

But now is the perfect time for me to sit down and thank you for reading. Why right now? Well, partly because my husband is outside staining the deck and I'm dragging my feet on putting on work clothes and helping, and partly because I can feel my editor staring at me from her office in the UK while she waits on me to write this.

There's nothing like a deadline to get me to sit down and work, I guess.

But before I venture outside in my paint-stained clothes, I want to thank you for sticking with me to hear the rest of Aimee's story.

If you've read my books before, you know that my psychological thrillers are all one-and-done. There's nothing like meeting new characters, getting to know them, and then experiencing the gut-wrenching shock when they're killed off or otherwise tormented.

Maybe it speaks to my psyche, but I love it.

Aimee, however, wouldn't get out of my head. She's really messed up in her own way and I didn't want to let her story end with *Uninvited*. She's strong, determined, and I wanted to see what would happen if I pushed her as hard as I could.

So I did. And she pushed back, didn't she? I'm not saying I want to be friends with her, but I'm totally cool with respecting her from a distance.

It was a bit scary writing a duet because *Unmarried* was written before *Uninvited* was released, and there was a little voice in the back of my head wondering what I would do if y'all hated the first book. Would you even pick up the second? Would I need to have a bonfire to burn the copies I ordered?

Well, all that remains to be seen, but I haven't picked up any packs of marshmallows yet... Unfortunately, I guess I do have to go stain the deck.

All that to say: I hope you loved *Unmarried*! If you did, I would be very grateful if you could write a review. I'd love to hear what you think, and it makes such a difference helping new readers to discover one of my books for the first time.

I love hearing from my readers—you can get in touch through social media or my website.

Thanks,

Emily

KEEP IN TOUCH WITH EMILY

authoremilyshiner.com

 facebook.com/authoremilyshiner

instagram.com/authoremilyshiner

bsky.app/profile/authoremilyshiner.bsky.social

ACKNOWLEDGMENTS

It would be impossible to thank everyone who had a hand in helping *Unmarried* become the book you just read, so let's hit the highlights: Kelsie Marsden, Donna Hillyer, Laura Kincaid, Lauren Stanfield, and my lovely daughter, Claire, were all instrumental in whipping this book into shape.

I tend to toss commas around like confetti, and I can't thank these amazing women enough for keeping me from looking like I didn't pass high school writing classes. I did, *I swear*, I just get excited and then commas happen more than they should, and in places they don't belong.

To my dogs, Macy-Grace and Pepper(oni), who alternate between snuggling while I write and playing with me in the yard so I don't lose my mind staring at a screen.

Because this book is for the girls: thanks to my mom for listening to me talk about tricky plot points; to my mail lady, Arkavia, who is an absolute delight when she brings packages to my door; to my sister; my best friends; and even my frenemy down the road.

We may not get along, but she has great pink hair.

And, of course, thanks to you, my readers. Y'all are the best!

PUBLISHING TEAM

Turning a manuscript into a book requires the efforts of many people. The publishing team at Bookouture would like to acknowledge everyone who contributed to this publication.

Audio
Alba Proko
Melissa Tran
Sinead O'Connor

Commercial
Lauren Morrissette
Hannah Richmond
Imogen Allport

Cover design
Debbie Holmes

Data and analysis
Mark Alder
Mohamed Bussuri

Editorial
Kelsie Marsden
Nadia Michael

RAISING READERS
Books Build Bright Futures

Dear Reader,

We'd love your attention for one more page to tell you about the crisis in children's reading, and what we can all do.

Studies have shown that reading for fun is the **single biggest predictor of a child's future life chances** – more than family circumstance, parents' educational background or income. It improves academic results, mental health, wealth, communication skills, ambition and happiness.

The number of children reading for fun is in rapid decline. Young people have a lot of competition for their time, and a worryingly high number do not have a single book at home.

Hachette works extensively with schools, libraries and literacy charities, but here are some ways we can all raise more readers:

- Reading to children for just 10 minutes a day makes a difference
- Don't give up if children aren't regular readers – there will be books for them!

- Visit bookshops and libraries to get recommendations
- Encourage them to listen to audiobooks
- Support school libraries
- Give books as gifts

There's a lot more information about how to encourage children to read on our websites: **www.RaisingReaders.co.uk** and **www.JoinRaisingReaders.com**.

Thank you for reading.

Printed in Dunstable, United Kingdom